TROUBLE COMES TO HARBOUR HOUSE

FENELLA J. MILLER

Boldwood

First published in Great Britain in 2026 by Boldwood Books Ltd.

Copyright © Fenella J. Miller, 2026

Cover Design by Colin Thomas

Cover Images: Colin Thomas, Shutterstock and [Delimata] Wikimedia Commons

A CIP catalogue record for this book is available from the British Library.

Paperback ISBN 978-1-80549-330-3

Large Print ISBN 978-1-80549-331-0

Hardback ISBN 978-1-80549-329-7

Trade Paperback ISBN 978-1-80656-197-1

Ebook ISBN 978-1-80549-332-7

Kindle ISBN 978-1-80549-333-4

Audio CD ISBN 978-1-80549-324-2

MP3 CD ISBN 978-1-80549-325-9

Digital audio download ISBN 978-1-80549-327-3

This book is printed on certified sustainable paper. Boldwood Books is dedicated to putting sustainability at the heart of our business. For more information please visit https://www.boldwoodbooks.com/about-us/sustainability/

Boldwood Books Ltd, 23 Bowerdean Street, London, SW6 3TN

www.boldwoodbooks.com

This book is for my son, daughter-in-law, grandson, brother and sister-in-law, niece and nephew, great-niece and -nephew plus my adopted niece and great-nieces. I'm so lucky to be surrounded by such loving, wonderful, caring people.

1

WIVENHOE, DECEMBER 1940

Emily Roby was staring morosely out of the sitting-room window at the freezing rain, trying to summon up enthusiasm for the end of term and approaching Christmas. This would be the first one for baby Grace, her little sister who was now nine months old, and the family was determined to make it memorable if they could.

There was little in the way of gifts, decorations, or anything exciting to eat in the shops because of rationing and all the bombs being dropped everywhere, but Lily Turner, their cook–housekeeper, had promised there'd be some edible treats to look forward to.

'Emily, just pop over to the shop, there's a sweetheart, and buy me some chocolate if they have any.' Cousin Lucinda lounged in front of the fire reading an expensive magazine.

'I'm not going out in the rain, and anyway you won't have enough points for any sweets.' This wasn't exactly polite but Lucinda's behaviour and selfishness had made her thoroughly disliked by everyone in the house. Even the cat hissed at this unwanted guest.

When Emily had first met her cousin a few weeks ago she'd liked Lucinda, had got on well with her. However, when they'd got home she'd realised this new arrival had brought trouble to Harbour House.

She was tall, elegant, really pretty with glorious golden hair, but had proved to be spoilt and selfish and had upset everyone including the boys.

'Rude child. If you're not going to do that then go and make me a coffee.'

Emily turned. 'I'm not making you anything, you've got legs of your own so why don't you use them? Anyway, the only coffee in the house isn't for you, it's for my parents.'

Emily wished this cousin hadn't come to stay, Grandma and Grandpa had been so much nicer. Lucinda had been with them since October and so far had done nothing but upset everyone. When Emily had complained to Mummy she'd been told to be more sympathetic, that Lucinda was hiding a broken heart and needed compassion, not criticism.

As far as she was concerned, someone had to earn compassion and respect and Lucinda was grown up and should have known better. Mummy's cousin had outstayed her welcome. The boys thought her stuck up and lazy as she didn't help at all and expected everyone to wait on her. Daddy was at work most of the time at the shipyard and didn't seem to mind that this cuckoo had fallen into the nest. Harbour House had been a lovely place to live even when her grandparents had been there, even when Grandpa had been a bit confused. Now, just because of Lucinda, everyone was on edge.

Emily left the room and closed the door loudly behind her. Despite the rain, Mummy had taken Grace out in the pram to either a WI or a WVS meeting. Her brother, George, must've heard the door bang as he appeared at the top of the stairs.

'Blimey, we can't even sit in our own sitting room without being tormented by that fiend. We thought we'd start making some decorations and Christmas cards. Lily said we can use the dining room as long as we put newspaper down on top of the tablecloth.'

'Perfect, we can be quite certain Lucinda won't want to join in so we'll not be bothered.'

Sammy, her other brother, peered over the banisters. 'It's blooming freezing in the dining room – do you think we could light the fire if all three of us are in there?'

'I'm not going to ask for permission,' Emily said firmly. 'The sitting room's enemy territory and we need a base for ourselves.'

Half an hour later, the dining room wasn't exactly warm, but it was bearable. They'd brought down the box of treasured bits and pieces from the attic and were ready to start making their decorations. There was absolutely nothing new to buy this year and Daddy had told them if they wanted to make the house festive, they would have to use what they already had.

'I'm going to make the flour and water paste,' Sammy said. 'How much do you think we need?'

'Well, we've already cut up two hundred coloured paper strips to stick together to make a long paper chain. Is there much more we can use in that box, Sammy?'

'I reckon we can make another four hundred strips if we don't intend to make anything else.'

'Okay, I know how much to do now. I won't be long.'

George pulled a face. 'Mummy has had Lily ironing last year's wrapping paper. I think we're lucky to have the bits we've got. I heard them talking the other night and we won't be getting much this Christmas, I doubt we'll even get a stocking. There won't even be any oranges to put at the toe as the government think oranges are non-essential.'

'Don't grumble, there's a war on. We're lucky, thousands and thousands of people all over the country have been bombed out and will be facing Christmas with absolutely nothing,' Emily said.

This could well develop into one of their regular rows – she and George often argued over the silliest things whereas she and Sammy never had a cross word to say to each other.

Sammy returned with the bowl of flour and water paste. 'I know how we can make Grace a gift, do you want to hear what it is or are you two going to fight?'

George grinned and she smiled.

'Go on then, she's the one who needs to have at least one decent present as this is her first Christmas ever,' George said.

'We need some small stones, a national dried milk tin and some string.'

Emily almost clapped her hands but she was too grown up to do that now. 'I know what you're getting at. You're forgetting that we'll need some paint as well and some sticky tape.'

George was looking mystified. 'What are you two going on about?'

Sammy beamed and Emily left him to explain. 'You wash the stones and the tin, then put the stones inside and seal the lid on. Then you paint it all a nice colour and put string round it and add a handle. Then a baby can shake it, roll it or pull it along the floor. I know where there's an empty milk tin, I'll ask Lily if we can have it,' Sammy said and rushed off.

'Mr Turner's got most of the men making little wooden animals, blocks and other toys from the scraps they're allowed to keep from the shipyard. Lily said that he's already made a cat, a dog and a cow for Grace as well as two dozen square blocks.' Emily had thought this was a lovely idea but then Lily and her husband were lovely people.

'That's spiffing,' George said. 'Grace will be spoilt for choice when it comes to toys. We don't believe in Father Christmas but we want her to.'

'Lily said there'll be enough wooden toys for every child in Wivenhoe to at least have two or three things. Isn't that marvellous?'

What she didn't tell him was that Mr Turner had made George a wooden Spitfire and Sammy a wooden Hurricane. They would be overjoyed when they saw those on Christmas morning.

By lunchtime, the paper chains were complete and draped over every available surface to dry. They'd each made a dried milk tin into a toy for a baby but hadn't had enough paint to do more than one. Mummy had returned and suggested that they cut up the remaining scraps of paper and stuck them all over the tins and then covered them with the flour and water paste.

'Won't they be all sticky, Mummy?' Sammy asked.

'No, the glue dries clear and hard. Like magic really. I'm very impressed with what the three of you have managed to achieve this afternoon. I know Grace will really enjoy playing with one of them. What are you going to do with the others?'

'Lily's offered to get them added to the toys that are being collected somewhere or other in the village. Mummy, we've talked about this, and we really don't need any gifts this year. As long as Grace gets something then that's all that matters.'

* * *

Usually, Emily got together with her best friends Penny and Doris who lived in Rowhedge, just a short ferry ride across the River Colne. The horrible weather this weekend had meant she wouldn't see her friends – obviously she'd see Penny at school but not Doris, who went to a different one.

The girls who'd been evacuated from her school were returning before the end of term. The governors of the school had decided that Colchester was perfectly safe after all. This would mean the classes would probably go back to how they were and her best friend Penny wouldn't be in her form any more. This hadn't been confirmed officially but that was what everyone was saying.

This wouldn't be so bad if things weren't difficult at home. She'd ask Daddy when the unwanted and difficult guest was going to leave Harbour House – it would be tricky to ask her mother as Lucinda was her cousin and Emily's sort of aunt – who she'd never met – had asked if this arrangement could continue until things had been smoothed over in London.

Emily wasn't exactly sure what this meant but having Lucinda Somiton staying was going to mean trouble at Harbour House.

* * *

Lucinda heard her cousin Elizabeth return with the baby and decided she'd better make an effort to be sociable, offer to help, pretend that she was enjoying being incarcerated in this dreadful little village in the middle of nowhere.

She'd been having such a super time in London when things had gone catastrophically wrong for her. After being trapped in a stuffy boarding school all her life, Pa had promised if she did well in her higher certificate then he'd fund a few months in Town. There was an apartment in Knightsbridge which an ancient relative had gifted to her and she had happily moved in.

Whilst in London, Lucinda had fallen in love with a man called Ralph, who'd told her repeatedly that he loved her, and that he wanted to spend the rest of his life with her. But, to her horror, Ralph had turned out to be married and his wife had discovered the affair and raised the most awful stink. Ralph was something very important in the War Office so before scandal overwhelmed his family and hers, she'd been parcelled off to Wivenhoe where she was to remain indefinitely. Heartbreak was proving to be more difficult than she'd ever imagined.

She'd lived here for almost a month now and was certain that if she found something or someone to become involved with then she wouldn't be so unpleasant to everybody. But there were no eligible young men within miles – no dashing RAF pilots to flirt with. Even an army officer would be acceptable in the circumstances. Anything to dull the pain of losing Ralph.

The door to the sitting room was already open when Elizabeth eventually turned up. Lucinda had heard her going upstairs with the baby – she knew nothing about babies but thought Grace was probably going for a late-afternoon nap.

'I've got news for you, Lucinda, but I doubt that you're going to be pleased with it,' Elizabeth said.

Surely her cousin wasn't going to evict her, not so soon before Christmas. Her parents wanted nothing to do with her after what had happened with Ralph and she knew she was fortunate that Elizabeth had agreed to take her in. She'd be homeless and penniless – as her generous allowance had been halted as well – and it would be entirely her own fault for being such an appalling houseguest over the past few weeks.

At least her father couldn't take away the inheritance from her grandparents. If she married before she was twenty-one then her trust fund would be released or, if she didn't, it would be hers when she was twenty-five. Her brother and sister, already adults when she was born, had also been left a substantial amount in trust. Her father had told her if she hadn't been born then the money would have been divided between her older siblings. This might well be why they so disliked her. Somehow, she had to find a way to support herself until she was a woman of substantial means again.

'From your expression, cousin, I'm assuming it's bad news for me and good news for you.'

'When I agreed to take you in I assumed it would be for a few weeks, that you would be a happy and helpful member of our family. The reverse has been true. I'm sorry, but you will have to make alternative living arrangements.'

Lucinda was shocked. She'd nowhere to go. Somehow she must persuade Elizabeth to give her a second chance, allow her to make amends, to be the sort of guest she knew she could be.

'I know you can't wait to send me away but although I might not seem to be appreciative, I really am. Please allow me to make up for my bad manners.'

'Hmm. If that's the case, Lucinda, then if you genuinely do wish to live with us you must make an effort to fit in.'

'I'm sorry, I'll really do better if you let me stay.'

Elizabeth smiled. 'Good girl, I'm sure that underneath the bad-tempered selfish person you appear to be there's someone lovely hiding.'

Lucinda was finding this conversation difficult as even though she knew she was entirely in the wrong, hearing it put so bluntly made her even more miserable than she already was. Somehow, she pinned on a smile and changed the subject.

'Cousin Elizabeth, now we've got that out of the way, what is it you have to tell me?'

'I think you'd better sit down. This is going to be a shock and possibly not a pleasant one.'

'Has someone died?' Lucinda's hands clenched and a sick feeling settled in her stomach whilst she waited for the answer.

'No, absolutely not. I'm so sorry, I didn't mean to upset you. You've gone quite pale, my dear, shall I get you a glass of water?'

Lucinda shook her head. 'No, if nobody has died then whatever you've got to tell me must be a huge improvement on what I feared.'

'Someone at the WVS meeting told us that there's about to be an official announcement from the War Office very soon saying that all young women between twenty and thirty are going to be conscripted.'

'When is this going to be enforced?'

'Not until the end of next year, but I thought you needed to know so you can decide for yourself where you want to go and not be sent where the War Office decides you should be.'

'I'm not twenty until February, but I want to do something useful before next December.'

'You will be doing something useful, you're going to be helping me,' Elizabeth said.

'I certainly am, but that isn't helping the war. I feel I should be making more of an effort.'

She frowned as she thought of what the choices she faced could be. 'I really don't want to join the army, khaki is a most unflattering colour. I get seasick in a rowing boat so the WRNS won't do which, I suppose, only leaves the WAAF.' She smiled and Elizabeth laughed.

'I don't think either reason is good enough to rule the WRNS or ATS out.'

'I'd like to do something that uses my intellect, I'm not sure being in the women's army would do that.'

'You're forgetting about the land army, Lucinda, but I think that would also be a waste of your intelligence. You matriculated with distinction in the summer – maybe the War Office could find you something more interesting than joining one of the services.'

'I have no language skills, apart from basic French, so I don't see how I could be of help in London.'

Just then Emily and her brothers emerged from the dining room, laughing whilst carrying arms full of brightly coloured paper chains.

'Can we put these up, Mummy? It is December and only two weeks more or less until Christmas,' Emily asked.

'I don't see why not, but the tree shouldn't go up until Christmas Eve. However, I think you need to ask your father before you start any hanging.'

'We'll put them in the boys' room for now, there's plenty of space under the window.'

They hadn't argued, they'd just wandered off chattering and enjoying each other's company. How Lucinda envied them the easy camaraderie, the obvious love they shared. Lucinda's parents had had her when they were much older and her siblings were adults and had left home before she was born. Ma and Pa had done their best but, being such older parents, had found her more a nuisance than a pleasure, which was why she'd spent most of her life away at school.

'Now, where were we? I think you can get the necessary documents by writing to the RAF as they handle the applications. But I'd suggest that you go up to London in person. I believe that the recruiting office is somewhere in Knightsbridge.' Elizabeth smiled brightly. 'As you lived in that district for a few months I'm sure you can find it.'

For the first time in weeks, Lucinda saw a glimmer of light at the end of the very dark tunnel she'd been in since leaving London heartbroken and in disgrace.

'I'll do that. In the meantime, I'd like to get involved in something a little more active than the Women's Institute or the

Women's Voluntary Service. Do you think I could become an ARP warden?'

'I know of girls who joined one of the services as soon as they were eighteen so you certainly could if you wanted to.'

Lucinda opened her mouth to say that she'd join up immediately but to her surprise said something quite different.

'If you don't mind, I'd much rather stay here until the weather improves and try and make up for my horrible behaviour. However, if you'd prefer that I leave as soon as possible I'll do that.'

'In which case, my dear, there's absolutely no need for you to dash off and become part of the military machine. Mr Hatch is the ARP person, and Mrs Hatch was bemoaning the fact nobody had come forward to join him in his patrols. I think it's very likely the appalling weather we've been having has something to do with it – who wants to be walking around in freezing rain during the blackout?'

Lucinda laughed – another thing that surprised her as she hadn't even smiled since the last time she'd been in London. This had been a few weeks ago when she'd been sent to collect Emily returning from a visit to her grandparents in Kent. Just being in the same city as the man who'd lied to her, but she thought she'd always love, and could never be with, had been enough to cheer her up.

'I'll go in search of him immediately. I don't care if I get drenched, it'll do me good and be suitable punishment for my bad behaviour here.'

'Good heavens, you can't go now, it's dark and Mr Hatch will already be on his patrol. He's also our postman so with any luck he'll knock on the door tomorrow and I suggest you invite him in for a cup of tea in the kitchen. He's bound to be delighted.'

'I expect he'll be delighted to be out of the winter weather rather than to speak to me, but thank you for suggesting it, Cousin Elizabeth.'

'Please call me Elizabeth, I know I'm almost old enough to be your mother, but I'd prefer us to be friends.'

'Thank you, Elizabeth, I'm going to make this a new start. I don't want to be any more trouble at Harbour House, I want to be an asset. I can certainly help the children with their homework if they'd like me to. I know Lily's overworked now that Enid's only doing the laundry and scrubbing the floors downstairs.'

'What are you suggesting?'

'I'll do upstairs from now on – including the fires and any chamber pots that need emptying.'

George, closely followed by his sister and brother, overheard her remark.

'Nobody uses them, we all come down.' He grinned and for the first time he looked friendly. 'I'll use mine if you—'

'George Roby, don't you dare continue. Horrible boy,' Elizabeth said, laughing.

'Well, you three, do you know how to play whist?' Lucinda asked.

'We don't, but I've heard of it,' Emily said, also looking more interested.

'Then after tea I'll teach you how to play if that's all right with you, Elizabeth?'

'Yes, I thought you might be going to offer to teach them to play poker and I'm not sure that would be a good idea. Do you play bridge, Lucinda?'

'I do indeed, I also play chess, but I prefer bridge.'

'Jonathan and I are attempting to learn from a book as our neighbours are keen for us to play with them. We're really not sufficiently skilled to play with anyone else. Do you think you could teach us? Playing the hand is relatively straightforward, it's the bidding we're having difficulty with.'

Lucinda went to bed that night feeling maybe her nightmare was over, that she was beginning to adjust to the loss of the man she loved who'd betrayed her and run back to his wife. Thousands of men had died in this beastly war. She was ashamed that she'd been behaving as if Ralph was one of them, she needed to pull herself together and be thankful he was very much alive but not with her.

2

Emily still wasn't convinced the sudden change in Lucinda, from sneering and cold to friendly and helpful, was real. The evening spent learning to take tricks and count cards was fun, but she wasn't as ready to forgive and forget as her brothers.

'I'm going to make the cocoa. It will be on the table in ten minutes, plenty of time to get washed and into your pyjamas, boys,' she said as Lucinda packed away the cards.

They'd been playing on the dining-room table as it was warm in there and easier than on the kitchen table.

'Do I have to get into my nightwear too?'

'I wasn't going to make any cocoa for you, Lucinda, as you've told me several times you didn't like it.'

'Fair enough. I'm happy to make some for the three of you.'

'Thank you but you don't know where anything is and don't know how we like it. I suppose I could make you a cup of tea.'

Lucinda looked a bit sad at this rebuff and Emily regretted being so abrupt.

'Actually, Emily, I do love cocoa, but having been so horrible to you when you offered to make me some I could hardly change my mind. I'm sorry to have been such a beast to you and the boys, I promise I'll do better from now on.'

Emily smiled. 'Golly, it's a Christmas miracle. I was dreading spending the holidays with you living here but now I think it might be fun.'

When the boys rushed in, four mugs of cocoa were waiting on the table and the two for their parents in the sitting room were on the tray with the best of the broken biscuits.

'I'll take this through, don't leave me with just crumbs, you two,' Emily called back, speaking quietly as raising one's voice wasn't sensible after Grace was asleep.

She hurried down the chilly corridor. 'Cocoa delivery, Mummy and Daddy.'

'Good, just what the doctor ordered,' he said and came to take the tray from her.

'Lucinda's all right now she's trying to fit in. I'm going to be nicer to her.'

'Good girl, she had a rotten time before she came to us but she seems to have got over it now,' Daddy said.

Emily wanted to know what this 'rotten time' might be about but knew better than to ask. As Mummy had mentioned a broken heart it must have been to do with a man. Perhaps her fiancé had died somewhere overseas, that would be more than enough to make her sad and bad-tempered. Maybe Lucinda might tell her when they were better pals.

* * *

With only ten days until the end of term, Miss King announced that the girls that had been evacuated with almost half of their teachers were returning the following week.

'As you know, the governors decided that as there's apparently no imminent danger in Colchester the school will be reunited at the start of the spring term. I'm sure, girls, that you must be as delighted as I am to know Greyfriars will be functioning as it should after the holidays.'

Emily exchanged a worried glance with her friend, Penny. If things were to go back to the way they were, it wouldn't be such fun. It had been so much better having all the scholarship girls in one class.

She glanced around and saw she wasn't the only girl concerned about this unexpected change of circumstances. However, nobody appeared to have the courage to put up their hand and ask. It would have to be her.

'Yes, Emily Roby, what is it that you wish to ask me?'

She was now on her feet and wished she'd not been so impulsive. Having everyone stare at her, a lot of them disapprovingly, wasn't enjoyable at all.

'I apologise for interrupting you, Miss King, but will the classes be put back the way they were, or can they remain as they are?'

'As always, a pertinent question. It hasn't been decided but am I to gather that you'd prefer things to remain as they are?'

Emily nodded vigorously and the other scholarship girls who were sitting, as they always did, together on the bench nodded just as enthusiastically. The headmistress looked along the row and then she too nodded.

'I think it can be arranged for you and your friends to remain together even if others are moved.'

'Thank you, Miss King, that's exactly the answer I wanted.'

There were a few more notices and then lower school was dismissed from assembly. As they trooped back to their form room in the required silence, she received several pats on the back and happy nods from the other scholarship girls.

* * *

There was no opportunity to talk about what had happened until morning break when the nine of them gathered at their end of the form room.

'Well done, Emily, no one else would have dared to ask but I'm so glad that you did,' Penny said and hugged her.

'I've been happier this term with the way things are arranged. We're the brains of the upper fourth and those that pay fees don't like that,' someone else said.

'They should never have relocated half the school in the first place,' Emily said. 'I know we still march down to the shelter whenever the siren goes but there've been absolutely no bombs at all dropped in Colchester or in Wivenhoe or Rowhedge.'

'We don't bother to go down any more at home,' Penny said with a grin. 'Too blooming cold in the cellar and my little brothers just plain refuse to get out of bed.'

The bell rang noisily outside the door and hastily they straightened their pinafores and returned to their desks, ready for the next lesson. It wasn't until the longer lunchtime break that Emily and Penny were able to find a quiet corner to talk.

'It's my brothers' birthday on Saturday. Do you think that your parents will still let the three of you come across on the ferry even if it's raining and the river's rough?' Penny asked anxiously.

'They promised we could come regardless. It's perfectly safe and the ferry runs in all weathers. The problem being that if we get drenched walking up to your house we're going to be wet and miserable and not enjoy the party.'

'Mum has that covered. She's managed to accumulate an assortment of clothes which will fit you. Not your usual smart things but guaranteed clean.'

'Spiffing news. If you have socks as well, then we can run about in those and if we put our things in the kitchen they'll probably be dry by the time we go home. I hope Doris is invited.'

'Of course she is, silly, she's part of our team. In fact, I see more of her out of school than I do you at the moment because of the weather. Mum insisted that we invite the older boy, Jimmy, from the big house. Heaven knows how that will work out as the other two will probably follow him. I'm going to collect him and speak to the parents of the others and say that they aren't invited.'

Three families who'd been bombed out of the East End had arrived to live in the huge, cold house in Rowhedge that had been left empty. The mothers were hopeless and Penny, Doris and herself had got to know the three smallest members of the household. They were neglected, unwashed and often not fed either.

'I didn't know you'd met any of the mothers or the nans.'

'I haven't and I forgot to tell you that the grandmothers went back to London. The three mothers are still here but the families haven't exactly made a good impression. The little girl, she's called Sally, is the worst as she'll steal anything she sees. The littlest one, Davey, is her brother and he usually has wet pants. Jimmy, the one with a mother who drinks, is the only one we trust in the house. So that's why he's invited and the others aren't.'

'How old is he? He seemed the most articulate and intelligent of the three although his mother was absolutely horrible,' Emily said. She shuddered as she recalled the time she'd been searching for someone to care for the three small children they'd just met. Jimmy's mother had been drunk in bed and had sworn at her and threatened to beat her.

'Jimmy's not exactly sure how old he is but he thinks that he's probably five. He should be going to school after Christmas if that's true, but I've a feeling he won't be able to because his mother's certainly not going to get him ready.'

'Couldn't you take him when you take your brothers down to the village school every day?'

'Mum's against that as she doesn't want us to be any more involved with those families than we are already. Anyway, as Jimmy doesn't know if he's actually five I expect nobody's going to notice if he's not there at least for another term.'

They heard the bell clanging in the corridor. Lunch break was over and this afternoon it was art and music – both subjects Emily loved.

* * *

Lucinda had got up the morning after spending time with the children determined to be cheerful in future but was finding it more difficult than she'd anticipated. If Ralph hadn't betrayed her by neglecting to mention that he was married with two small children, then maybe it would be easier to get over what had happened.

Ralph's wife had somehow discovered her husband's infidelity and with whom he was committing it, but instead of speaking to Ralph, she'd gone straight to Lucinda's parents. The wronged wife had also passed the information on to a gossip column so not only her family knew, but everybody else in her circle did as well and Lucinda was branded a scarlet woman.

She scowled at her reflection in the speckled mirror over the sink in the WC downstairs. She'd lost weight and she'd been on the thin side of slender already. Now she looked as if she was suffering from some dreadful illness. At least her crowning glory, as Ralph had always called her golden locks, remained lustrous and shiny. She needed to be in the sitting room to catch the postman and hurried down the chilly passway and into the room.

The only positive about this debacle was that she hadn't been pregnant – that would have been just too awful. She did want children but obviously not before she was married. If Ralph hadn't been so handsome, so charming, so irresistible, if she'd had any sense at all she wouldn't have slept with him. No decent man would want anything to do with her now her reputation was in tatters. Ralph's wife had made sure of that.

She blinked back unwanted tears. Life was so unfair to women! Ralph had returned home to be welcomed with open arms, whereas she was now a social pariah. The fact that he'd been unfaithful, had broken his marriage vows, had lied to her and his wife, didn't seem to matter. He was a man, and the rules were different for them.

She'd been hovering at the sitting-room window, waiting to see if Mr Hatch came with any post, and there he was about to trudge up the path, head bowed, water dripping off his hat.

The front door was open in a flash. 'Mr Hatch, if you care to come around to the back door I've got a lovely mug of tea waiting for you.'

'Righto, cuppa tea would go down a treat. Ta, Miss Somiton.'

He'd only taken one step down the path so just turned around, carefully closing the gate behind him, in order to make his way down the side of the house and in through the back door.

Lucinda flew to the kitchen. 'Mr Hatch is on his way, Lily. Mrs Roby said I could make him a cup of tea. I hope we won't be in your way.'

'No, Miss Somiton, you go ahead. Pour one for me when it's ready, I'll be getting on with things in the scullery.'

A kettle was always simmering on the range, a sturdy brown

teapot warming beside it. By the time the postman knocked on the door, the tea was made and brewing.

'Come in, Mr Hatch. Shall I take your outdoor garments and hang them near the range? I don't suppose they'll dry but they'll be considerably warmer when you put them on again.'

He nodded, dropped his bulging postbag in the corner and then handed her his dripping navy-blue greatcoat and peaked cap.

'Here you are, love, kind of you to invite me in. Not happened before, but I ain't complaining.' He grinned, showing the large gap between his front teeth.

'You've guessed that I've an ulterior motive, but I hope when you hear why I want to talk to you you'll be pleased you interrupted your round to speak to me.'

She poured the tea into three large enamel mugs, a working man wouldn't want to fuss about with a porcelain cup and saucer.

'Excuse me a minute, Mr Hatch, I'm just going to pop in with Lily's tea. Help yourself to sugar and biscuits.'

She joined him at the table and took a couple of crisp broken biscuits. Lily had managed to get a pound of these damaged biscuits this morning from the general stores over the road so the tin was brimming.

'I want to become your assistant ARP warden, Mr Hatch. I'm hoping to join the WAAF or possibly find a position at the War Office next year but I'm all yours until then.'

He held out his empty mug hopefully and she hastily filled it up again.

'That's champion, love, I'm finding it a bit much out all day delivering the letters and that and then every night doing a patrol. Not that there's much to see or do in Wivenhoe, law-abiding lot we are, and not a blooming bomb dropped, thank the good Lord.'

'Is there much training involved? Is the uniform easy to come by and is it expensive?'

'Bless you, love, we ain't got a uniform, not really. I was issued with a bluette overall last year, and a tin helmet and armband. I wear me own clothes and Wellington boots.'

'Gosh, that's a relief. Will I get the overalls, helmet and armband?'

'You certainly will. When can you start?'

'Tonight, if you like. I've got rubber boots, warm slacks, and a thick coat. If you can supply me with the other three things then I'm tickety-boo. I have to be honest and admit that I don't exactly know what you do apart from make sure the blackout's being observed.'

'You need to come out with me a few times until I'm sure you know what's what. I've got a pamphlet I can give you but I can tell you as it's common sense really.'

He raised his hand and began to tick off things as he told her.

'Enforcing the blackout, advising the public, firefighting, rescue and first aid, monitoring and reporting and maintaining order.' He nodded as if reciting this list made everything transparent.

'Are you in the most dreadful hurry to get back to your round, Mr Hatch? If not, can we just go through those things quickly before you leave?'

'As long as I get everything delivered by lunchtime I'll not be in any bother. What is it you want me to explain?'

Half an hour later, Lucinda thought she knew enough to join him that night without making a complete fool of herself. She also knew where he lived in Station Road and had agreed to be there at six o'clock sharp to collect her own metal helmet, blue overalls and official armband.

'Will I be working every night, Mr Hatch?'

'Once you know the ropes I'd be that grateful if you'd do the weekdays and then I'll do the weekend. How does that sound?'

'Just the ticket, Mr Hatch, I won't let you down.'

'Why did you decide to volunteer for the night patrol? Young lady like you would be better off working the day shift.'

'I understand that there are already more than enough daytime volunteers and absolutely no one to help you.'

He'd been talking to her long enough for his coat to be gently steaming and his cap was already dry.

'Crikey, I nearly forgot, I better give you the post for the house before I go. My youngest works at the yard, he's a joiner and they don't work late in the winter. I'll send him with the overalls and that so you'll be ready when you turn up.'

Lucinda ushered him out, excited by the prospect of doing something useful for a change.

'Lunch will be late, it's a good thing it's only you, Mrs Roby and the baby today.' Lily seemed a bit upset that she'd been unable to get into her own domain for so long.

'I'm so sorry but I'm starting as an ARP warden tonight and really needed to know exactly what I had to do in the event of any of the emergencies.'

Lily's expression changed. 'That's different, Miss Somiton, Dougie Hatch works too hard and you sharing the work with him will make things easier for him.'

'What can I do to help you as I've hindered you for the past half an hour?'

'Nothing at all, thank you, Miss Somiton, but I appreciate the offer.' Lily pointed at the half a dozen envelopes on the table. 'Don't forget those, they go on the hall stand by the telephone.'

Two days ago Lucinda would have taken umbrage at being told something she already knew but today she just nodded and smiled. As she walked along the passageway towards the table outside the sitting-room door, she flicked through the letters.

Her attention was immediately caught by the expensive cream envelope amongst the brown manila ones. Her heart thudded uncomfortably. She'd received several letters that looked just like that.

She carefully placed the post addressed to Mr Roby in the wooden box before turning over the odd one out. It was addressed to her, had been posted in London yesterday, and she recognised the writing. Why was Ralph writing to her?

This wasn't a letter she wanted to read and she was tempted to throw it straight into the sitting-room fire. Instead, she pushed it under the inlaid wooden box where the post was kept and forgot about it.

3

Emily and her brothers were drenched by the time they got home and to make it even more miserable it was already dark. She just hated creeping about with no streetlights as the tiny beam they were allowed on their torches was scarcely any use at all.

When it was wet, they always went in through the back door so they could leave their coats and macintoshes to dry on the rack in the kitchen. The front door was hardly used at the moment as even Daddy came in and out this way.

To her surprise, Lucinda was waiting for them. 'Here, give me your things and I'll get them hanging up ready for tomorrow. I expect you're wet through so bring down your uniform when you've changed and I'll deal with that as well.'

'Thank you, we usually do it ourselves but if you're prepared to do it for us tonight then all the better,' George said.

'I'm liking this new version,' Emily said to her brothers as they ran down the cold passageway in their socks and headed up the stairs.

As Emily slept in the attic, it took her longer to get organised than her brothers as she had to light the oil lamps before she could do anything at all. There was no electricity upstairs, which was a nuisance sometimes, but her room was warmer as the chimney breast from the big range ran up one of the walls. Fires weren't allowed in the bedrooms unless the occupant was unwell – of course baby Grace was different.

'Hello, Ginger, have you been on my bed all day?'

The big cat purred, stretched and rolled onto his back, waving his legs inelegantly in the air, demanding she tickled him. He didn't do this for any other member of the family and if they were silly enough to attempt to touch his tummy then he immediately grabbed their hand with his claws. Sometimes he bit them for good measure.

'Silly boy, let me get my wet things off and then I'll spend a few minutes with you.'

Although he couldn't possibly understand what she'd said to him, she thought that sometimes he did as he immediately rolled back onto his front, continued purring, whilst watching her with his gorgeous golden eyes.

As Emily always put out her warm winter slacks, flannelette blouse and thick jumper ready to change into when she got back from school every night, it didn't take her long to get ready. She dropped onto her bed, scooped Ginger onto her lap and immediately recoiled.

'Oh, no, you horrible cat, not another dead mouse.'

This small rodent had been hidden under Ginger, apparently deceased, but as soon as the cat's weight was removed, the mouse revived. Emily wasn't really afraid of mice or rats, but the sudden movement made her grip tighten just as Ginger realised his prey was escaping.

He did what all cats do when incensed or restrained, and dug his claws into her before pouncing. She yelled at him and the mouse shot under the chest of drawers. Ginger flattened himself and attempted to squeeze under to catch his prey.

Emily had more sense than to try and pick him up as this was the only other time she was likely to get scratched or bitten. The top of her legs and her arms hurt where he'd scratched her and she was pretty sure he'd drawn blood.

The racket must have been heard by her brothers, whose room was directly beneath hers. They thundered up the stairs and burst into the room.

'Crikey, Armageddon in here, Emily, from the sound of it,' George said, dancing about as he watched the increasingly futile and furious attempts of the cat to reach the mouse.

Sammy was less impressed and sidled up beside her. 'You yelled, Emily. Did he bite you?'

She shook her head. 'No, thank goodness, but he did scratch me and I can feel the blood trickling, so I'd better find the first-aid tin and do something about it.'

George was all for staying but she insisted that he left the cat to do his job. 'If the mouse has any sense it'll stay under the chest of drawers until Ginger gives up or needs to go outside.'

'That cat will never give up. The mouse is doomed to a grisly death and I want to see him perish.'

To her surprise, Sammy punched his brother and it wasn't a gentle one either. 'You're a cretin to even think something like that. What's that little defenceless mouse ever done to you?'

George didn't retaliate but rubbed his arm and pulled a face. 'Fair enough, sorry, Emily, I got a bit carried away. I know I can't stay in your room without your permission.'

He walked out and ran down the stairs whilst she exchanged a worried glance with Sammy. George hadn't apologised for wishing to watch the mouse die, just for the fact that he'd said he was going to remain in her bedroom.

'That's not like him, he's never been a bloodthirsty boy,' Emily said.

'He's changed, Emily, he's not the boy he was last year when I first met him. I shouldn't really tell you this, but he's been involved in a few fights lately and has been coming out the winner every time. So far the boys he's been fighting have been a bit older than him which means that they've got the blame.'

Her legs and arms were really stinging but she had to hear the rest of this. 'Are you saying that George instigated these fights with bigger boys?'

'He goes out of his way to antagonise them into lashing out. Emily, he's got really aggressive these past few weeks and when the teachers eventually realise it's his fault I'm really worried that he'll be expelled.'

'Oh dear, that's not good news at all. Leave it with me, I'll find out what's going on. I really must do something about my scratches as I don't want to ruin my slacks or my blouse by bleeding all over them.' George had always had a volatile temper but this was something different, something really worrying.

* * *

Again, Lucinda surprised Emily by taking charge of the medical emergency, if a few deep scratches could be considered one. She told the boys to play in their bedroom until they were called down and after a few grumbles they did as she asked.

'I have my St John first-aid certificate, Emily, all sixth-formers had to do it. I can take care of this for you if you'll allow me to.'

'Good show. I'll take everything off and sit by the range in my knickers and vest.'

'Goodness, they are quite deep,' Lucinda said as she began to dab the injuries with Dettol which stung like billy-o.

'Ouch, that hurts. I hope you don't think Ginger's a vicious cat, he's not. It was my fault, he saw a live mouse and I held onto him. Of course he dug his claws in.'

'Your cat isn't fond of me, but then neither are any of you. Hopefully things will be different soon for all of us.'

'Where's Lily? I don't want her walking in on me like this.'

'She's gone home early tonight, I said I'd do supper before I leave for my first shift as a trainee ARP warden.'

'I don't envy you out in this awful freezing rain, but I'm glad you're doing something useful.'

'So am I. It's about time I did my bit for the war effort. Now, just a couple of plasters on these two scratches and I'm done.'

As Emily was dressing, she wondered why Lily had left early. 'Is Lily unwell? I hope not.'

'She's tickety-boo, Emily. I offered to help and she was happy to accept.'

'Thank you for helping me. I'll fetch my wet uniform as I forgot to bring it down with me.' This sudden change by Lucinda was rather confusing, but nice. Emily wondered if it was genuine or because Mummy had threatened to send her away?

The boys' short school trousers, purple blazers and other things were waiting to be hung up. Lucinda had put away the first-aid tin and was washing her hands in the scullery.

The kitchen door opened and Mummy came in carrying Grace, who was in her nightie and ready for bed.

'Are you all right, darling? You should have told me about Ginger scratching you.'

'It's nothing a bit of Dettol couldn't fix, Mummy, and Lucinda did it for me. I knew you were getting the baby ready for bed.' Emily held out her arms and Grace threw herself into them. Fortunately, she was ready as her little sister had an unnerving habit of doing this.

'I wish she didn't launch herself at us, Emily, she's going to be dropped one of these days,' Mummy said, smiling at them both.

'She doesn't fling herself at Daddy or the boys, I wonder why that is?'

Lucinda reappeared and Grace hid her face against Emily's shoulder.

'I'm doing supper tonight, Elizabeth. I spent one summer in the kitchen learning how to make the most of what's available, and I'm actually quite a good chef,' Lucinda told them. 'I know that seems rather unlikely, but my parents were happy as it kept me out of trouble during the long break.'

* * *

Emily waited until she heard the light go out in her brothers' bedroom and then crept down the attic stairs. She paused outside her parents' room and could hear someone moving about – she guessed it was her mother and that Daddy was still in the sitting room. It was him that she wished to speak to.

When Sammy had told her about George and his fights, she'd been horrified and decided immediately she would have to tell Daddy about it. He was less likely to overreact, and it would be better if he spoke to George – man-to-man sort of – than either she or Mummy doing so.

This might be a difficult conversation and she almost changed her mind. The sitting-room door was closed and although there was no need for her to knock for some reason she thought she ought to. The sound of band music filtered through the door and this gave her the necessary courage. If he was listening to Joe Loss and his orchestra he'd be in a good mood.

She tapped on the door, didn't wait for him to call out, and opened it. 'I'm really sorry to come down when I know I should be asleep in bed, but I need to speak to you most urgently.'

Daddy was beside her before she'd finished her sentence. He didn't ask why she was there, what it was about, just hugged her.

'Don't hang about in the passageway, come into the warm. Sit with me on the sofa and when you're ready tell me what's wrong.'

After a few steadying breaths, Emily blurted out everything Sammy had told her and what had happened upstairs with the mouse. He listened without interrupting as he always did. Then he smiled and the lump in her chest began to go.

'There's no need to worry, sweetheart, your mother and I know about this. The school got in touch with us a couple of weeks ago. Fighting is so out of character for George that even though he wasn't thought to be the instigator they were initially concerned he was being bullied by the older boys.'

'Have you spoken to him? Asked why he wants to fight? I know we've had a few scraps in the past but he's never been a violent boy.' She frowned as something else occurred to her. 'Where did he learn to punch people? If he's been winning fights against bigger boys then he must have learnt from somewhere.'

'He joined a boxing club at school at the beginning of the school term. It seems he's rather good at it and the boys he's been fighting are older club members.'

This didn't make any sense to Emily. Why was Daddy so relaxed about things? 'I don't understand why George didn't tell me. Sammy didn't mention the boxing club – I'm assuming he doesn't go to it.'

'They had a choice and George chose boxing and Sammy does fencing. I'm surprised you didn't know that. We've noticed that you've grown apart recently and that's a shame.'

'I've one foot in the grown-up camp whereas George and Sammy are still boys. I spend my free time with my own friends now. Also, as we've stopped visiting Nancy until the nights are lighter again, the boys and I hardly spend any time together at all.'

'I'll speak to George about being so bloodthirsty. He's been warned that fighting anywhere but the club's forbidden. The three of you are going over on the ferry on Saturday to that party so you'll have plenty of time to talk about it then.'

A gust of wind and rain made the sitting-room windows rattle. 'Golly, I don't envy Mr Hatch and Lucinda being out in this weather. I think I'll put a hot water bottle in her bed so I'm going to do it now. Then it'll be cosy when she goes to bed.'

* * *

Lucinda wasn't exactly regretting her impulsive decision to become an ARP warden as since she'd started spending the nights patrolling the blacked-out streets of Wivenhoe her life at Harbour House had become so much better.

Every morning when she tottered into the house, a thermos of cocoa and a sandwich wrapped carefully in greaseproof paper was waiting for her on the kitchen table. There was also a rubber hot water bottle – not one of the china ones – warming up her bed and a fire would be burning, making her bedroom absolute bliss after trudging round the streets in the blistering cold all night. Jonathan must have made an exception for her as fires weren't usually allowed in the bedroom.

On Friday night, as she pulled on her overalls over her clothes, Emily came into the scullery with the last of the plates from the dining room.

Lucinda had no idea who was making her life so much easier by lighting the fire in her bedroom and making her a hot water bottle. This angel must be getting up at dawn to do this and also to fill up the thermos with cocoa and make the sandwich which were always waiting on the kitchen table.

'Is it you making my life so comfortable, Emily? I can't tell you what a difference it makes to know someone's thinking about me whilst I'm miserable and cold and doing my duty all right.'

'It is, but I don't want your thanks as you deserve it. I'm not sure I'd have volunteered. When you become a WAAF next spring it'll seem like a walk in the park after what you're doing now.'

'I jolly well hope so. I know it's unpatriotic, but I sometimes wish there would be a fire, a bomb dropped somewhere, an accident – anything to break the monotony would be good.'

Emily giggled. 'I still think on balance you're better off being miserable and wet on your own than knitting socks for sailors with the WI or doing something even more boring with the WVS.'

Lucinda joined in the laughter. 'My idea of absolute hell. I hope the weather improves for you tomorrow or the three of you are going to get as wet as I do every night when you go over to Rowhedge for your party.'

'Penny's mother has found us all a change of clothes so it won't matter if we do get wet. Hopefully, as we're going to be there a long time, our own things will be dry when we need them.'

Lucinda plonked her black metal helmet on her head and pulled the chinstrap tight. If she didn't do this it would fall off. 'Right, I'd better get going. I'm hoping that at least I'll get a few houses showing illegal light so I can shout at them. I've had only two of those so far. I bet there would be more in London.'

'There would, but you would also have bombs dropping on you every night and on balance I think it's better to be bored than blown up. Are you up for a game of Monopoly tomorrow night?'

'Absolutely, but only if I can be the top hat.'

* * *

It took Lucinda an hour to complete her patrol and on her second circuit she got her wish that something exciting would happen. She was just walking past the Greyhound, which sounded livelier than usual, when the noise level escalated.

Something was going on and it sounded as if there was a fight. She wasn't a member of the constabulary, therefore it wasn't her business to interfere in anything apart from ARP business.

She was watching from the other side of the street in front of the tobacconist when the door to the lower bar crashed open. The light poured out into the street, closely followed by three drunken locals attempting, from the look of it, to kill each other.

'Close the door. Do you want a bomb dropped on you, you stupid men? The Germans will be able to see you from miles away.' Her voice carried wonderfully and someone inside had the sense to slam the door shut.

However, despite the freezing rain and the fact that it was as dark as a dungeon, the three idiots from the pub sounded as if they were continuing their brawl.

Lucinda pulled the tape from the end of the torch so she got the full beam. Being able to see trumped the remote chance a German bomber would be flying overhead and see the light.

One of the men was sprawled half on the pavement, half in the road. He wasn't moving. The other two continued to yell and aim wild punches at each other.

She ran across and kicked one of them in the backside as hard as she could. This got his attention wonderfully well. He swung a beefy fist at her and his language made her ears burn. She'd been expecting a reaction like this and jumped aside easily.

'Stop this right now. I don't care who's to blame or what it's about, but the other man is unconscious and needs urgent medical attention.'

It was as if she'd tipped a bucket of icy water over their heads. Both belligerents scrambled to their feet and followed the beam of her torch.

'Den, come on, don't play the fool, open your eyes, you silly bugger,' one of them said as he dropped to his knees.

'Excuse me, sir, I'm a trained first-aider and I need to examine him. One of you go immediately to Dr Cousins and say that the patient's unconscious and has possibly a severe neck injury. Ask him to call for an ambulance.'

'I'll go, miss, sorry for the language.' The man was up and running, his heavy boots clattering on the road. Everybody knew where the doctor lived, and it was only a minute away.

The other man had staggered across to Clifton Terrace and, from the sound of it was being very sick indeed. Lucinda shuddered – she could deal with cuts, broken bones, and blood but not that.

She checked that the man had a pulse, he had but it was thready and weak. She carefully ran her hands along his limbs, making sure she didn't move him. As far as she could tell he hadn't broken anything but he'd hit his head on the kerb when he'd gone down and head injuries were the very worst.

From her knees, she leaned up and hammered on the door. 'There's a man critically injured here. Possible severe neck injury. I need blankets to try and keep the rain off him.'

'We'll bring him in, miss, he'll do better inside,' the shadowy figure hovering by the blackout told her.

'No, he mustn't be moved until the doctor has examined him. He has to stay here.' She pointed at the sandbags piled on either side of the door. 'Give me those and I'll use them to stabilise his head.'

* * *

By the time the doctor arrived with his bag in one hand and a torch in the other, the unconscious man had been painstakingly covered in blankets and then a tarpaulin had been tucked under him and wrapped around so he wasn't lying in a puddle or getting any wetter from the rain. The men who'd helped her understood that the slightest jar to the unfortunate man's neck could prove fatal. The sandbags had, she prayed, provided the necessary support.

The doctor bounded up beside her. Lucinda explained what she'd done. 'I know I shouldn't have moved him at all but I was worried that being wet through and cold would lessen his chances of surviving.'

He pointed at the sandbags. 'Good girl, you've done exactly the right thing,' Dr Cousins said as he crouched beside the patient and carefully checked him over. 'We can't move him until the ambulance arrives. A doctor from the hospital will bring a cervical collar – I don't have one myself.'

'There's not a lot one can do for this sort of injury, is there? If he recovers, will he be paralysed?'

'If his neck's broken then he's unlikely to recover. However, as you had the good sense not to move him, he might survive this. Would you shine your torch so I can administer some pain relief? I don't want him to move if he does regain consciousness.'

'I don't know if I'm supposed to stay here as this is a real emergency or if I should be continuing with my patrol.'

'I can take it from here, Miss Somiton, you continue with your patrol.'

She was turning to go when she remembered the other man. She could no longer hear any hideous retching noises.

'I'd better check on the man who was vomiting. He's ominously quiet.'

'No, I'll get someone from the pub to do that. It's not in your purview.'

'Thank you, Dr Cousins, I'd better put the tape back on my torch before I go. I've been breaking every regulation for the last twenty minutes.'

She was walking past the Station Hotel when she was pretty sure she heard the ambulance arrive. Obviously, there was no need for them to ring the bell as there was no other traffic. Also, sound carried at night and possibly could be heard thousands of feet above them by a passing German bomber or fighter.

* * *

The remainder of that night's patrol was uneventful, but when Lucinda eventually staggered into Harbour House it took her some time to enter the details of the emergency in her logbook. Gratefully, she drank the entire flask of cocoa and gobbled down the sandwich before stumbling up to her warm bed.

4

Emily woke up determined to enjoy every minute of the day ahead. It was still dark but she was pretty sure it was no longer raining and the wind had dropped too. That probably meant it would be much colder going to Rowhedge, but that was preferable to being wet as well as cold.

Not wanting to wake anyone else, she dressed quietly in her warmest clothes and then, in slippered feet, crept down the attic stairs. Grace was beginning to grizzle. She'd collect the baby and take her down and give her parents a much-needed lie-in. Daddy had finally arranged to have a weekend free – it had been months since he'd had even a whole day off.

'Good morning, little one, do you want to go downstairs and have some breakfast?' Emily said to the baby, who immediately stopped crying, rolled over and began to pull herself upright on the cot bars.

'Clever girl, but I think you're a bit whiffy. I'm going to change your bottom and get you dressed before we go down.'

Grace gurgled happily and held out her hands to be picked up. Emily held her at arm's length, trying not to gag. An extremely unpleasant ten minutes later, her sister was in a clean nappy. Rubber pants went over the top to keep the worst of the wet from seeping out.

'Right, Grace, if you'll stop wriggling for a minute I'll put on your vest and leggings.' Emily put the baby on the ground to crawl about whilst she selected a romper suit. A frock was no use at all now the baby was so mobile.

The one she chose was pink, with long sleeves and a Peter Pan collar and had hand embroidered ducks and geese on the bodice. On top of that went a thick knitted matinee jacket in a darker shade of pink.

'There, all done, sweetheart, let's get to the kitchen which will be warmer and you can sit in your highchair whilst I get the range going.'

Grace was quite happy to bang the tray of the highchair with a wooden spoon whilst Emily worked. The scullery window clattered which meant Ginger was back and she hoped he hadn't brought in anything alive like he had last week. Dead ones she could manage, but not anything alive.

The baby recognised the sound too and tried to swivel around in her highchair, squealing with excitement. She loved the cat and now she was bigger Ginger seemed to be taking more interest in her.

The cat stalked in, tail erect, and whatever he'd brought in with him he'd sensibly left in the scullery. Lily would deal with it when she got here at seven. The kitchen clock showed it wasn't quite six o'clock – nobody would be up for another hour at least.

'Good morning, Ginger, I'm just making porridge. Would you like some?'

The cat wove in and out of her legs, making it difficult to work. Emily wasn't exactly sure if porridge was good for cats but Ginger loved it. Probably it was against the law to feed human food to a pet – it was certainly forbidden to put even a crust out for any birds.

She carefully tied on Grace's voluminous bib and tucked it firmly between the baby's tummy and the highchair. Her sister was at the age where she wanted to try and feed herself, but it was a messy business. Usually, Mummy spooned whatever it was into Grace's mouth but this morning Emily decided to allow her sister to have a go.

After pouring herself a much-needed mug of tea, spooning an overgenerous amount of porridge into the cat's dish in the scullery, she was ready to face the inevitable chaos caused by Grace being allowed a spoon and a bowl of porridge.

* * *

It took longer to clean the mess from every surface within throwing distance of the highchair than it had to make it.

'There, not a speck on you, the furniture or the floor. Here's your spoon, darling, you bang it whilst I make us both some toast.'

Emily took the baby into the sitting room where the fire was lit and the fireguard hooked into place, when Lily appeared at the door with a lovely mug of tea.

'It's perishing out there, but at least it's not raining today. I've got a tray for your parents, Emily, I'll watch the baby for you whilst you take it up,' Lily said.

'What a treat for them, I can't remember when they last had the luxury of early-morning tea in bed. Ginger brought in something, but I haven't dared look.'

'Rabbit pie tonight for all of us. I brought three eggs from our chickens, and I'll make a nice Victoria sandwich.'

'Sounds scrumptious.' Emily took the tray from Lily and was

surprised there was no sound of anyone moving around in any of the bedrooms. Lucinda would sleep until lunchtime after her late-night patrolling, the boys always had a lie-in at the weekend, but her parents were usually up by now.

She hesitated outside the door, not sure if she should leave them to sleep or wake them up with the tea. Nothing should be wasted so there was no option but to knock.

'Mummy, Daddy, I've got tea and biscuits for you. Shall I bring it in, leave it outside or take it back downstairs?'

There was no answer for a few moments and then Daddy called out. 'Bring it in, sweetheart, if you don't mind.'

Emily carefully balanced the tray on one arm whilst she unlatched the door. 'I got Grace up at half past five and she's had breakfast and is playing with her bricks whilst Lily watches her in the sitting room.'

The hall light spilled into the bedroom and she almost dropped the tray. Daddy was sitting up in bed and had absolutely no clothes on his top. Mummy remained hidden under the covers and didn't say a word.

'I'll put the tea on this table. No need to hurry down,' she said and backed out, her cheeks scarlet.

Doris had explained to her in some detail what a man and a woman did together in bed. It all sounded awkward and embarrassing and not at all to her taste. However, she did know it required both participants to remove their garments.

She was halfway down the stairs before her heart stopped hammering. Imagine if she'd walked in without knocking – that would have been even more embarrassing. Lily must have seen how pink Emily's face was but didn't comment. Having to explain would have been even worse than what she'd seen.

'Ta for getting things ready in the kitchen, Emily. Did you hear any movement from the boys?'

'No, all quiet. Lucinda didn't rinse the flask and plate as she always does. I hope she's all right.'

'I'm not surprised after the night she had.'

Emily listened wide-eyed as Lily told her what had occurred outside the Greyhound.

'Golly, she said she wanted something exciting to happen but I'm sure it wasn't that. I hope whoever it was that was so badly hurt is okay. Does anyone know what the fight was about?'

'My Patrick was in the pub playing darts when it happened. The three were drunk; he said they only arrived in the village a few days ago so he doesn't know much about them.'

'Are they some of the new men who have come to work in one of the yards? Daddy told us he's short of men as there's so much work now Vospers, the other shipyard downriver, is running as well.'

'They aren't at Patrick's yard so must be at Vospers. Right, I'd better get on, are you and Grace having a second breakfast?'

'Yes, please, I only managed half a slice of toast but Grace doesn't need anything substantial, just a biscuit and some warm milk would be lovely.'

'The boys asked if they could have the rest of the apple crumble for breakfast, there's enough for three, would you like that or more toast and porridge?'

'Yes, please, Lily, I need something filling before braving the foul weather and the ferry.'

* * *

Emily and her brothers, warmly wrapped in winter coats, wellingtons on over two pairs of socks, balaclavas pulled down over their heads, set out for Rowhedge before their parents came down. Grace had been returned to her cot for a nap and when she woke Mummy or Daddy would take care of her. She wondered if they'd deliberately stayed upstairs to avoid seeing her. Whatever the reason, and she tried not to think about it, by the time she returned it would have been forgotten.

* * *

Lucinda was woken by a soft tap on the door. Lily called out to her.

'I've got your lunch on a tray, Miss Somiton. Mrs Roby thought you might like to have it in bed today.'

Lucinda yawned loudly and hopped out of bed. 'Thanks, Lily. That's so kind of all of you. Hang on a minute, I'm coming.'

She collected the tray, thanked the housekeeper, and put it on the table she used as a desk. The room wasn't exactly warm but definitely not freezing, even though the fire that had been lit before she came home had almost gone out. There were a few logs in the coal scuttle and she threw all of them on the embers and prayed that they'd catch.

Before examining the tray, she arranged her two pillows, plus one of the cushions from her armchair, against the headboard so she had something to lean on. Only as she settled back with her lunch with the tray across her lap did she notice the letter from Ralph was tucked under the mug of tea.

She wasn't going to let her delicious lunch go cold just to read that man's letter. There was a steaming bowl of vegetable soup as well as a plate of bubble and squeak with lashings of chutney.

She devoured every morsel and drained the mug. After carefully putting the tray on the floor, she picked up the envelope, still undecided about opening it or burning it. If Ralph was no longer important to her then why was she hesitating? What could he possibly say that would be of any interest to her? She might as well open it and see for herself. There were three closely written pages, he obviously had a lot to say.

Lucinda,

If you haven't torn this up and thrown it into the fire then I hope that curiosity if nothing else has led you to read it.

There's nothing I can say that will make things better. What Leone did was unforgivable – you were the innocent party and yet you took all the blame.

I was obliged to go home to sort out the mess as best I could. I made the necessary financial arrangements to support my wife and children and then told her that I wanted a divorce. I was the guilty party so she could do so without sullying her reputation.

As we'd been living apart for more than two years – not officially separated but no longer cohabiting – I thought that she'd be prepared to go along with this, to accept the generous settlement, and set me free from a marriage that was a mistake from the start.

How wrong I was – she refused to countenance a divorce or even a legal separation. She told me quite plainly that I'd never be free of her, that I could never marry you as I want to.

I've left her anyway; I have told friends, family and my employers at the War Office that I've left her. I would have it printed in The Times *if I thought that might help.*

I should never have fallen in love with you, had an affair with you, it was reprehensible behaviour and I know that you'll never forgive me.

I just wanted you to know that I intended to tell you the situation before we became intimately involved but events overtook us and then it was too late.

I ruined your life, I know that. I returned to London in the hope of seeing you, of trying to explain my perfidy, only to find that you'd been banished.

It has taken me five weeks to find out where you are. I know of Jonathan Roby; he's a good man so I can be sure that he is taking care of you.

I understand that I can't see you again whilst I'm still a married man. I just wanted you to know that when I said that I loved you, I meant it, I'll always mean it.

I have instructed my solicitor to start divorce proceedings. I'm hoping that when I'm no longer married you will give me a second chance.

Lucinda read the letter several times before its contents registered. She flopped back on the pillows clutching the paper, couldn't prevent the tears and wasn't sure why she was crying. She'd vowed not to shed another tear over that man and here she was doing exactly that. Once she'd started, she couldn't stop, and weeks of pent-up emotion poured out in ugly gasping sobs.

'Oh, my dear girl, what's wrong?' Elizabeth must have heard the crying and come to investigate.

Unable to answer through her tears, she held out the letter. Her cousin took it and sat on the end of the bed to read it. This gave Lucinda time to recover her composure, blow her nose and wipe her face.

'I thought I'd lost him, Elizabeth, that I'd never see him again. I can't believe he's going to get a divorce so he can marry me.'

Elizabeth carefully folded the pages and pushed it back into the envelope before speaking. 'Do you know what's going to happen when this gets to court?'

Lucinda shook her head. 'I expect my name will be mentioned but I'm already a scarlet woman so I can't think it matters. There are more important things happening right now than me being named in the divorce petition.'

'I don't think you quite understand, my dear. If Mrs Castleton doesn't want to be divorced then it will go to court and you'll have to appear. You'll be cross-examined, what little reputation you have left will be stripped from you.'

This wasn't the reaction she wanted or had expected. 'You don't understand, Elizabeth, he's giving up everything for me. It won't just be my reputation that's talked about, it will be his.'

'I'm sorry, Lucinda, but I think if Mr Castleton genuinely loved you then he'd at least let things settle down for a year or two and not be forcing the issue so publicly.'

Lucinda was about to argue but Elizabeth held up her hand.

'Think about it, no decent man would have put you in that position in the first place. You didn't know he was married but he certainly did and yet he still seduced you. No, don't shake your head, you were seduced. That's what it's called when an innocent girl ends up in bed with an experienced older man.'

Hearing what she thought of as a wonderful, loving relationship described so coldly put things in a different light.

'I suppose when you state the facts so baldly it must make me re-evaluate what happened. But surely, Elizabeth, if he's risking getting dismissed from his important position it proves that he loves me?'

'There's a grain of truth in that. Maybe I've underestimated his character, but I haven't changed my mind. He might love you as much as he says he does, but it's a selfish kind of love. Jonathan would never put me through what he intends to put you through.'

'Can I stop him? Can I refuse to appear in court if it comes to that? I really don't want to bring further embarrassment and disgrace to my family, especially you and Jonathan who have been so kind to me.'

'I don't actually know whether you can prevent him naming you in the petition. I'll talk to Jonathan and see what he says. It might be better if I did it whilst you're up here – less likelihood of things being said in the heat of the moment.'

Obviously, Elizabeth didn't mean that Jonathan would say something intemperate, but that Lucinda was likely to if she heard something she didn't agree with.

'All right. Do you think I should reply to the letter or throw it in the fire?'

'Neither, Lucinda, it might be needed as evidence later on. I'll take it with me so Jonathan can read it. I'm sorry that just as you're getting over all the unpleasantness Mr Castleton has upset you again.'

Her cousin had the letter in her hand as she stood up. It was a personal letter, showing it to Elizabeth was different as she was family and a woman. Having Jonathan read it was quite another thing and Lucinda wasn't going to let that happen.

'No, please, Elizabeth. I'd rather Jonathan didn't read it. It's private, it's not up to you to show it to anybody else.'

'I beg your pardon, I overstepped. Here you are, put it some-where safe just in case you need it later.'

* * *

Lucinda regretted having shown the letter to Elizabeth. This wouldn't have happened if her cousin hadn't walked in whilst she was sobbing. But there was nothing she could do about it and right now the contents were being shared with Jonathan as well.

Instead of getting up, Lucinda turned out the bedside light and snuggled back under the blankets and eiderdown. She'd only had seven hours' sleep and another two or three would do her good.

Eventually, she rose, washed and dressed. She always cleaned her teeth in the washroom and WC downstairs and headed that way as soon as she was ready. She was halfway down the stairs when she remembered she'd left her tray so reversed and went to fetch it.

The house was quiet. The children, she remembered, were out for the day visiting a friend over the river. Grace must be asleep and Lily only worked for the morning on Saturday. Presumably, Jonathan and Elizabeth were in the sitting room – as the door was kept closed to keep the heat in she could nip past and use the facilities without having to speak to them.

She was busy in the kitchen making herself a sandwich and a pot of tea when Elizabeth arrived.

'Good, are you feeling better after your lovely sleep?'

'More rested, yes, thank you for asking. I've just made tea – do you and Jonathan want a cup?'

'No, thank you, we had one a little while ago. We were beginning to be concerned when you didn't come down.'

'I'm tickety-boo now, I needed the extra time in bed to make up the hours I've missed over the week. I can't tell you how happy I am not to have to go out for two nights. I don't know how Mr Hatch was managing to be a postman every day and be out every night.'

'He only delivers the morning post so was able to sleep in the afternoon. But you're right, he's not a young man and having you take over the weeknights will make his life so much easier. The young man that you rescued last night hasn't broken his neck, thank God, he's just suffering from a severe concussion. Dr Cousins came round and told us what you did – we're very proud of you.'

'I'm a bit proud of myself. I'll drink my tea and eat my sandwich and then come through. Would you like me to meet the children from the ferry? It won't be running after dark so they'll have to come back by four.'

'Are you sure? That only gives you half an hour to eat.'

'I'd be happy to. I'll also take charge of supper. I know it's rabbit pie, vegetables and that scrumptious-looking Victoria sandwich for dessert.'

Keeping busy kept her from thinking about the letter. She also wanted to show her family that she was a reformed character, that the Lucinda she was now was the real one.

5

Emily and her brothers didn't enjoy the freezing, rough crossing from Wivenhoe to Rowhedge across the River Colne on the ferry that Saturday morning.

'Blooming heck,' George said as they disembarked their teeth chattering. 'Coming back's going to be even worse. I've changed my mind, I'm going home now before it gets rougher and colder.'

Sammy grabbed his arm and yanked him away from the hard. 'No, you're not, you're coming with us as we've promised to go to the party.'

Emily intervened before it became physical. George had already clenched his fists.

'It's too late, George, as Doris is already waiting for us.'

The boys liked Doris, especially Sammy. Emily thought her friend reminded him of his previous life in London's East End.

George looked even more grumpy but didn't turn tail and hurry back to the ferry before it returned to Wivenhoe.

'Good to see you, Doris, I'm almost looking forward to this so-called party. We've got indoor shoes and homemade cards, plus the boys have very kindly donated a jigsaw as a gift.'

'You twisted my arm, Emily, or I wouldn't have given it. Anyway, it's a picture of teddy bears on a picnic and we're too old for it,' George said grumpily.

This was hardly gracious and she was about to tick him off but he ran on ahead with Sammy, leaving her to walk with Doris.

'Crikey, he's in a bad mood. Who pulled his chain?'

'He's in trouble for fighting in the playground and has been suspended from the boxing club until next year.'

'He doesn't look like no fighter, but he does have a temper on him. He'll ruin the boys' party if he's grumpy all day.'

'We're all really cold after the crossing. I'm hoping he'll be fine as he warms up – running all the way to Penny's house should do the trick.'

'It's perishing, and Nan reckons it might snow this afternoon. I ain't running, but you go ahead if you want to.'

'No, I'd rather talk to you. Anything new from the big house?'

'I should say so, it's the talk of the village. Those women had half a dozen soldiers up there for a party the other night. They never went home until the morning neither. Nan was scandalised and said those women are tarts and shouldn't be allowed to have those kiddies living with them.'

'I'm not sure what a tart in that context means, I'm guessing that they're being intimate with men for money.'

'Spot on, Emily. I'd not want to do it, not for money nor nothing else,' Doris said. 'When I get married I'll have to, but I ain't indulging in any hanky-panky before then. Jill's sister just had a baby and there's not a husband in sight.'

'Sorry, do I know Jill?' Sometimes Doris talked about village friends, forgetting that Emily didn't know any of them.

'Right, Jill's a bit slow, if you get my drift, but ever so nice. She lives in the cottage next door to us and is a bit older than me. If someone was going to get caught out like that I'd have thought it would be her.'

'I see, what will happen to the baby?'

'I reckon they'll keep it, it's a boy, not been one of those in the family for years.'

Emily knew roughly how babies were conceived but not the actual details. Why would a girl want to do it when there was a risk there could be an unwanted baby? Doris was more worldly than her and took such things in her stride.

They arrived outside Penny's house and were surprised to find the boys waiting for them.

'Why didn't you knock and go in?' Emily asked.

George grinned and looked his old self. 'Wanted to wait for you two slow coaches. Sorry for being so ratty, I don't like being cold.'

'No one does, let's get inside. I hope the twins aren't overexcited by it being their birthday,' Emily said to the back of his head as he raced to the door and hammered loudly on it.

* * *

The day was such good fun, if a little noisy. There was jelly and custard as well as cake to go with the jam sandwiches. They played pass the parcel, blind man's buff and musical chairs. Penny's mum had to re-wrap the same things in the same brown paper so that the twins could play pass the parcel four times. Blind man's buff and musical chairs were equally popular and even the overactive twins were exhausted by three o'clock.

'Thank you so much for coming,' Penny said as the three of them got ready to leave. 'It's a pity little Jimmy didn't come – I wonder why as he was very excited when I invited him the other day.'

'I'll call in on me way home and see what's what,' Doris offered.

'Thank you, that would be kind. I'm going to keep his piece of cake here for him to collect.'

'We better get a move on, Emily, so stop yapping with your friends,' George said. 'It's going to be dark in twenty minutes and we promised we'd be back by then.'

'I'm coming. Thank your mother for inviting us, Penny, and I'll see you at school on Monday.'

Emily first hugged Penny and then said goodbye. Doris was waiting in the middle of the lane. 'It's your turn to come to me next Saturday, Doris, so if you can't make it will you please tell Penny?'

'Nothing's going to stop me, I love coming to Harbour House. Shame Penny can't come next week as well.'

'They've got an ancient aunt visiting from Colchester. She's not seen the twins for over a year as they're too volatile to take on the bus.'

Even the boys hugged Doris as they really liked her. The three of them almost ran down the hill and only just made it as the ferry was about to leave.

'Look, Lucinda's come to meet us. I didn't like her at first,' George said as they were approaching the riverbank where the ferry would drop them. 'But I think she's okay now.'

'So do I,' Sammy agreed. 'She's a bit of all right, very glam and posh. Not like the back end of a bus like what some of them girls are.'

Usually her adopted brother sounded exactly like George when he spoke but occasionally, after he'd spent time with Doris, he sometimes reverted to his East End vocabulary.

Lucinda had a scarf wrapped around her face and a woolly hat pulled down over her ears so she was barely recognisable. It was her mink coat that made her stand out in a crowd. Emily wasn't quite sure how she felt about someone parading around in Wivenhoe in a coat that was worth more than most people made in wages in an entire year, if not a decade.

The boys raced off, eager to get home and out of the cold, leaving her to walk at a more ladylike pace the short distance from the river to the house.

'Why don't you sell your mink, Lucinda? You could buy a lovely one made from rabbit fur and then you wouldn't be short of money,' Emily suggested.

'I say, that's a spiffing idea. I don't know why I didn't think of it myself. There's no point in trying to sell it here, I'll take it up to London next Saturday. It came from Harrods and I'm pretty sure they'll be delighted to buy it back from me.'

'There was plenty of party food, but I didn't eat much, I wanted to make sure the boys and the twins had what they wanted.'

'That was kind of you. I'm in charge of supper tonight and I promise it's going to be scrumptious. Is that what you wanted to know?'

'I suppose it was. I can't remember the last time we all sat down together to a meal and I can't wait. Actually, I don't really like jam sandwiches and jelly and custard so doing without wasn't a hardship.'

As they were walking down Alma Street – or The Cut as this end was called – Ginger suddenly jumped onto the wall and meowed. Emily shot sideways, collided with Lucinda and for a few seconds they stumbled about, trying to regain their balance.

'You ridiculous cat, why do you do that?' Emily said once they were upright and reached out to stroke him. His purrs echoed down the road.

'I'm more a dog person myself, but your Ginger's beginning to grow on me. He's definitely got a sense of humour.'

To her surprise, the cat jumped onto Emily's shoulder and draped himself around her neck like a big, warm, orange scarf. She was glad it wasn't very far to the back door as he weighed a ton but she didn't like to turf him off when he was being so friendly.

Emily left Lucinda in the kitchen and, after carefully hanging up her coat and putting her wellingtons in the correct place, she headed to the sitting room to see her parents and hopefully her baby sister too.

* * *

Lucinda sat at the dinner table, surrounded by chattering family, and for the first time in her life felt loved and that she belonged. The children took it in turns to go to the bottom of the stairs and listen out for the baby without being asked. It didn't matter to them that they were a decade or more older than their new sibling, they loved her more if anything. Unlike Lucinda's older sister and brother, who had not exchanged more than a few sentences with her ever.

'Lucinda, is there any more gravy lurking in the kitchen so we can finish up this splendid pie?' Jonathan asked.

'There is. I left it to keep warm in the saucepan on the range so what I've got to do is fill up the gravy boat again. I won't be a minute.'

The huge ginger tomcat greeted her with a purr and tugged at the leg of her slacks. 'What do you want, silly boy?'

The cat nudged her still with a mouthful of her trousers. Light dawned.

'You want something to eat. I'm sorry, I should have fed you and I quite forgot I'm not quite au fait with everything in the kitchen.'

Emily spoke from behind her. 'You're definitely one of the family now whether you like it or not, Lucinda, as Ginger's decided he likes you and you're talking to him just like one of us.'

Lucinda, for the first time in her life, felt she belonged somewhere, that she was genuinely loved and wanted.

'I wonder if you'd be allowed to come with me next Saturday, Emily, we could have lunch at the Savoy if I managed to sell my coat.'

The girl shook her head. 'I'd love to, but it's just not safe. No one goes to London unless they absolutely have to – I should never have suggested that you did. There's a smashing department store, Williams, in Colchester and they've got a very grand section where all the rich ladies go to buy expensive things. I bet they'd be delighted to buy your mink coat – you might not get quite as much as you would at Harrods, but you wouldn't have to put your life at risk, which must be worth a lot more than a few pounds.'

'What a sensible young lady you are – I was still a giddy girl at your age with the most enormous crush on the head girl at my boarding school.'

'I don't think I even know the name of the head girl at my school as the lower school is in Greyfriars House and upper school is at the top of North Hill. The head prefect at our school is only a couple of years older than us so maybe the babies in the prep school have crushes on them but we certainly don't.'

'Heaven knows why we're talking about school when we came out here to get gravy.'

'You do that, Lucinda, I'll feed the cat. I know what he likes.'

* * *

As it was a special occasion – the first time they'd all sat together and Lily had made a cake – Jonathan said the adults would have coffee to go with it. Emily triumphantly carried the cake to the table to a round of applause and she brought up the rear with a tray holding a magnificent silver coffee pot and matching paraphernalia.

'Here, my dear, let me get that, it weighs a ton,' Jonathan said as she stepped into the room.

'Thank you, I'll just fetch the second tray with tea for Emily and her brothers.'

The cake was even more delicious than it looked and having it with real coffee and not the vile liquid ersatz coffee, Camp, made mostly from acorns, rounded off the meal perfectly.

Lucinda had promised to play Monopoly and expected to be doing it in the dining room but Elizabeth had other ideas.

'It's much warmer in the sitting room and Jonathan and I are going to play as well. It will be the first time since we purchased our Monopoly game that we have six players so all the tokens can be used.'

'We've got a cannon, boot, battleship, top hat, iron and thimble,' George announced proudly. 'It's a good job Mummy and Daddy bought the game before the war, otherwise we'd have cardboard or wooden pieces to play with.'

'I've the most frightful admission to make,' Lucinda said. 'I've rarely played and don't know a lot about it. The only board games we had at school were snakes and ladders, ludo and chess.'

'It's very easy, very long and usually very exciting,' Emily told her. 'I can't remember a game where one of us doesn't get extremely cross. The first time George played he tipped the board over because he lost and was sent to bed in disgrace.'

George wasn't upset by this revelation and grinned. 'I was only seven, I wouldn't do it now.'

Sammy nudged him. 'No, but you would cheat if you could get away with it.'

'I can't promise that I won't do so again, sometimes being devious is the only way to win.'

'Horrible boy,' Jonathan said, laughing, and ruffled his hair. 'I'm going to make you sit between your mother and me and that way we can keep an eye on your shenanigans.'

It didn't take long to clear the table as Lucinda, Elizabeth and Emily did it together. They stacked the dishes in the scullery sink as the washing-up would be done in the morning before church. The cake was put in the tin, not to keep the mice away as there weren't any, but to make sure that Ginger didn't take a bite.

They transferred to the sitting room in high spirits and Jonathan and the boys had already set the board up on the coffee table which was now placed in the centre of the carpet in front of the fire. There were six cushions to sit on and the only thing left to do was decide who would have which little metal playing piece.

'Each of us will roll the die,' Jonathan said. 'Highest number has first choice – if you roll the same number as somebody else then you roll again.'

George looked a bit cross but accepted this was the fairest way to do things. Lucinda was the only one to roll a six and chose the battleship. Sammy got the cannon which he was pleased about and George got the iron. Only the two boys really cared what they had.

'I'll swap with you, George, if you promise not to cheat,' Lucinda said and winked.

'Done, I always win if I get the battleship so I won't need to cheat.'

* * *

The children retired exhausted but happy, especially Sammy who, for the first time, had triumphed in the game, much to George's disgust. This gave Lucinda an opportunity to talk to Jonathan and Elizabeth.

'I've decided not to answer Ralph's letter. Also, as he works in the War Room, I don't think going there myself to work would be a good idea.'

Jonathan agreed. 'Sensible decision, Lucinda. Will it be the WAAF? There are several interesting trades available for someone with your academic qualifications. You'd fit in well.'

'Did you know that I learned to fly when I was in the sixth form? I can also drive a car, lorry and a tractor.'

Both Elizabeth and Jonathan were paying Lucinda more attention suddenly.

'I've been reading a lot lately about something called the Air Transport Auxiliary. Women have been allowed to join and are helping the RAF with deliveries of parts, people and planes. I'm going to apply to be one of them. They started at the beginning of last year and are now actively looking for new women pilots to join.'

'I've seen pictures of them and they look very smart in their navy uniform. Is it one of the services?' Elizabeth asked.

'No, it's a civilian one. There were originally RAF pilots doing it, but they were needed on active duty,' Lucinda told them. 'They're actively recruiting experienced women pilots right now, and I spent a whole summer flying, have 400 hours in my logbook. I also know how to service a Tiger Moth. I'm hoping that they might think I'm a good choice. I'm going to post my application this week. I don't expect I'll get a test flight, but you never know.'

Jonathan was impressed. 'A pilot, a driver and a mechanic? Not many girls your age have those qualifications. Good luck, I hope they want you.'

'I'll have to prove I can fly well enough first. They'll certainly not contact me before Christmas but I hope I hear soon afterwards. Therefore, I can be an ARP warden until I do hear. Even getting called in for an interview and flight test doesn't mean they'll accept me, but it's worth a try.' She smiled. 'I spent ages over my application letter, I'm hoping Miss Gower, who's in charge, will be impressed.'

'Why didn't you mention this when we talked about what war work you wanted to do the other day?' Elizabeth asked.

'I did know about the ATA but until the other day Miss Gower wasn't taking on any new recruits. As soon as I knew there was a chance for me I applied.'

'It certainly is worth applying. Now, you mentioned earlier selling your mink coat. Take it to Harrods, my dear, if you go up first thing next Saturday then you'll be home before there're any raids,' Elizabeth said. 'You'll get twice the money in Town than you will in Colchester.'

'Emily asked to come with me, but I wouldn't be comfortable taking that risk. That's really why I agreed to go to Williams instead.'

'I thought that was probably the case. You must go on your own,' Jonathan said.

'Then that's what I'll do. Thank you for your support, it means a lot to me.'

* * *

As she fell asleep that night, Lucinda was thinking about the letter and came to an unexpected decision. She'd contact Ralph and ask him to meet her in London. She wanted to tell him how despicable he was, writing a letter wasn't good enough. Face to face was the only way to bring an end to the episode. Whatever she'd said to the contrary, she'd not be able to move on, put the affair behind her, until she'd spoken to him.

6

Emily had been disappointed Lucinda was taking the coat to London and not to Colchester and was worried, after what had happened when Lily and her family had tried to go to Town, that there might be an air raid. Lucinda had left about half an hour ago on a very early train. Hopefully, the mink would sell for tons of money and she'd be pleased. The house was much happier now this new member of the family was making the effort.

Cancelling the visit to Colchester had meant Emily could spend today with her friends as planned. Doris loved being at Harbour House and it would have been mean to deprive her of the visit.

'I'm just going to meet Penny and Doris, Lily, but will come straight back so you can show us what to do for this evening's meal.'

'I managed to get some real sausages, it's amazing what you can exchange for a few cracked eggs.'

'I thought all sausages were real,' Emily said grinning. 'Are you telling me that these ones have some meat in them and aren't mostly breadcrumbs?'

Lily laughed. 'From under the counter, love, they look smashing and smell even better. Do them with bubble and squeak and gravy. No one will complain about that for tea.'

Emily thought that having things from under the counter wasn't as bad as being on the black market, but she wasn't comfortable with the idea that the butcher had saved these sausages for Lily when somebody else who'd got sufficient points should really have had them.

'Don't worry, love, it's all above board. Don't forget your family has a stake in a porker which will be slaughtered in time for Christmas. We'll all have lots of lovely bacon, ham and that then.'

'Please don't talk about it, I love meat, but I don't like the thought of an animal being killed so we can eat it.'

George had wandered into the kitchen in his pyjamas and overheard her last comment.

'Crikey, are you going to be one of those peculiar vegetarians? Imagine – there are people who just eat plants. Can't see how that works.'

'I know feeling sorry for animals is silly. There's absolutely no chance that I'm going to become a vegetarian so don't look so horrified. Why aren't you dressed? I'm going down to the ferry in a minute and you'd better be up when I get back.'

He stuck his tongue out. 'Sammy and I are having a lazy day. It's too foul to go out even to play football so we're staying upstairs. We've got permission to light the fire as well.'

'In which case you're going to get very hungry and thirsty as we're certainly not bringing food to you on a tray and you can't come down to eat as you are.'

His eyes narrowed and for a second Emily didn't recognise him. Since he'd been suspended from his boxing club he'd become even more edgy and bad-tempered than usual.

'I'd like to see you try and stop us coming down as we are.'

'I've no intention of attempting anything physical. I suggest you consider how our parents will react when they hear of your behaviour.'

He shrugged. 'Don't give a hoot, they've already taken away the one thing I really liked. They can't do anything worse than that.'

Emily turned her back on him. When he was in that sort of mood he didn't listen to reason and his bad behaviour would escalate. Then she was flying forward and crashed painfully into the wall and was sliding to the floor. George laughed.

'Serves you right. I hope I hurt you.'

Lily had seen what happened. 'I don't know what's come over you, George Roby, you used to be a nice boy but not any more.' She helped Emily to her feet. 'If that had been my Daphne behaving like that she'd have been put over my knee. Are you hurt, love?'

George, after pushing her over, had vanished upstairs. If he'd still been within arm's reach she might have forgotten her pacifist inclinations and slapped him very hard.

'Only my dignity and my knees, thank you.' Emily straightened, rubbed her knees, and nodded. 'I'd better get a move on or my friends will arrive before I get there.'

* * *

The ferry was just docking at the hard. 'Good morning, you two, thank goodness it's not raining today,' Emily called out as Penny and Doris scrambled out of the boat.

'A bit parky, and my nan still thinks it's going to snow soon,' Doris said.

Emily hugged her friends and they agreed to run back to Harbour House. As soon as they were inside and warm she told them what had just happened with George.

'We'll just keep out of his way, Emily, he's got more sense than to try and bully us,' Penny said.

'He wasn't bullying me, he wouldn't dare, and I wouldn't let him, he was just being absolutely foul. He thinks that having been suspended from his boxing club is the worst thing that can happen to him but after this he'll be in for a very nasty surprise once I've told our parents.'

Lily called them into the kitchen where she'd made a large jug of cocoa.

'Here you are, girls, and it's made with all milk and sugar. I've just made some ginger biscuits and they're warm from the oven especially for you.'

'Golly, that's kind of you. What a treat,' Emily said as the three of them pulled out chairs and sat down.

'Where are your parents and baby sister?' Penny asked as she dipped her biscuit into the cocoa.

'They went into Colchester. I've no idea why, but I think they might be going to see Nancy and Annie.'

Doris had a chocolate moustache and removed it with her hand. 'Both of them worked here a while back, didn't they? I'm that grateful for these slacks what they made me. Ever so kind of them.'

Whilst they were finishing their drink and the biscuits, Lily explained what Emily would have to do for supper. Her friends would already have gone home by then so this didn't really concern them.

'I've made a lovely pot of vegetable soup for your lunch and as a special treat there'll be homemade rolls to go with it.'

'We can do the vegetables, Lily, so once you've finished your other chores why don't you go home? We can take care of everything else,' Emily suggested.

'Ta, I'll do that. Are you going to be all right with the boys?'

'Don't worry about them, there's three of us and we're a lot bigger. I think Mummy said they'd be back for lunch too and I'll hand them over to Daddy to deal with. They certainly won't get any breakfast or any lunch unless they get dressed.'

'I should think not,' Lily agreed.

'We're going to take our cocoa and the last of the biscuits into the sitting room and listen to whatever's on the wireless,' Emily told her.

Once they were settled comfortably in front of the fire, they chatted about the disgraceful families now living in the biggest house in Rowhedge, what was going on in the war and what their plans were for Christmas.

'It's a shame that George and Sammy have blotted their copy books so thoroughly today as we've permission to put up the paper chains and other bits and bobs. I was so looking forward to doing it, to having you both helping, and now George has spoilt it.'

'Do you think that your Sammy's too scared to argue or is just going along with it?'

'You're right, Penny, he might be as disgusted as we are by George's behaviour. He's not aggressive or rude and he might be trapped up there. I think we'd better go and investigate.'

'I ain't going anywhere until I finish me cocoa and biscuits. I reckon these are even better than the ones me nan makes on high days and holidays.'

Ten minutes later, Emily led the way upstairs. She paused outside the boys' door. 'I can hear them talking but not what they're saying,' she whispered.

'I reckon we need to be away from the top of the stairs just in case,' Doris said.

Emily agreed. If George pushed any of them down the stairs that could be really serious.

* * *

Lucinda sat with her precious mink coat, disguised by its silk cover, in her lap in first class. Jonathan had insisted that she didn't travel in second or third in case someone realised what she was carrying and waited to steal it from her when she got off the train. He'd also given her sufficient to take a taxi for the same reason – that's if she was fortunate enough to find one outside the station.

Steam and smoke from the engines filled the air when she alighted at Liverpool Street but there was another smell she didn't at first identify. She glanced at the roof and saw there were large panels of glass missing, the girders that supported them twisted and broken. The station had been bombed recently and there was rubble, broken concrete and the line on the other side of the platform where she'd disembarked was unusable.

Lucinda shivered, regretting her decision to come to London. She didn't really need the money, and she should have waited until things were safer. She clutched her precious parcel to her chest, wondering if she should catch the next train back to Wivenhoe.

Then she looked around at the other passengers. There were a handful of businessmen, dozens in uniform, but as many smartly dressed women in tweed suits, ridiculous hats, and in some cases mink coats, mingling with them and not one of them was in a frightful panic like her.

Slowly her heart returned to normal and she could breathe.

She headed for the taxi rank outside the station. There were two grey-haired matrons just in front of her. She thought she'd ask if they might be going to Harrods too. Oxford Street had been heavily bombed and although the big department stores remained open, Knightsbridge was safer.

Although they looked formidable, they looked at her and smiled. 'Indeed we are, young lady, are you going there too?'

'I am, could I possibly share your cab if you manage to get one?'

'Absolutely, we don't intend to stay more than an hour. Would you like to return with us as well?'

'That would be top hole, thank you so much. I've only got one thing to do as well.'

They emerged into the street and had the good fortune to arrive just as the taxi pulled up. It was one of the ancient pram-hooded cabs with a driver that looked even older than his vehicle.

Lucinda took the pulldown seat as she thought it would be rude to squeeze in between the two smart ladies. As they started and stopped through the streets, she was appalled at the damage that surrounded the station but as they went towards Knights-bridge things were different. So far the Luftwaffe hadn't dropped as many bombs on the wealthy side of London.

The uniformed doorman at Harrods jumped forward to open the door and Lucinda scrambled out first. 'I'll pay for the return journey. Shall I wait here one hour from now?'

'Yes, my dear, do that. I'll arrange for this taxi to return for us. It might be somewhat dilapidated, but beggars can't be choosers,' the lady in the burgundy hat said.

* * *

Lucinda knew exactly where the fur coats were sold and hurried off, praying that someone there would be happy to buy back the coat that she'd selected for herself when she'd left school last year. Her father had paid but as far as she knew he'd not set eyes on the coat.

The carpet was deep, luxurious, and her ankle-length heeled boots sunk into it. She stalked across the expanse of open floor as if she belonged there – she did but no longer wanted to be part of this world. Not because she wasn't a wealthy young woman, even if temporarily short of funds, but because she'd changed and preferred the less rarefied atmosphere of Harbour House and her new family.

An oily salesman glided up to her. 'Can I be of assistance, madam?'

Lucinda was slightly taller than him and enjoyed looking down her nose. 'I don't know, can you?'

She was being deliberately obtuse and he blinked and looked a little less sure of himself. She took pity on him.

'I have a mink coat that came from here last year but I don't need it. I'm about to join the WAAF, I hardly think that anyone in the services owns or wears something of this quality. I have the receipt here.'

His expression changed. 'Please, come this way. Mr Griffiths, the department manager, will be delighted to speak to you.'

He ushered her into the inner sanctum and when the salesman explained the reason for her visit she was greeted warmly. Lucinda handed over the receipt.

'Yes, I remember this purchase. If you'd be kind enough to allow me a few minutes to examine the coat I can tell you what it's worth to us.' He snapped his finger at the salesman who was still hovering in the doorway. 'See that Miss Somiton has coffee and pastries while she waits.'

'Yes, sir, I'll do that immediately. Would you care to follow me, Miss Somiton? You can sit comfortably in the viewing room as it's not being used at present.'

The coffee arrived promptly and was quite delicious, the pastries a little dry but tasty nonetheless. She was just pouring herself a second cup when Mr Griffiths bustled in, beaming.

'Miss Somiton, I expect that you came to us today because you know that we are desperately short of good furs. The demand is still there but we've been unable to offer the selection we usually have.'

Lucinda sat up, trying to look calm, as if she had indeed come in knowing this pertinent fact. 'Well, Mr Griffiths, my mink is top quality. I've rarely worn it so it's like new.'

He nodded so vigorously that his gilt-framed glasses slipped down his nose. 'Exactly so, which is why I'm able to offer you three thousand guineas – more than your father paid for it.'

She almost choked on her biscuit but managed to cough the crumbs into her handkerchief. 'Excellent, then we're both delighted with the transaction.' She smiled; she couldn't help herself. 'Tell me, Mr Griffiths, do you really have women prepared to pay thousands of guineas for a coat in the middle of a war? It hardly seems credible.'

'I cannot tell you her name, but a member of the aristocracy is at the head of our waiting list for a coat exactly like yours. I've examined it minutely and as you say it looks as it did when you purchased it last year.'

'If you could be so kind as to make out a banker's draft in my name, Mr Griffiths, I have a taxi waiting. I am working as an ARP warden at the moment and need to be back on duty as soon as possible.'

'I anticipated your decision, Miss Somiton, and I have it here. Thank you for bringing it to us as I can assure you that any furrier in Town would have been just as eager to buy from you.'

She checked the contents of the envelope, it was correct, and then put it in her handbag. She shook hands with Mr Griffiths and sailed out, scarcely able to believe her good luck. The first thing she needed to do was hide the envelope, leaving it in a handbag was too risky as somebody could snatch it from her. Maybe inside the velvet gas mask cover would be better as nobody would try and take that.

Once safely behind a marble pillar where nobody could see her, she removed the envelope and pushed it inside her blouse, tucking it firmly underneath her bra. It would be uncomfortable but absolutely safe there, even safer than in her gas mask cover.

She glanced at her wristwatch, she was in good time, so could saunter through the department store admiring the expensive items on display. The glass shelves and counters were less full than they had been before the war, but if you had the money there was still plenty to buy.

There were no longer the extravagant displays for pedestrians to gawp at as they walked past, but the window dressers still produced something to look at. The fact that the plate glass was crisscrossed with ugly tape meant it was hard to see what was behind it anyway. The windows couldn't be lit at night which was another reason to keep displays simpler.

When she emerged, the taxi was there but there was no sign of the two ladies she'd travelled with. She walked up to the driver.

'How long are you prepared to wait?'

'Five more minutes, miss, and then we'll have to go.'

'What if I give you half a crown to wait a little longer?'

'Then I'll wait ten minutes. Coppers will be after me if I'm here any longer than that.'

'Thank you. I'm paying this time so shall we sort that out now and save the fuss when we get there?'

She thought if she kept him occupied looking for change they might be able to stay more than the ten minutes he'd agreed.

In the nick of time, the other two passengers hurried up. 'Thank you so much, my dear, for persuading the taxi to wait. We really weren't looking forward to having to catch the underground or, even worse, a bus.'

This time they insisted that she sat between them on the more comfortable leather seat. 'We guessed that you were selling something, was it a very grand coat?'

'It was a mink, full length and silk lined. It seems that the aristocracy is still desperate to have such a thing and are prepared to pay a ridiculous amount to own one.'

'Where are you returning to, my dear?'

'I need to catch a Clacton train.'

'As do we, so we can sit together and you can tell us all about yourself.'

The woman in the ridiculous burgundy hat did all the talking but her companion nodded and smiled appropriately. The last thing Lucinda wanted was to reveal her name or where she lived. She was notorious; even though there hadn't been a photograph of her in the papers her name had been plastered all over the gossip columns.

'That would have been delightful, ladies, but I'm meeting a friend in the refreshment room. A gentleman friend, he's being posted overseas very soon and this might well be the last time I ever see him.'

They smiled, nodded and left to catch the train. Lucinda had written to Ralph and asked him to meet her at midday. If he'd got her letter, she wasn't sure he'd come. She'd deliberately chosen the refreshment room at the station as it was public and would allow her to leave if things become difficult. Ralph could be rather controlling at times and despite her wish to end things properly, tell him she'd no intention of being named in his divorce, she rather regretted arranging this meeting.

What had seemed a reasonable idea in the safety of Harbour House now seemed anything but.

7

Emily banged loudly on the bedroom door. 'Sammy, I want to speak to you. Come out immediately.'

The door was flung open and not by Sammy. George, still not dressed, glared belligerently at her. 'He's not speaking to you and neither am I. You can bugger off, all of you.'

His appalling language made her lose her temper. Her hands shot out and she grabbed him by his pyjamas and lifted him from his feet. She dropped him on the floor in front of Doris and Penny.

'You stop right where you are, you nasty little toad,' Doris said and glowered down at him. 'You move an inch and I'll clobber you. Got it?'

George's face paled. His scowl vanished and he shrank back without a word. He understood that Doris wasn't like his sister, she would thump him without hesitation.

Emily rushed into the bedroom and found Sammy flinging on his clothes. 'I'm sorry, Emily, I never wanted to stay up here. He's gone mad, he scares me. I don't want to share with him when he's like this.'

'Good, hurry up and then you can come down and spend the day with us. He can remain in here until our parents return and can deal with whatever's going on.'

Sammy didn't answer, he ran from the room in bare feet, his socks and slippers in one hand. He fled past George and the girls and was downstairs in seconds.

'You'll stay in your room until our parents return. Daddy can deal with you,' Emily said to George.

'I don't have to do what you say, you're just my sister.'

Doris poked him hard with her foot. 'You do as you're told, matey, or you will have me to answer to. I'm not nice like your Emily.' Doris leaned down and picked George up by the front of his dressing gown. 'You get my meaning?'

He didn't answer but didn't argue either. Penny had opened the bedroom door wide and Doris tossed George in. Her brother landed on his knees; that served him right as he'd done the same to her but with more venom.

Emily slammed the door shut, making things rattle inside. 'He won't come down whilst you're here, Doris, thank you for that. I don't know why he's behaving so badly. I don't recognise him as my little brother, he's like a different person. I'm not surprised that Sammy's frightened of him.'

They'd moved away from the door so could converse without being heard by the culprit. Penny said what Emily was thinking.

'I doubt that he'll try and come after us but unless somebody's permanently watching the stairs he could sneak out the front door – or if we're in the sitting room he could go out of the back.'

'Then let's work out how we can stop him doing that. He's being absolutely horrible at the moment but I don't want him wandering about outside in this weather. Last year Sammy's brother almost died after being outside in the cold all night.'

Penny was examining the door. 'I think if we put some wedges on this side he won't be able to push it open. Do you have anything that would do?'

'There are a couple in the drawer in the kitchen table – the one where we put all the bits and bobs that we don't know what to do with,' Emily said.

Leaving her two friends to guard the door, she raced downstairs, almost colliding with Sammy who was lurking halfway down the passageway that led to the kitchen.

'Goodness me, I could have sent you flying. I've just got to get something from the kitchen and then we'll all be down here. Don't worry, George won't be joining us.'

'I think he's gone doolally, Emily, he's not like my brother any more. Do you think the boxing, being punched in the head, has made him like this?'

'I doubt it, but something's certainly wrong. Our George's still in there somewhere, we won't give up on him, will we?'

Sammy didn't answer, he looked away.

'Has he been bullying you? Has this been going on for a long time?'

Sammy nodded. 'It started when you went to Kent. At first I thought he was just jealous because he hadn't gone, then it got worse when Lucinda started being nice.'

'Are you saying that whilst Lucinda was being so beastly to all of us George stopped being nasty to you?'

'I am, he liked the fact that she was unpopular with everyone.'

'I see. Anyway, it's nothing for you to worry about. I'm sure Mummy will say you can move into one of the empty rooms until things have been sorted out.'

* * *

The little wooden wedges did the trick and Emily was certain George wouldn't be able to escape even if he wanted to. She was concerned that he'd had no breakfast, had nothing to drink in his room, but it would only be until lunchtime, and she was quite sure nobody died from hunger or thirst in so short a time. If he needed the loo then he had the necessary item under his bed.

Although they tried to enjoy their time together, knowing George was upstairs in disgrace, probably hungry and miserable, put a damper on the morning. Emily returned from putting the rolls in the fast oven of the range to bake to find Penny and Doris hovering by the sitting-room door.

'We've decided to go home, Emily, we don't want to be here when your parents get back. It's not fair on George,' Penny said.

'I don't blame you, I'm really sorry as we were all looking forward to spending the day together. Thank you, I didn't like to ask you to leave but it's definitely the best thing for everyone.'

She embraced her friends and they hurried through to the back corridor to collect their outdoor garments and boots. They didn't come back and she heard the door close behind them.

Sammy was huddled in one of the armchairs pretending to read a book. He looked up. 'I like your friends, but I'm glad they're gone. Is it going to be very bad for George? Will he be sent away like my other brother was?'

Emily dropped to her knees and hugged him. 'Of course he won't, silly, he's not a bad boy. Something's wrong but I'm sure our parents will discover what it is and be able to put it right.'

'Does that mean he won't be getting into dreadful trouble?'

'I'm afraid not. He'll have to face the music first and then when he's been forgiven by all of us hopefully, he'll be able to tell us why he's behaving so badly. Bullying you is almost unforgivable – I'm not exactly sure how Daddy will deal with what's happened.'

Even the appetising smell of freshly baked rolls wafting from the kitchen couldn't restore Emily's appetite. Her stomach was churning and she was both dreading her parents' return but also eager to see them.

'I'm going to go for a walk,' Sammy announced as they heard the train that they'd be on steam past the house.

'No, you're not, you've got to be here so you can tell them what's been happening. They need to know everything, not just about today. This is going to be absolutely horrible for all of us and I just hope that Lucinda doesn't come back in the middle of it. We really don't need anyone else to witness this family disaster.'

The next half an hour dragged most dreadfully. 'They'll be back in a few minutes. Let's get the dining-room table laid and everything ready for lunch.'

'We're going to have to tell them before we have lunch, otherwise they'll want to know where George is.'

'I'm not going to serve anything, just get it ready. If we're nervous, imagine how George is feeling right now? He's not a monster, he's our brother and he must be absolutely terrified.'

The pram had to come in through the back door and a few minutes later they heard the door open and the banging and bumping as it was manoeuvred over the step and into the scullery. Sammy pressed himself close to her and Emily put her arm around him.

Daddy walked in and took one look at their faces and his happy smile vanished.

'Your mother's taking Grace up to have a proper nap upstairs. What's going on? Where's George?'

* * *

Lucinda found an empty table tucked away in the corner and ordered a pot of tea for two from the waitress who didn't look old enough to have left school, let alone be waiting at the table.

'You thirsty then, miss?' the girl said with a grin.

'I am, but I'm meeting a friend who should be here at any minute. So please make sure I do have two cups.'

The girl wrote the order painstakingly on her pad with the nub of a well-licked pencil. 'Do you want any toast? We've just had a tray of buns – what about a couple of them?'

'Yes, I'd love two buns, but no toast, thank you.'

'That'll be threepence for the buns and sixpence for the tea. Ninepence altogether.'

Lucinda handed over a shilling. 'Keep the change, thank you.'

'Cor, ta ever so,' the waitress said and dashed off to collect the order.

The tea and buns arrived a few minutes later but there was still no sign of Ralph. Lucinda glanced at the large clock on the wall – it was now ten minutes past midday. She decided that she'd drink her tea and eat the buns and if he hadn't turned up by then she'd leave and never think about him again.

'I'm so sorry, Lucinda, for keeping you waiting. I can't tell you how happy I was to receive your letter.'

She slopped her tea onto the table. 'Goodness, I didn't see you coming. You're only fifteen minutes late and the tea's still hot.'

Whilst he was removing his gloves and trilby she was able to sneak a glance at him. He looked different somehow; she couldn't quite put a finger on it. He didn't use Brylcreem, so his hair wasn't slicked back, his brown curls were flopping over his forehead as usual.

'You've lost weight,' she said as he sat opposite, his usual charming smile absent.

'I have; it's been a difficult few weeks as you might imagine.'

'Certainly for me, as I was the one who was castigated and pilloried, sent to live in the country in disgrace.' Her tone was sharp and something she didn't recognise flashed in his eyes.

'I'm aware of that, of course, and offer my unreserved apologies for a second time that my wife chose to reveal our affair in such a public way.'

'You asked me to marry you before we slept together. I thought we were unofficially engaged, that you were just waiting for the opportune moment to speak to my parents.'

He didn't answer and to fill the awkward silence she strained his tea into the waiting cup and pushed over one of the buns. 'Here you are. I shouldn't have come but I wanted to hear why you'd deceived me. To look you in the eye whilst you tried to explain.'

His knuckles were white, his posture tense. In the few months they'd been together he'd been nothing but loving, charming, funny – this was the first time she'd seen him like this. She wasn't sure if he was angry or embarrassed by her attack.

'I'm going to try and explain why I behaved the way I did. I'd been separated from my wife for several months before we met and had no idea I was going to fall in love with you – I thought we were just going to go out to dinner a few times, see a show, dance at a nightclub. That's why I wasn't honest and when things changed between us it was too late.'

'I see. I still don't understand why you seduced me, you knew I was inexperienced, that if I got pregnant you wouldn't be able to marry me and yet you still did it.'

'I just told you; I was hopelessly in love with you, I wasn't thinking straight. Honestly, I was plucking up the courage to explain when it all blew up in our faces.'

'How old are your children?' Lucinda wasn't sure why she'd

asked this so abruptly but she wanted to know. A decent man wouldn't have abandoned his family in the first place.

'I have two daughters, five and four. I can assure you they don't care either way about my marital situation.'

The children were so young. She was shocked at his casual dismissing of them. Did she want to become a stepmother when she was not even twenty years old?

Suddenly he pushed the bun across to her. 'I'm too upset to eat but you're obviously not.'

'I'm too angry to be upset. I don't want my name plastered over the papers again, I don't want my name mentioned in any divorce petition. If you can manage that, then I might consider seeing you again when you're a free man.'

'Only consider? Please, I need to know that you'll be waiting for me on the other side of this nightmare.'

'I can't promise that I'll resume our relationship, but I will see you again if you manage to do what I've asked. Goodbye, Ralph, good luck.'

His eyes widened. He swallowed and pushed himself to his feet as if he was an old man. 'I wish I hadn't come today, Lucinda, as if I hadn't, I could still hope there might be a chance for me.'

He brushed what could have been a tear from his cheek, rammed his hat on his head and with his gloves in his hand he strode out. She watched him go, wanting to call him back but knowing that would be wrong. She must be strong – have nothing to do with him until he was no longer married.

Her heart was thudding painfully, she wanted to get up and run after him, but it was too late. She was astonished that she actually felt sorry for him when she was the injured party.

The waitress sidled up to the table. 'Shall I put your bun in a bag, miss?'

'Yes, that would be kind. I'll eat it on the train. My friend had to leave for an important meeting.'

There'd been no need to explain Ralph's sudden departure and Lucinda wished she'd not said anything. He'd been different, not quite as she remembered him, but then so was she. Her disgrace and his betrayal had changed her – she wasn't as gullible as she'd been before. That said, he was still a very attractive man and the months they'd been together had been most enjoyable.

Would she be able to trust him if they renewed their relationship? She remembered her nanny saying, 'Once a liar, always a liar.' She had not really understood what this meant as she'd only been a few years old then but now she did, and it gave her pause for thought.

The girl returned with the bag and Lucinda smiled her thanks, tucked it into her capacious handbag, and hurried off across the station in the hope of finding a train that stopped at Wivenhoe.

She glanced at her wristwatch and realised that it was less than twenty minutes since the two ladies had walked off to find a train. Ralph had only been at the table for five minutes – he'd not even touched his tea – but at least she had his bun safely in her bag.

She stopped a porter and asked him when the next train to Clacton would be leaving.

'Five minutes, miss, it should have left half an hour ago but like everything else in this blooming war it was late. You'll get on it in good time.' He pointed towards a row of carriages only a few yards ahead of her.

'Thank you, I thought I might have to wait an hour or more.'

She showed her ticket to the guard and then walked along the platform – it made sense to sit at the front of the train as then the person disembarking at Wivenhoe would be right next to the exit.

As she hurried past a carriage roughly in the middle, somebody knocked on the window. She looked over and saw it was her companions from the taxi. The lady in the alarming hat beamed and beckoned her.

Lucinda nodded, jumped onto the train and made her way down the narrow passageway to the compartment they were sitting in. It was a ladies-only compartment which was perfect.

'Come in, my dear, I doubt that anyone else want to sit with us so we'll have this compartment to ourselves. We travel to Thorpe, where do you get off?'

'Wivenhoe. My friend didn't come, I expect his posting came sooner than he thought.'

'I'm sorry to hear that, my dear, was he a very close friend?' burgundy hat asked.

'No, not really. I just wanted to wish him well and promise him that I'd write. The young men serving overseas really appreciate any correspondence from home.'

She was not revealing any details about her life. They might well remember reading about her in the paper and she couldn't bear to see their friendly smiles turn to disapproval. Telling white lies was acceptable, at least she hoped so.

* * *

When the train rocked to a halt at Wivenhoe, Lucinda realised they still hadn't exchanged names. She did know the two ladies had husbands somewhere, children also, but strangely none of them had exchanged any details of their lives. This suited her as it was quite likely they'd have recognised her name if she'd given it to them.

Instead they'd talked about the war, rationing, the land army and the home guard. One thing she had told them about herself was that she intended to apply for the ATA and they'd been suitably impressed.

She'd left home at nine o'clock and now it was just after two and she was looking forward to telling her new family how successful she'd been. She didn't cross the bridge and go along Station Road but took the steps that led up to Clifton Terrace. The post office was on the corner of Queen's Road and she wanted to draw out three pounds. A lot of money, but she was a woman of wealth now and could afford to have more than a few pennies in her pocket in future.

She couldn't open a new bank account without her father's permission but hoped a letter from Jonathan might be sufficient in the circumstances. If that was the case, then she'd go into Colchester one day next week and deposit the banker's draft.

She was halfway along the path that ran next to the railway when she remembered it was Saturday and the post office would have closed at lunchtime. She could pay the money in on Monday so that didn't matter. She was smiling as she headed home, eager to share her good news about the mink coat and also tell Elizabeth what had happened when she'd met Ralph.

* * *

8

Emily didn't know where to start. Daddy sensed she and Sammy were upset and put his arms around their shoulders and gently guided them into the sitting room.

'Sit down, take a deep breath, and tell me what's going on.'

Sammy sat squashed against her and didn't say a word whilst she explained what had happened earlier and also about George bullying Sammy. Daddy listened without interruption – he was good at that – and let her stumble to a halt.

'I really don't know what to do, what to think, and I know how serious it is because my friends went home early as they didn't want to be here when this was going on.'

Mummy had joined them halfway through and she too just sat quietly listening.

'Okay, sweetheart, son, this has been an upsetting and horrible experience for both of you. Your mother and I will take it from here. Why don't you both go into the kitchen and have some lunch and then perhaps go for a walk – the tide will be up and maybe you can get us some tasty sardines for tea.'

The last thing Emily wanted was lunch or sardines, but she

nodded. 'Thank you, the soup and rolls will be ready for you later. George hasn't had any breakfast and as far as I know he's still in his pyjamas.'

'No longer your problem, Emily, you've handled this with maturity and we're both very proud. Sammy, I'm sorry about what's been happening to you. In future, please come to one of us immediately and don't let it drift on like this.'

Sammy hadn't spoken at all and didn't answer this time either. He just nodded, held onto Emily's hand and they left the sitting room.

As soon as the kitchen door was closed, she felt a rush of relief. 'I wasn't sure I wanted any soup but the rolls do smell lovely. Let's have some and then do what Daddy suggested and go down to the quay.'

'I didn't like sardines the first time I had them but I do now. Do you think George will be allowed to eat any if we get them?'

'Of course he will, he's not going to be locked up on bread and water like a prisoner. I don't know what our parents are going to decide but whatever it is I'm sure it'll be the right thing to do.'

She tried to sound cheerful, positive, but she feared George would be sent away to boarding school. Then something occurred to her.

'The Royal Grammar School you attend has boarders as well, doesn't it?'

'Yes, we've got three in our class.'

'Then maybe that's what they'll do, make George a boarder until he learns how to behave sensibly.'

Sammy sniffed and rummaged in his pocket for a grubby handkerchief to blow his nose. 'I don't want him to be sent away. I love him, he's my brother, he's a better brother and you're a better sister than the ones I had before. We've got a spare room, maybe things would be better if we had our own rooms.'

This was the most he'd said on any subject as he didn't talk as much as either she or George did. Before she could stop him, he was out of the door. She'd been in the middle of serving the soup and dropped the ladle with a clatter on the table and ran after him.

Sammy hadn't stopped to knock on the door but burst in. She was close behind him.

'I don't want George to be sent away to be a boarder even at the grammar school. If I have the spare room—'

'Clever boy,' Mummy said and held out her arms, he flung himself in. 'We were just thinking the same thing. When you come back from your walk, I'm sure that George will be ready to apologise to both of you. Now, go and eat your lunch and let the grown-ups deal with this.'

Emily grabbed Sammy's hand and led him back to the kitchen. His impulse had been to run upstairs and tell George he wasn't going to be sent away which wouldn't help at all.

Surprisingly they enjoyed their lunch and left for the compulsory walk just as the sun came out.

'Look at that, it's a good sign, isn't it, Emily?'

'I hope so. It's going to be difficult for the next few days, don't expect everything to go back to normal tomorrow.'

'Will you help me move my things? Don't want to do it on my own.'

'I don't think either of us will have to be involved. Our parents will do everything. I'm glad that Lucinda wasn't here. Goodness knows what George might've said to her when he was in such a rage.'

* * *

It was a high tide and the water had come over the hard and was several inches deep outside the canning factory.

'Thank goodness we put on our rubber boots, Sammy, or we wouldn't be able to go and buy some fish. Imagine how horrible it must be for the ladies who work here when the tide's as high as this.'

'I'm not going near the edge as I might fall in.'

'I should think not, far too dangerous. Come on, let's speak to one of the ladies gutting the fish. They look like sardines on her table.'

A short while later they paddled back down Quay Street with Emily carrying a newspaper-wrapped parcel of nicely cleaned sardines. Daddy would cook them for tea tomorrow under the grill of their lovely new gas cooker.

Sammy was dragging his feet as they exited West Street into the High Street opposite the church. 'Do you think we should stay out a bit longer? I don't want to hear them telling George off.'

'I'm sure whatever they had to say it will be said by now. Isn't it lucky that our parents don't believe in corporal punishment, otherwise George would have been beaten.'

'That's why I don't want him to board at the school. They cane the boys that live there far more often than they do the day pupils. George got the cane – he said I wasn't to tell anyone.'

Emily stopped so abruptly, her toes crushed against the end of her boots. 'How could he not have told us? The school must have informed Mummy and Daddy. What dreadful thing did he do?'

'After he'd been warned not to get involved in any fights, he did it again. Do you think that's why he's been so horrible to me?'

'I don't know, it could be. How absolutely awful, Daddy will be furious. He made it very clear when you went there that neither of you were to be physically punished, whatever the rules were.'

They ran the last few yards and burst into the house. Mummy was feeding Grace some soup but there was no sign of George or their father.

'George got the cane for fighting again, Sammy said that's when he started being horrible,' Emily said.

'Good gracious, no wonder he's been difficult. Sammy, did he tell you not to tell us?'

Sammy nodded miserably. 'Never mind, you're a loyal and good brother. Emily, will you continue to feed your sister whilst I go upstairs?'

Her mother vanished and must have taken the stairs at a run from the clatter she made. Emily exchanged a smile with Sammy.

'I think things are going to be all right. Now we know there's a good reason for George's dreadful behaviour it will be so much easier to forgive and forget.'

* * *

After the baby had been fed, Emily put the sardines in the meat safe so the cat couldn't get at them and Sammy played with Grace. She couldn't hear anything going on upstairs and was becoming more and more worried the longer her parents were absent.

She didn't like to say to Sammy that it was possible their father might decide to remove both of them from the RGS after what had happened. They could hardly return to the village school, which was horribly overcrowded and not nearly as good.

What seemed like hours later, Daddy came in looking a lot better than he had last time she'd seen him.

'George wants to know if you really want to move out of the

bedroom, Sammy? He wants you to stay there as he loves sharing with you.'

Sammy was on his feet and out of the door almost before the sentence was completed. 'I don't want to move either.'

Grace had crawled over and was hanging on Daddy's trousers, hoping to be picked up. He leaned down and scooped her into his arms.

'What are you going to do about it, Daddy? Will the boys stay there?'

'That is a conundrum indeed, sweetheart. All schools, even the village one, believe that corporal punishment is perfectly reasonable when a pupil misbehaves. Your mother and I are in the minority when it comes to objecting.'

'Are you saying that they might as well stay where they are as it would be the same wherever they went?'

He nodded. 'We've explained to George that although we don't approve of the use of a cane, if he'd behaved himself, if he'd not disobeyed a direct order, then he wouldn't have been beaten. It's up to him to toe the line.'

'Will you make a frightful stink on Monday that they punished him without informing you?'

'That I will do. In fact, I'm going to go in with the boys and speak to the headmaster in person. It seems that George has been on the receiving end of a beating more than once and neither he nor the school informed us. Even Sammy didn't know about the other two occasions. The fighting other boys came after the first of the incidences.'

'It's all such a muddle, but I'm so relieved we know why George hasn't been himself recently.'

* * *

Lucinda arrived to find the family in the kitchen eating a very late lunch. 'I say, I don't suppose there's any of that delicious soup left for me, is there?'

Emily was on her feet at once. 'There certainly is, Lily left us an absolutely enormous pot. The boys are just going upstairs to do a jigsaw together so there's plenty of room at the table.'

Lucinda glanced at George and was shocked to see that his eyes were red and puffy – he'd obviously been crying a lot. Something had happened but it wasn't her business and she'd no intention of asking. If they wanted her to know then somebody would tell her.

'I sold my coat for the most ridiculous amount of money. I'm hoping, Jonathan, that you can act in loco parentis and write me a letter of introduction so I can open a bank account in Colchester.'

Like a magician producing a rabbit from a hat, she delved into her blouse and removed the envelope. Jonathan's eyebrows vanished under his hair. Elizabeth laughed and Emily giggled.

'I'm sorry, I should really have turned my back to do that. Look inside and see for yourself what I was paid.'

'Good God, that's a small fortune, Lucinda,' Jonathan said. 'I'll certainly write that letter. When do you intend to deposit this draft?' He showed Elizabeth and her eyes rounded.

'I'm sure it's perfectly safe here but I do think the sooner it goes into the bank the better. I'll decide what I'm going to do with it once it's secure. I'll be able to pay for my keep in future. I don't want be a financial burden to you.'

'You're not a burden, you're family,' Elizabeth said. 'Keep your windfall for yourself. If you get into the ATA I expect that you'll have to pay for your own uniform, find your own billet and so on.'

Jonathan laughed at Lucinda's expression. 'I know, we've been doing some research. We're most impressed that you can fly a plane.'

'Thank you for caring.' She smiled at Emily. 'That soup was good. I thought you and your friends were going to be taking care of the catering this afternoon.'

Emily bit her lip. 'I'm going to help the boys with something. Excuse me,' she said and rushed off.

'Come into the sitting room and we'll tell you about the latest family drama,' Elizabeth said.

'I suppose the previous one was caused by me.'

'It was, Lucinda, but all sorted and forgotten. It's going to take longer to resolve this one,' Jonathan said.

They stood up and waited politely for her to join them.

'I'll tidy the kitchen and then join you. I'll take care of the evening meal as the girls aren't here to do it.'

They didn't argue and wandered off, leaving her alone with the lunch dishes. She was stacking the soup bowls on the rack on the draining board when Emily turned up.

'Sorry, I should be doing this. Saturday is my day.'

'It's done now. Do you need a hand with tea later? I'm part of the family; I must pull my weight.'

Emily explained what they were having and Lucinda grinned. 'I love bubble and squeak. Shall I do that, and you do the gravy and bangers? I can smell fish. Will that keep until tea tomorrow?'

'It will keep in the pantry, it's freezing in there. Daddy cooks them for us and we have fresh bread and butter with them – scrumptious.'

* * *

Elizabeth was occupied playing with the baby. Jonathan was happy to fill Lucinda in on the events of the morning.

'At my boarding school if we broke the rules we got caned on the hand or slapped but not beaten like George was. Usually, punishments for serious offences were loss of freedom, removal of privileges. Lesser misdemeanours resulted in us writing lines and having to stand in a corner for hours.'

'I think I'd have preferred a couple of smacks on the legs to any of those,' Elizabeth said.

'To return to George's misbehaviour, how is he being punished?'

'Confined to the house until after Christmas, in bed before eight o'clock and not being allowed to join in family games,' Jonathan told her.

Lucinda deftly diverted the conversation, talking about poor George's disgrace was upsetting for all of them.

'If you don't mind, I'd like to tell you what I did after selling my coat.'

They listened and to her relief didn't seem shocked that she'd replied to Ralph's letter.

'It was brave of you to see him, my dear. How was it? Do you still feel the same way about him?' Elizabeth asked.

'Not quite the same, but I do still find him dangerously attractive and am glad he rushed off as if he hadn't, I might have agreed to see him again before he's divorced.'

'How long do you think a divorce would take, darling?' Elizabeth looked at Jonathan.

'How should I know? I'm pretty sure that it costs a small fortune and I imagine could take months rather than weeks. The lawyers young enough have been conscripted, or volunteered, leaving only the older men to deal with everything.'

'I intend to put him out of my mind, for now at least. I'm going to concentrate on being the best ARP warden I can until the New Year. By the way, I posted my letter of application to

Pauline Gower at Hatfield airbase when I was in Town. I'm hoping I'll be one of the first to apply. However, I suspect lots of eager young women will have responded after the article asking for recruits was in the paper.'

'I hope you hear soon, although not before Christmas,' Elizabeth said.

'I might not hear anything as she might well recognise my name and not want someone like me in the ATA. I'm hoping that the four hundred solo flying hours in my logbook might do the trick.'

'Let's hope so. I imagine that how any of the young women perform in the test flight will decide if they're good enough,' Jonathan said.

The conversation was interrupted by the harsh clang of the telephone. It rang twice, indicating the call was for them. If it was once, then it was for the doctor as they shared a party line.

'Shall I answer that?'

'Please do, Lucinda, I'm far too comfortable in this armchair,' Jonathan replied.

'Harbour House, to whom do you wish to speak?'

'Darling, thank God, I was going to put the phone down if it had been anyone else.'

She almost did exactly that. 'Ralph, how did you get this number? I'm sure I didn't tell you where I'm living.'

'I'm in intelligence, so I used mine. I want to see you and I won't stomp off like a child next time.'

Everything she said could be overheard in the sitting room and possibly upstairs as well. Why had she blurted out his name? Now she couldn't pretend it was a school friend or something else less embarrassing.

'I thought I told you I don't want to see you until you're single.'

His warm laughter sent a well-remembered thrill down her spine. 'I know you did, but it's about achieving my divorce that we need to talk.'

Jonathan was now standing at the door. He raised an eyebrow. She shook her head and smiled her thanks. He retreated and closed the door behind him.

'This is all very awkward, Ralph. Now my family know I'm talking to you.'

'Good, I'd like to meet them.'

Her horrified squeak at his suggestion made him laugh again. She loved his laugh; it made her tingle all over. Despite her reservations, despite being well aware of the dangers involved, his charm was working its dangerous magic.

'Seriously, darling, we do need to talk. I thought you'd prefer it to be away from London, somewhere you feel safe.'

His deep dark voice reminded her of smoky night clubs and passionate nights. Ten minutes ago she'd been determined not to see him but found herself saying the opposite.

'All right, hang on a minute, I'll speak to my family. If they agree, then you can come.'

She put the telephone receiver down and walked away but didn't go into the sitting room. This was her decision – if she didn't want to see him then she'd say that Jonathan had vetoed the visit. If she did, then she'd say he'd given his permission.

She rejoined her family a few minutes later, still unsure if she was going to regret what she'd just told him.

9

Ralph was smiling as he replaced the receiver. He'd achieved his objective. Lucinda had agreed that he could come to this godforsaken village in Essex and they'd arranged for him to visit next weekend which suited him perfectly. It was imperative that the meeting went well, that he made a good impression on her provincial relatives. For without her consent to have her name listed as the co-respondent on the divorce petition he couldn't file it. He hoped to convince her that as her reputation was already in tatters, she'd nothing left to lose and everything to gain as he'd then be free to marry her.

He couldn't legally name her without consent but was certain he'd be able to persuade her. Leone, his wife, would never divorce him willingly, although she had the grounds. She wanted him to be as miserable as she was, to ruin his life as well as Lucinda's. Unless he got Lucinda's signed permission, he'd be unable to wrench his freedom from the woman he'd never loved but who he'd married for her fortune.

He was virtually penniless, only had the money from his work as an intelligence officer to live on, and he wasn't going to live in penury. The few hundred pounds annuity he received was scarcely enough to pay his bar bill. It didn't suit him to be scratching around, having to watch his expenditure, like an ordinary person. He owned his tiny flat near Horse Guards, but it was too small and he wanted somewhere more his style.

Lucinda's Knightsbridge place would suit him perfectly. Her massive trust fund would be released when she married, therefore he had to get this bloody divorce arranged and then marry her as soon as the decree absolute arrived.

He nodded. She'd have no option if she agreed to him dragging her through the courts, as then she'd be a social pariah, her only recourse to recover even a smidgen of her reputation would be to marry him. His family could trace their lineage back to the Tudors; he might not be wealthy, but he was definitely top drawer.

His smile faded as he sauntered downstairs – Ralph Castleton didn't run for anyone, even the important people he worked for. This affair hadn't been the first of his dalliances, Leone had locked him out of the bedroom after the second baby, and a gentleman had his needs, after all.

Lucinda initially had just been a silly girl, easily seduced into his bed. He hadn't intended to fall in love with her and that was why things had gone so wrong. This time his eagle-eyed wife had sensed the difference, had known he was in love. As soon as she discovered Lucinda's name, she'd sent the information to all the gossip columnists, not even told him what she was going to do. She'd also informed Lucinda's elderly and very stuffy parents. It had taken him all his charm to smooth things over with the War Office as having an affair was perfectly acceptable, having it public knowledge was not.

His brother held the title and the purse strings, but the Castleton name would be more than enough to restore Lucinda's tarnished reputation. The fact that he had no nephews meant he'd inherit the title if his brother died. He'd got two daughters, as had his brother, which was why he intended to have several children with his next wife. Surely a boy would arrive eventually and cement his claim to the title?

He hadn't been lying when he'd told her that he was hopelessly in love with her, that was true. This time he wouldn't be marrying for solely mercenary reasons. He would make her happy, wouldn't be unfaithful. She was young, stunningly beautiful and was easily manipulated. Her huge trust fund would be his to use as he wanted, she would be content to be his beloved wife and remain at home taking care of all the children they would have.

'Hey, Castleton, you're wanted downstairs,' Humfrey, another spook, yelled at him across the office.

'On my way, no doubt yet another crisis only I can resolve.'

* * *

Emily, like the other members of the family, pretended that everything was tickety-boo at home. It certainly wasn't as George's behaviour and his subsequent well-deserved punishment had cast a black cloud over Harbour House.

Daddy had accompanied the boys to school on Monday but she didn't know what he'd said or the outcome of his visit. Certainly, George wasn't any happier and neither was Sammy. She was relieved that tomorrow she'd be spending the day with her friends over the river as she really didn't want to be in the house when everyone was so miserable.

Sammy sidled up to her as she was getting ready to leave to catch the ferry.

'Can I come with you? I won't be a nuisance, promise, I just don't want to be here at the moment. I think I preferred George when he was angry and bossing me about, I hate how subdued he is. I hope that our parents let him off his punishment before Christmas or it's going to be horrible for all of us.'

The only good thing to come out of the shocking events of last weekend was the fact that Sammy was now talking freely like all the other Robys.

'I'm happy to take you, I'm sure Penny will be delighted if you agree to play hide-and-seek and so on with her brothers. I'll ask Mummy – I think Daddy would definitely have said no but fortunately he's at work.'

She returned smiling. 'Yes, you can come. You've got two minutes to get your boots and coat on. I warn you it's going to be beastly on the ferry and you might well end up with an icy wet backside.'

'I don't care, as long as I'm not spending the day here you can throw a bucket of water over me and I'd be happy.'

* * *

Doris usually met her on her own as Penny didn't like to bring her little brothers down in the bad weather. Today not only was Doris there, but also Penny, her brothers and little Jimmy from the big house. What on earth was he doing here?

There was a lad waiting on the hard to help everybody disembark from the ferry but she and Sammy were out without assistance. Jimmy was hiding behind Penny, peeping nervously around her, obviously expecting to be shouted at for coming.

'Hello everyone, hello, Jimmy. What a nice surprise to see you.' It was certainly a surprise, but Emily wasn't quite sure if it was nice or not.

'My mum's buggered orf with some bloke she met. We ain't seen her for days and I'm on me own now.'

'Goodness, that's really bad news. At least you've got the other mums and their children to play with. They'll look after you, won't they?' Emily said.

The little boy was wearing clothes that didn't fit him, his shoes were too big as well and tied onto his feet with string. She wasn't sure how old he was but thought he couldn't be much more than four, he was much smaller than the five-year-old twins.

Sammy turned his back on Jimmy. 'Right, hop on, I'll give you a piggyback.'

Jimmy hesitated. 'I'll lift you, then you'll know what to do next time,' Emily said.

She was shocked at how light he was, this hadn't been obvious because of his overlarge clothes.

The twins ran on ahead; Sammy followed at a jog and Jimmy was screeching with laughter.

'Penny, did he come across to you or did you go and fetch him?'

'He was shivering outside the door when we left and I could hardly leave him behind. I'm not sure what my mum will say if she hears that I've taken him in. He's bound to have fleas and possibly nits as well.'

Doris was scowling. 'I think it's rotten that a little scrap like him has no one to take care of him. Why aren't the other mums doing a better job?'

'I suppose we should take him to the police station,' Penny said, 'I'm sure that my mum said that's who deal with neglected children in the first place.'

'What about the NSPCC? The National Society for the Prevention of Cruelty to Children,' Emily suggested.

'I reckon we should go and speak to them mums before we do anything. We don't want to get the welfare involved as they might take all the kiddies into an orphanage.'

'I'd better hurry after the boys, explain to my mum what's going on, and ask her to let Jimmy spend the day with us whilst you two go round to the big house and speak to someone there.'

Doris nodded. 'Then it'll be quicker if we go up the other lane. Come on, Emily, it's taters, Nan's still saying it's going to snow – maybe she'll be right this time.'

* * *

Emily knocked loudly on the front door, half-expecting it to remain unanswered. She was wrong as a youngish woman with metal hair curlers in her stringy, dyed blonde hair heaved open the door. She didn't look particularly pleased to see them.

Emily thought it was as cold inside the house as it was outside. What a miserable existence everyone in the house was having. It was all very well sending East End families down here to get them away from the bombs, but she rather thought that they might prefer to take a chance and be somewhere warmer and more familiar.

'Excuse me, ma'am, I am Miss Emily Roby, and we need to talk to you about Jimmy.' She realised that she didn't actually know his second name and this was essential if they were going to take the matter further. 'I'm sorry, I don't know your name or Jimmy's family name. Would you be so kind as to supply it?'

'None of your business what me name is. And he ain't nothing to do with me, nor with Thelma. His bleedin' ma buggered off a couple of weeks ago and left the little sod behind.'

'It doesn't matter if his mother abandoned him, he's living under your roof so he's under your protection. He's obviously not being fed or clothed. I've just called in to inform you that Jimmy's with us and we're going to take him to the police station when we go home this afternoon. I'm quite sure that the welfare office will be making an investigation.'

The woman's face twisted and her eyes narrowed. 'Don't want no nosy parkers round here. You bring him back, don't take him to the coppers, I'll give him a good wash and find him something decent to wear. I reckon his ma will come back when the bloke she went off with kicks her out.'

'Thank you. However, I come to Rowhedge every other weekend and I'll be checking up on him. If his condition hasn't improved then you know what will happen.'

Emily nodded and marched down the steps, knowing she'd made the wretched woman think twice about what was going on.

'Cor, you told her and no mistake. The poor little perisher will be better staying here as long as she sticks to her word. No kiddie wants to be in one of them orphanages if there's an alternative,' Doris said.

'I'm not sure we did the right thing. I'd have thought even being in an orphanage would be better than where he is now – at least he'd be fed and clothed and educated even if he isn't given the love he deserves.'

'It ain't our concern really, Emily, you've got enough on your plate with your George being in trouble and all that. We don't know how old little Jimmy is, he might be older than he looks because he's so thin.'

'He certainly talks well so I think you might be right. His language leaves a lot to be desired, but living where he does that's hardly surprising. I'm hoping that Penny's been able to find some of her brothers' outgrown clothes that will fit him.'

'Poor little mite, it ain't fair that someone so little is having such a hard time.'

* * *

One of the twins was waiting by the door, ready to let them in; she wasn't sure whether it was Thomas or Toby. The sound of Jimmy screeching echoed down the stairs.

'Penny's giving Jimmy a bath – I don't think he likes it very much.'

'I don't suppose he's ever had one. He'll feel a lot better when he's clean,' Emily said.

'He smells nasty, his mum doesn't look after him properly.'

'No, she doesn't, so it's not his fault.'

The little boy looked up at her and grinned. 'I'm Toby, Thomas is helping with the bath. I stayed down here to let you in.'

'Ta ever so, Toby, much appreciated,' Doris said as she hastily closed the door to keep out the icy wind.

'Penny said that you've got to put the kettle on and make some tea. We don't drink tea so we have hot milk with honey in it.'

* * *

Doris found some stale bread in the pantry and whilst she and Toby were doing the toasting Emily found some marge and jam to go with it. When Penny returned with Jimmy and Thomas, the kitchen was filled with the appetising smell of hot toast.

'Golly, you look very smart, Jimmy,' Emily said when she saw the little boy in his new outfit, hair washed and face free of dirt – hopefully free of livestock too.

'I ain't never looked so good, real posh I am now.' He pointed to his feet. 'Look at these shoes, they ain't got no holes in nor nothing – they almost fit me too.'

Doris dropped to her knees and gave the little boy a hug. 'Just the ticket, Jimmy, now you can have some nice toast and hot milk.' She glanced at Emily and then continued. 'What's your other name, do you know it?'

'Course I do. I'm Jimmy Sugden cos me ma's called Mrs Sugden.'

The children scrambled onto the chairs at the kitchen table and whilst they devoured several slices of toast and drank the milk and honey, Emily, Sammy and her friends had a mug of tea.

'Jimmy, do you know how old you are?' Penny asked.

'I ain't never had a birthday, but I reckon I'm four or five. My ma never said when I was born. She never said who me da is. I don't reckon I've got one of those neither.'

Thomas nudged Jimmy, almost knocking him off his chair. 'You're stupid, everybody's got a dad. My brother and I are five – you came to our party. You're much smaller than us so you can't be five.'

Penny stepped in firmly. 'Apologise at once, Thomas, Jimmy's our guest and not only should you not have pushed him, you certainly cannot call him stupid.'

Before Thomas could reply, Jimmy did.

'I ain't stupid, I've been able to talk since I was a baby. Even me aunties says I'm a clever one, so there.'

'Thomas, I'm waiting. You won't be playing hide-and-seek but spending the morning in your bedroom if you don't apologise,' Penny told him.

Instead of doing the sensible thing, Thomas pushed Jimmy even more violently and this time he and his chair tumbled backwards. Sammy managed to catch the chair before it crashed onto the tiles.

Jimmy wasn't upset but laughed. 'Bugger me, I never expected any rough stuff in this house. I get a lot of it over there.'

Penny picked up Thomas, smacked him hard on the back of the legs, and carried him kicking and screaming out of the room.

Emily held her breath, waiting for his equally volatile brother to create a second scene, but Toby just carried on eating his toast.

'I think there's some cake in the pantry, I'll get it, shall I, Emily?'

'Yes, I think we could all do with a piece of cake. I need another cup of tea after that nonsense. Do you boys want more milk?'

'I ain't fond of milk, not really, but I'm gasping for a cuppa,' Jimmy said solemnly.

* * *

As the warmest room in the house was the kitchen, Emily decided it made sense for them to remain there until Penny came back. Rushing about the place playing hide-and-seek hardly seemed appropriate in the circumstances.

They were involved in a riotous game of Simon Says, which Jimmy had never played before, when her friend returned, a subdued and apologetic Thomas with her.

'I'm very sorry, Jimmy, for being so horrible. I want you to be my friend.'

Jimmy grinned. 'That's all right, water under the bridge, mate. You joining in this silly game?'

They took it in turns to be Simon until they'd laughed so much they were exhausted. Emily kept looking at the dark red handprints on the back of Thomas's legs and wished her friend hadn't smacked him. This was the first time she'd felt uncomfortable with Penny and hoped that it wouldn't spoil their friendship.

Sammy took the three little boys to the WC, leaving her with Penny and Doris.

'Penny, I have to say that I was shocked that you smacked Thomas so hard. My family don't approve of physical punishment and I thought that you agreed.'

'I know I shouldn't have done it, but he could have killed Jimmy and I reacted without thought. It was the wrong thing to do. I regretted it immediately and apologised to him. I'll tell my mum and she'll be really cross. I'm ashamed of myself.'

Emily immediately hugged her. 'I'd hoped it was something like that. Shock makes you do things you regret later. More than once I've almost slapped George and I know that my parents have barely restrained themselves on occasion.'

Doris was looking at them as if they were speaking in French. 'Crikey, all this fuss about a couple of slaps. Never did me no harm and it won't do that little lad neither. I reckon a smack is better than having to stay in your room all day, but that's just my opinion.'

'I know children at school are regularly smacked, caned and beaten,' Emily said.

'Not all at the same time,' Doris said, 'that would be bad even for the worst teachers.'

*   *   *

The rest of the day passed without incident and when it was time to leave Emily said she'd take Jimmy home. She expected him to be sad, reluctant to go to what was obviously a miserable life, but the little chap smiled bravely.

'I can go over sometimes on me own, Penny said, if her ma agrees. That'll do me. It ain't much cop in that big old house, Emily, all of us is sleeping in the big room near the kitchen. It's too bleeding cold everywhere else.'

'Please try not to swear, Jimmy, because if you use words like that in front of Penny's mother, she won't let you come again.'

'Why not?'

Doris answered for her. 'Because them little terrors, the twins, will start to copy and decent people don't use bad language. I don't swear, and I'm not posh neither.'

Jimmy pulled a face. 'No, you're not. I like you, Doris, can I come and see you sometimes?'

'No, sorry, me nan and grandad wouldn't be happy.'

10

Lucinda continued with her ARP duties and by the end of her second week she was less exhausted. She and Mr Hatch patrolled the lower half of Wivenhoe but there were two others that patrolled the rest. It was unlikely that those two ever had anything to do apart from shout about the blackout law being broken, most of the pubs and families likely to cause problems lived below the railway bridge in overcrowded little cottages.

This weekend Emily and her friends would be at home which was going to make Ralph's visit a little awkward. She could hardly entertain him in her bedroom, and the children would be roaming about putting up the Christmas decorations.

The schools would be breaking up for the Christmas holiday on Friday and even though there wasn't going to be much festive jollity this year, Lucinda was sure everyone would try with what little they had.

She decided it would be better to meet him in Colchester where there were a few cafés, a British restaurant and at least three hotels that served a decent lunch. She posted a letter to his flat near Horse Guards saying that she would meet him at twelve thirty for lunch at the Red Lion in the High Street.

Despite the fact there was a war raging, rationing making it hard for the less fortunate to put a decent meal on the table, the Postal Service was still working splendidly. Ralph would get her letter in plenty of time.

* * *

Whilst she was getting ready on the Saturday morning, she heard George and Sammy arguing next door. Elizabeth and Jonathan were downstairs with the baby and Emily had gone to the river to meet her friends off the ferry.

Today would be the first day that George was allowed to join in family activities. Under normal circumstances she would have ignored the shouting, but things were different now.

'Boys, what's going on in there? I'm coming in,' Lucinda said after she'd knocked on the door.

George wasn't dressed, Sammy was, and she thought this was the cause of the row.

'Don't you want to put up the decorations, George? Your mother has agreed that the tree can be decorated tomorrow.'

'I'm not interested in Christmas, I don't believe in God, we won't be getting any presents this year, so why should I help put up a few tatty bits of paper?'

'This is a time of year when you think about other people, not yourself, young man. Your parents have very kindly rescinded your punishment and allowed you to rejoin the family. Even if you don't believe in any of it, you should join in enthusiastically to try and make up for all the trouble you've caused.'

His expression was murderous. How could a child of barely ten years old be so angry at the world?

'I wish my grandparents would come back. I really miss them.' Then he collapsed on the bed and burst into tears. 'I don't think I'll ever see Grandpa again. They got a letter the other day saying he was fading. That means dying, doesn't it?'

Sammy got to his side before her and hugged the sobbing boy. Lucinda wasn't good with physical affection so raced downstairs and into the sitting room.

'Quickly, George's desperately upset. He must have overheard you talking about Major Roby being very unwell.'

Elizabeth was sitting on the rug playing bricks with the baby. Jonathan dropped his newspaper and was out of the door before Elizabeth reacted.

'Is your father-in-law dying, Elizabeth?'

'He seems to be slowly slipping away, he's not eating much, spends a lot of his time asleep, but he's not unhappy. His confusion hasn't got any worse, it's his physical health that's the concern.'

'Is Jonathan going to see him? I heard that the shipyards were going to close for Christmas Day this year, couldn't he take a couple of days off then?'

Elizabeth smiled sadly. 'He could but he wouldn't be able to get to Kent as there'll be no trains running for civilians. He's been given permission to use an official car after Christmas, and they've even agreed to have a driver bring it down. I just pray that it won't be too late.'

* * *

Jonathan returned and smiled reassuringly at Elizabeth. 'When I told him that we're going to Kent after Christmas he stopped crying. He's getting dressed but I'm not sure how today will progress. I wish we hadn't decided to punish him by keeping him away from us all. He's a very unhappy and disturbed little boy at the moment.'

'He behaved so badly it seemed right at the time. I agree, we should have given him more love, not kept him apart. I hope we haven't damaged him permanently.'

Lucinda had listened to this conversation but didn't understand the reasoning behind it. 'You could have sent him away to boarding school, that's what my parents did to me, so I think he got off lightly.'

'Being sent away didn't improve your behaviour, did it?' Jonathan said.

Lucinda was going to reply angrily but something made her reconsider. 'No, you're right. If I'd had a loving home, been a wanted child and not an embarrassment, I'm sure I'd never have become so wild and disruptive. George's lucky, all your children are, to have such a happy home and parents who want them.'

'I'm sorry, that was uncalled for. You've got a loving home now and even though neither Elizabeth nor I think it's a good idea for you to meet Mr Castleton today we trust your judgement and support your decision.'

Tears welled but Lucinda brushed them away. 'Thank you, I can't tell you how much that means to me. Joining the ATA is my goal, but I suppose I should see what he wants. I can't imagine it's anything important but just in case, I'm going to go. It will be the last time, I promise you.'

'Good for you, you'll look absolutely splendid in the navy-blue uniform. It's fortunate that you're so tall, I should imagine that flying an aeroplane would be difficult if you weren't,' Elizabeth said.

'I read somewhere that you can't be a fighter pilot if you're over six foot tall; I've not heard that there's a lower limit, but you might be right,' Lucinda replied.

* * *

The two boys and three girls put the boxes of paper chains, folded tissue paper bells and balls, glass baubles, and tarnished silver tinsel on the dining-room table. Even George had cheered up and appeared to be enjoying the jolly occasion.

Jonathan had gone to work immediately after the incident but Elizabeth was keeping an eye on things. The children took it in turns to entertain the baby and Grace was enthralled by the coloured paper and activity.

When Lucinda left to catch the train just before midday, the bright festoons of homemade paper and the other tissue paper decorations were mostly up. Being the tallest by far, she'd done most of the high stuff, pinning dozens of bits and pieces wherever instructed by the children.

The boys had staggered in with the tree which had been in the shelter for the past week waiting to be brought up and decorated.

'Will you be back this evening?' George asked Lucinda as she was leaving. 'Mummy's agreed we can do it tonight and not wait until tomorrow. I love it when the little electric lights are switched on.'

'I'll absolutely definitely be back to help with this momentous occasion. I've never helped decorate a tree so am not going to miss the opportunity. I'll also see if I can find anything to add to it – you never know, I might even find a bar of chocolate somewhere.'

It was bitter outside and Lucinda was glad she'd put on her warmest clothes, sturdy boots, woolly hat, gloves and scarf. She was smiling as she reached the station, thinking that her lack of glamour would no doubt offend Ralph.

If she'd been thinking of one day perhaps starting again then she'd be wearing court shoes, a fashionable outfit, and not slacks and a twinset. The train was almost as cold as the platform and today there was no mass of bodies to give some warmth. There was no point in looking for a seat as the train only stopped at Hythe before steaming into St Botolph's station.

She was forced to push her way through housewives with bulging baskets full of vegetables, meat, fish, and quite likely a few precious items for gifts for Christmas next week. Today was market day so these would be shoppers returning home.

She'd had the forethought to telephone and reserve a table for two at the Red Lion hotel – being market day it would be busy and especially as it was the last Saturday before Christmas. There'd never been much under the tree for her – one year there'd been nothing as her parents had gone away, leaving her with her nanny and the staff. Despite the lack of gifts, it had been the happiest Christmas she could remember as she'd spent it downstairs in the kitchen and servants' hall and been thoroughly spoilt.

Lucinda paused at the door of the restaurant, admiring the greenery and candles that decorated every unused surface. She waited patiently for the head waiter to seat her. It gave her a few moments to gather her thoughts and remove her outer garments.

'I hope you have a reservation, miss, we are fully booked for lunch today,' the black-garbed old gentlemen said as he came up to her.

'Yes, a table for two at twelve thirty in the name of Roby.' She was still reluctant to use her own name in case somebody recognised it from the scandal.

'Excellent, if you'd care to follow me, I'll take you to your table.'

She and Ralph would be sitting by the window and Lucinda

wasn't sure if that was a good thing or not. Did she want passersby to see them together?

'Someone will bring you the menus, can I get you anything whilst you wait for your guest?'

'I'd like a large pot of real coffee, cream and sugar.'

Lucinda was enjoying her second cup when she saw Ralph hurry past the window, trilby pulled down low over his forehead, his expensive trench coat neatly buttoned and looking every inch a city gentleman. What he didn't look was happy – was this because of the weather or because she'd insisted they meet at the Red Lion?

Ralph hadn't enjoyed his journey to this benighted place – this town might be the oldest one in England, but it had absolutely nothing to recommend it as far as he was concerned. He'd travelled first class – of course – but there'd been no taxis available to take him the two miles from the station to the centre of Colchester and he'd been obliged to catch a bus along with the other plebs.

As he entered the less than impressive Red Lion, through the archway that had once been used for coaches, he straightened his shoulders, pinned on his customary charming smile and walked confidently into the restaurant.

He saw Lucinda immediately. Even if he hadn't been coming to meet her he would have noticed her – she was the best-looking young woman in the room without a doubt. For a second his smile slipped. What in God's name was she wearing?

On seeing him enter she'd stood up and he'd seen at once she wasn't dressed in one of her usual expensive, elegant ensembles but was wearing, of all things, a blue cardigan and slacks. What had possessed her to meet him dressed like a housewife?

He pushed these unwelcome thoughts to the back of his mind, widened his smile, raised a hand in salute and then turned to hand his things to a hovering waiter. He didn't acknowledge this person but strode across to greet Lucinda.

'Thank you for agreeing to meet me, I do appreciate the fact that you've come,' he said, hoping he sounded sincere.

She nodded and resumed her seat without answering. Once he was sitting opposite, she handed him the menu.

'I'm afraid I've drunk most of the coffee but I'm sure they can bring you a pot if that's what you want. I don't need to look at that as everyone comes here to eat one of their pies and I intend to do the same.'

It was hard to stay charming when faced with such indifference. 'In which case, Lucinda, I'll have what you're having.'

He was about to snap his fingers, knowing that someone would run to serve him, but she was smiling at an old waiter who shuffled over immediately to take their order.

'Another pot of coffee, please, and we'll each have one of your excellent pies and whatever vegetables are available.'

'Yes, Miss Roby, you'll not be disappointed. Chicken and ham today with sautéed potatoes, braised carrots and buttered cabbage.'

'Thank you, that sounds absolutely delicious and exactly what we want on such a cold day.'

'I was going to ask for a real drink, but I've no option but to have coffee as you've ordered it. What made you choose this hotel for our meeting?'

'It has an excellent reputation, and I'm sure you didn't expect somewhere like the Savoy.'

He smiled. 'Of course I didn't, this is charming and old-fashioned. I'm sure I'm going to enjoy my lunch.' He leaned forward, intending to put his hand on hers but both of them vanished under the table. This wasn't going how he'd hoped.

'Shall we talk now or wait until we've eaten?'

'After lunch. The pies will be ready and brought out immediately.' For the first time her smile was warm. 'Don't look so disgruntled, Ralph, I know this isn't somewhere you'd have come from choice but I promise you the food's excellent.'

'I'll have to take your word for it, but just being here with you makes this a special occasion as far as I'm concerned.'

The ancient waiter tottered up, pushing a trolley. The food was plated, not something he was accustomed to. In his opinion the waiter should have used silver service so one could select the vegetables one wanted and the quantity.

At least it smelt appetising and there was a jug filled with aromatic gravy placed between them. This was followed by the coffee jug and the other paraphernalia associated with this.

'Good God, are we to serve ourselves? Why didn't that wretched waiter pour our coffee for us?'

She raised an elegant eyebrow. 'I think we've established, Ralph, that you're not at the Savoy. Things are different in the country and better for it in my opinion. Don't worry, I'll pour the coffee for you. Do you want me to cut up your pie as well or can you manage that on your own?'

He couldn't prevent a flash of anger at her impertinence. How could this girl have changed so much in the few weeks since they'd been together? She'd never spoken to him like that before or poked fun at him, and it dawned on him that persuading her to do as he wanted was going to be a lot more difficult than he'd anticipated.

'No, thank you, darling, I might be twelve years your senior but not so old I can't cut up my own food.'

She laughed, even when he was angry with her the sound still sent waves of desire flooding through him.

He surprised himself by enjoying the meal, clearing the plate, and the apple crumble and custard that followed was equally acceptable.

'I apologise for my doubts, that was one of the best lunches I've had in a long time. Mind you, I'd have preferred a decent glass of claret rather than coffee to wash it down.'

'I'm glad you enjoyed it, I certainly did. I'm sure you noticed that the waiter addressed me as Miss Roby. I still daren't use my own name in case anybody recognises me. I'm absolutely not going through that a second time.'

'If my wife won't divorce me and you won't have your name on the petition then we can't get married. I love you; don't you want to be my wife?'

'No, I don't, I certainly did when we were together but since being apart from you and living here, things have changed. I'm going to join one of the services voluntarily, the WAAF or the WRNS, or I'll be conscripted into the women's army or something equally awful next year if I don't sort out something for myself.'

She'd no intention of telling him about her real plans, she didn't trust him not to interfere in some way.

'Are you mad? Conscription for women doesn't come in until next December. If you agreed to be named in my petition, then I'd be free in a few months and we could be married.'

'Being married wouldn't stop me being conscripted, Ralph. Women with small children are exempt but I don't intend to be one of those.'

'Are you telling me that you don't want children?' He tried not to sound as horrified as he was but from her expression he failed.

'Not every young woman wants children. Obviously, if I was

married to the right person then when the war's over that would be different. I intend to do my bit, not sit at home doing nothing useful.'

He dropped his napkin in disgust and stood up. 'I don't know you any more, Lucinda, you're not the lovely young woman I fell in love with and I'm not sure that I want to marry you.'

She looked at him, not cowed by his harsh words but calm and confident. 'Excellent, because I've already told you that I certainly don't want to marry you. Meeting you today has just confirmed my decision that having an affair with you was a mistake – I intend to put it in the past and get on with my life.'

For the first time ever he was speechless. When she smiled at him as if he was a simpleton, he wanted to throttle her.

'Goodbye, Ralph, I'm sorry you had a wasted journey. I really could have told you this in a letter, but I wanted to see you one more time to be sure.'

'I won't forget this meeting, Miss Somiton, I hope you don't come to regret treating me so disrespectfully.'

When he reached the door, by some miracle there was a waiter holding out his garments. He shrugged into his coat, tied the belt, rammed his hat on his head, his gloves on his hands and strode out.

What he thought had been love for Lucinda had turned in an instant to something else entirely. She wasn't going to get away with rejecting him, treating him as if he was of no account. If he couldn't have her then he was going to make sure nobody else would want her. He had powerful friends and intended to use them.

His lips thinned. His first job would be to ruin her name with those who took on girls for the WRNS or the WAAF. His second would be to ingratiate himself with his wife and persuade her that being reconciled would suit them both. Leone was still young enough to produce a couple more babies and maybe one of them would be a boy.

No one crossed him and didn't live to regret it. Lucinda would be no match for him. When her pathetic little life began to fall apart, she'd not know why, not realise he was behind it. He'd sit back and watch the destruction, pleased she'd got her come-uppance.

11

Emily and the boys escorted Penny and Doris to the riverside mid-afternoon. It got dark early, and the ferry wouldn't be running once the shipyard workers were finished for the day. On the way back, Sammy saw Lucinda cross the road in front of them back from wherever she'd been in Colchester.

'Hey, Lucinda, we've got everything ready to dress the tree. We're waiting for you,' he yelled, causing a baby being pushed past them in a pram to scream and an old lady on a bicycle to veer dangerously towards the hedge.

Not stopping to apologise, he took off and flew into Lucinda's waiting arms. Emily smothered her giggle, not wishing to offend the mother or the elderly cyclist, and even George smiled.

'No manners at all, he deserves a good spanking,' the old lady said loudly.

'I'm sorry, ma'am, he's just excited to see our cousin who's been away,' Emily said.

The mother had soothed the baby and walked on without comment.

'Let's run, Emily,' George said. 'It's perishing, or taters, as Doris would say.'

They raced to the front door and arrived in a heap and a tangle of arms and legs just as it opened. Mummy was holding Grace and the baby screeched and waved her chubby arms about.

'What a lot of noise, you three. Hurry up and come in so I can close the door, the wind's icy.'

'Sorry, Mummy,' Emily said, and her brothers echoed her. 'We're excited to be doing the tree. Lucinda's never done this before and it's Grace's first time too.'

* * *

'Lucinda, as this is your first time decorating the tree, why don't you put the angel on the top?' Mummy said later. 'Grace can do it next year as I'm certain she couldn't manage it this time.'

'Are you sure? I'd love to but I don't want to tread on anybody's toes.'

George grinned. 'You've done that several times already, so go ahead, we want you to. We've all had a turn – Sammy did it last year.'

With due solemnity, Lucinda stretched up and pushed the angel with the wonky wings on top of the tree. Emily sighed. She was so lucky to be living here surrounded by her family and to have two best friends just across the river.

'I expect you've noticed our angel is far from perfect,' she said. 'George trod on it when he was little, but we still love it. Putting it up's a family tradition.'

'We won't switch on the lights until we're all here. Is the table laid in the dining room, boys? Daddy will be back at any moment and I like things to be ready for him.'

Emily headed for the kitchen. Lily had left a Woolton pie, potatoes to roast, carrots and cabbage to boil, ready for tonight's meal. Pie with no meat wasn't as tasty as one with rabbit or chicken in it, but a precious onion made into gravy would make the meal tickety-boo.

The pie and parboiled potatoes went in the hot oven in the range, and she put a saucepan of water on to simmer for the carrots. When they were done, she'd fish them out with a slotted spoon and put the cabbage into the same water but for less time.

Grandma had taught her how to cook vegetables so they weren't soft and tasteless. Thinking about her grandma and grandad, and the proposed family visit after Christmas, made her come to a surprising decision.

She went in search of her mother to put the idea to her – she didn't want to mention it to her father unless Mummy approved.

'I went to stay with them a few weeks ago and I said my goodbye to Grandad then. I think George and Sammy would be better off without me there; it wouldn't be fair for me to come again. I'd like to stay here with Lucinda, if that's something you think acceptable.'

Emily braced herself for a rebuff but got the opposite. 'I'm so proud of the young woman you're turning into, darling girl, your father and I would never have suggested you stay behind but in the circumstances I think it would really make things easier for George.'

'How long will you be staying? I'm perfectly capable of getting myself to school and back if you're not back when term starts. That's another thing, I don't want to miss any more lessons.'

'We can't stay as long as you did, but will be gone for a week, maybe a day or two longer. The Admiralty surveyor working at Vospers shipyard will manage both whilst we're away. If we leave the day after Boxing Day, which would be the soonest anyone would bring the car down from London, then we should be back before term starts.'

'It's going to be strange having everybody together again after almost half the school relocated to somewhere in the country. It was a relief Miss King's keeping us scholarship girls together, I'm not exactly sure which form we'll be in, but we won't be separated as we were originally.'

Lucinda wandered in with a large box of Liquorice Allsorts and handed them to Emily.

'I promised I'd try and get something for tonight so here you are.'

'Golly, how did you manage to get those? I hope we don't have to keep them for Christmas, having some tonight would be absolutely super.' Emily looked hopefully at her mother who laughed.

'Shall we compromise, my darling girl, eat the top row and then put the box away until Christmas Day? That's only four days away, after all.'

'I need to get back to the kitchen. It's almost completely dark so I'm sure Daddy will be here at any moment.'

Lucinda smiled apologetically. 'I promise I'll come and help you dish up but I need to speak to Elizabeth first.'

Emily politely closed the door behind her, knowing it was a grown-up conversation. George and Sammy had completed their task and the dining room looked splendid, the fire crackling in the grate, all the cutlery in the right places for a change.

'We're going to sort out the Monopoly box, Daddy said we couldn't play again until we've done it,' George said.

'It wouldn't be in such a mess if you hadn't tipped everything on the floor when you lost last time,' Sammy said.

'I don't like losing.'

'Nobody does, George, but remember you're on your last

warning. If you do something silly again you won't be allowed to play with us,' Emily said.

His cheeks flushed. She shouldn't have reprimanded him. He was still a bit overwrought and threatening him had been absolutely the wrong thing to do.

'There's something I need to tell you. I'm not coming to Kent, I went last time and you had to stay at home, so our parents have decided it wouldn't be fair if I came again.'

This wasn't exactly true, but it did the trick. George relaxed and his colour returned to normal.

'Are you really fed up about that?'

'No, I had my turn and now you and Sammy can see where our father grew up, play with the dogs, spend time with our grandparents.'

'You're a good egg, Emily, I know it was your suggestion. I don't deserve to have such a lovely sister,' George said and his eyes glittered.

'You deserve to have everything wonderful in your life as we all do. Can I tell you something a bit sad and a little bit happy?' The boys nodded. 'Grandad will be pleased to see you, but he doesn't get up now, it's as if he's getting ready to go to heaven. Grandma will be sad too, but when he does go, she'll come back to live with us permanently.'

'Crikey, that'll be good, Grace will have to stay in the box room if she does come,' Sammy said.

'Lucinda might well be leaving here in a few weeks if she gets into the ATA. I don't think she told you she's hoping to join them and to be collecting and delivering fighter planes for the RAF eventually?'

This had their full attention. 'No, she didn't tell us. What's the ATA? I don't think I know anything about it.'

The boys followed her into the kitchen and sat at the table.

She told them what she knew about this association whilst she dashed about doing the final preparations for the meal. Emily was proud that Lucinda could fly an aeroplane and would be doing something so important to help the RAF.

* * *

Ralph wasted no time in setting his plans in motion. Three hours after his disastrous meeting with his erstwhile mistress, he was stepping out of a taxi outside his palatial family home.

Whatever Leone thought about the matter, she couldn't stop him living with her – the estate and house belonged to him – if the thousands she'd brought to the union were safely in his hands then he'd not need to ingratiate himself. Her money remained hers, apart from the household expenses which she paid. She was pretty enough, but had no sparkle, no wit, and talked of nothing but the children, fashions and the deprivations she was suffering because of the war.

The only reason the marriage had lasted as long as it had was because she was content to remain in the country which allowed him to do as he pleased in London. God knows why she'd kicked up such a stink about Lucinda, how she'd even known about this affair was a mystery to him. Someone must have seen them together at a nightclub or a party and rushed off immediately to inform on him.

His two equally dull daughters, Cynthia and Sybil, would be with their nanny so no danger of them interrupting his conversation with their mother.

Only visitors entered through the front door, family used the garden door which was where he headed.

His wife had two little snappy dogs, he loathed them, and they knew that if they got within his reach they'd be unceremoniously kicked aside. This didn't stop them yapping and barking from the other side of the large entrance hall.

Leone appeared, her expression uncertain, her smile nervous. 'Ralph, I didn't expect you this weekend.'

'I know, I should have telephoned to let you know I was coming. I have had time to think, my dear, and now understand why you did what you did. You made things difficult for me, but I forgive you. I was at fault, I'm hoping we can put things right between us and leave that unfortunate business in the past.'

He'd hoped she'd look delighted, rush into his arms but she did the reverse and retreated several steps.

'I don't know, Ralph, a few weeks ago you were demanding a divorce, telling me you loved this Lucinda Somiton and wanted to marry her. You said some horrible things to me.'

'I did, and I apologise for that. Understand, Leone, I am not a man who is used to being thwarted. This girl was no more important to me than the others. If you hadn't made the matter public the affair would have been over and we could have continued as usual.'

'I'm not sure if that's supposed to make me feel better or worse, Ralph. I'm not sure that I want to be reconciled, to be forced to live with a serial philanderer who cares nothing for me or our daughters.'

This was hardly the place to hold such a private conversation and he herded her into the drawing room and closed the door firmly behind them.

'I want to try for a boy, Leone, secure the title and estates for us. When Hugh dies everything comes to us but without a son it will eventually go to some remote second or third cousin.'

She was listening with more interest now and from nowhere he thought of the clincher. 'I've not been well since the debacle and visited a doctor in Harley Street. He sent me to a cardiac consultant who informed me that I have a rare and complicated heart malformation. I could have a fatal attack at any time.'

'Oh, my word, Ralph, how absolutely dreadful. Have you told Hugh?'

'God, no, I don't want to worry them. According to the chap I saw I might go on living a perfectly normal life for many years so why tell him? It also means that we've got time, if you agree, to have another baby and pray that it might be a boy, not just for my sake but for the family.'

'This is all a dreadful shock, I'm not sure I can go through the heartbreak of you having another affair. I'd rather live as if I was a widow than go through that again. You think you were humiliated, can you imagine how I felt?'

Ralph stepped in and gathered her close. He stroked her hair, her back, murmured encouragement and loving words and she relaxed against him. She'd always been easy to manipulate, unlike that bitch Lucinda.

'I'll not let you down again, darling, knowing what I do about my health has changed me. From now on I'm going to live every day as if it's my last, no more nonsense, I'll be an exemplary husband and a loving father.'

She looked up at him. 'Do you love me?'

'I've always loved you, Leone, you're my wife. I'm a man and I have needs that you weren't prepared to meet after our second daughter was born. I'm not proud of being unfaithful, but I never loved anyone but you, whatever I might have said in the heat of the moment.'

His false sincerity convinced her. 'Then, yes, I'd love to have another baby. Are you sure that doing something so energetic won't trigger a fatal event?'

'Absolutely certain, my love, I explained the circumstances to the doctor and he reassured me. In fact, he advised me to live my life as usual, put this dire news aside, and try and forget about it.'

'I am in the middle of my cycle. You've returned at the perfect time if we wish to start another baby.'

He knew she wasn't suggesting they tumbled into bed right now but he pretended he'd misunderstood. He swept her up into his arms and strode to the door.

'I love you, my darling Leone, and intend to show you just how much.'

Making love to his wife wasn't as exciting as making love to Lucinda but he was sure he did what was necessary and Leone certainly didn't complain about his efforts.

He remained by her side for half an hour talking nonsense as that's what she expected.

'It's going to be the most wonderful Christmas, Ralph, the girls will be so excited to have their father here. I promised that we could decorate the drawing room this afternoon and do the tree tomorrow.'

He hid his irritation as the last thing he wanted was to be involved in anything as mundane as decorating the tree or, even worse, the house with hideous paper chains and other gaudy items.

'That's why I came home today. I want us to be a happy family again. I thought as there are no toys to speak of available even in Harrods that we could find something in the old nursery. I'm sure our girls won't mind if anything we find is old, especially if we tell them it had once belonged to their grandmother.'

'I've managed to acquire a few small things to go in their stockings but your suggestion is quite brilliant. I can't wait to explore with you – we can do it after the children go to bed and before we dine.'

* * *

Lucinda explained to her cousin what had happened between her and Ralph. 'I don't know how I ever thought I loved him. Do you know, Elizabeth, he threatened me with some sort of repercussions for rejecting him?'

'What do you mean?'

'He said he hoped I wouldn't regret what I'd done, and it scared me. He comes from a powerful family, remember I told you that his brother is Sir Hugh Castleton, and Ralph's something important in intelligence.'

'Oh dear, I think you're right to be concerned. He could make things very difficult for you, possibly prevent you from getting an interview for the ATA.'

This was hardly encouraging. Lucinda had hoped Elizabeth would reassure her, tell her that she was overreacting.

'He doesn't know that I've applied there, I told him I was hoping to get into the WAAF or the WRNS. Thank God, I never told him that I had a private pilot's licence. Even then I must have sensed it was something he wouldn't approve of; he wanted me to be submissive and feminine and flying an aeroplane is neither of those.' She sat back, her stomach curdling, as things she should have noticed when they were together made sense. She'd been too innocent, besotted, to consider that Ralph's behaviour wasn't loving but controlling.

'Clever girl, your instincts were right. By the time he realises he's putting his energy into the wrong places you might already be part of that wonderful organisation. We can only hope so.'

'Perhaps you'd be kind enough to tell Jonathan what happened, get his advice. When we go to church tomorrow then I'll certainly be praying but probably not for the things I should be.'

Lucinda tickled Grace under the chin before heading for the door. 'Excuse me, I need to help in the kitchen. I'm pretty sure I heard the tramp of heavy boots outside just now so the shipyard workers are on the way home which means Jonathan will be here soon.'

She joined the children and they greeted her with unusual enthusiasm.

'Emily told us your exciting news about joining the ATA,' George said. 'Please will you tell us everything you know about what you might be doing if you get taken on?'

They proceeded to bombard her with questions that she was happy to answer. Ten minutes later the back door banged, Jonathan was home. Everything stopped when the man of the house arrived, the children rushed to greet him, she heard Elizabeth and the baby coming down the passageway.

This just reinforced Lucinda's determination not to be married, not to be at the beck and call of a man and unable to make her own decisions. She smiled; unless she met someone as wonderful as Jonathan.

12

Lucinda took Jonathan's advice and went into Colchester in order to collect application forms for both the Women's Royal Navy Service and the Women's Auxiliary Air Force, better known as the WRNS and the WAAF. These could be collected at the library. She went first to the Midland Bank in the High Street with the bank draft and the letter from Jonathan.

A supercilious man dressed in a navy pinstripe suit accosted her as she walked in. 'Do you have an appointment, miss?'

Today Lucinda hadn't made the mistake of dressing down and almost wished she still had her mink coat as that would really have impressed them.

'I don't, what I do have is a letter from my guardian and a bank draft for three thousand guineas. I wish to open an account.'

His expression changed. 'If you would care to take a seat, I'll see who's free to arrange this for you.'

She could put the money in the Trustee Savings Bank, or into National Savings, but she needed a substantial sum in her post office account so she could withdraw or deposit from this without having to come into Colchester.

Mentioning the huge amount of money she had to deposit had meant she suddenly became a desirable customer and not a nuisance to be fobbed off. What really annoyed her was that if she was married she'd be considered an adult but would still need her husband's permission to do anything financial.

A different, older, less smarmy, suited gentleman came over to her. 'Mr Peabody should have asked your name. I am Mr Sargent.'

'And I am pleased to meet you. Shall we go into your office?'

If he was disconcerted by her evasion he didn't show it. In fact, his eyes twinkled and he smiled. She was conducted to a plush office and he indicated a comfortable chair by the fire, not the upright one in front of his desk.

'I've taken the liberty of assuming that you prefer coffee to tea, I also hope that you enjoy a freshly baked pastry.'

'I do, Mr Sargent. When I tell you that my name's Lucinda Somiton, does that mean something to you?'

He sat opposite and his expression was serious. 'I do recall seeing your name in the gossip columns a few weeks ago. However, that has nothing to do with your financial probity. I'll be delighted to open an account for you.'

The conversation was temporarily interrupted as a very young woman came in precariously balancing a tray on one arm. Lucinda was about to stand up and assist but Mr Sargent was on his feet first.

'Mabel, let me take that from you before you drop it. Mr Peabody should have been there to open the door for you. I shall have words with him about his poor manners.'

The girl grinned, nodded at Lucinda, and retreated. He put the laden tray on the coffee table in front of them.

The pastries were delicious and freshly baked, the coffee hot and strong, and Mr Sargent was, she discovered, the actual bank manager.

'Now, Miss Somiton, shall we get down to business? You have a very substantial amount of money. Do you have your own ideas about how to manage this or would you like me to give you some advice?'

'Mr Roby, my guardian, and I have discussed this at length. I thought to put £1,000 into war bonds, keep £350 in my personal account, and I have other plans which I'll explain to you later. Would you approve of that?'

'I would have advised more or less the same. I assume that you have a post office book?'

She nodded.

'Then I'd suggest you have perhaps a hundred pounds in that so you can take out what you need on a day-to-day basis wherever you are. I'll have the cash withdrawn from your account as soon as it is set up.'

'Thank you, how long will the paperwork take to be organised? I have an errand to run which should take me about twenty minutes – will the paperwork be ready for my signature by then?'

'Absolutely, Miss Somiton. Thank you for choosing my bank, I hope we have a long and satisfactory relationship.'

Lucinda smiled, stood up and brushed the crumbs from her skirt. The bank manager held her coat whilst she slipped her arms into it and then escorted her to the door.

'Mr Peabody will be waiting to bring you back to my office when you return.' He smiled. 'Take as long as you want, Miss Somiton, you are now a valued customer and we are at your disposal.'

'There's one more thing, Mr Sargent, I'd like to set up a trust fund for the four Roby children. I know you can't do that today, but that's what I wish to do with the remaining thousand pounds.'

She handed him over the necessary information which she'd kept in her pocket. She hadn't quite decided if she wanted to put everything with this bank but he'd proved to be someone trustworthy so the children's money would be safe at the Midland.

Lucinda was smiling as she walked out. What a difference having a large sum of money made to the way one was treated.

* * *

As there was no rush to return to the bank after she'd collected the application forms, she decided to fill them in immediately. Once that was done, she posted them at the main post office, conveniently situated next to the town hall further up the High Street.

A little over an hour after arriving in Colchester, Lucinda was on a bus back to Wivenhoe. The necessary forms had been signed and she had the cash to pay into her post office account safely in her handbag.

The bus stop was outside the Greyhound pub, just a few yards from the post office so she'd deposit the cash when she got off. As she'd been walking around with a massive amount of money in a bank draft that anybody could have deposited if they'd stolen it, having a hundred pound in banknotes didn't bother her at all.

The post office, like every other shop, closed for lunch but she was there in ample time. She now had a satisfactory amount of change, a ten-shilling note and a pound note, more than enough for her day-to-day expenses.

Mr Sargent said he would write to her when the trust fund had been arranged which was when he'd require her signature.

Until she'd signed, she'd no intention of telling the family what she'd done in case they tried to stop her. The bank manager had promised the papers would be ready early in the New Year. This meant the announcement would have to wait until the family returned from Kent.

* * *

The house was quiet – Jonathan would be at work, Elizabeth was probably at one of her endless women's meetings, the children were in Rowhedge, but where was Lily? Normally at this time she'd be bustling around the kitchen ready to serve lunch to whoever was home to eat it.

Lucinda removed her outer garments, hung them up, carefully put her boots into one of the boxes beneath the pegs, and stepped into her slippers. The housekeeper wasn't downstairs, that was obvious, maybe she was upstairs tidying?

'Lily, Lily, are you there? Is there anything I can do for lunch?'

Her voice echoed down the empty passageway and got no response. Lunch was eaten just after midday, apart from on a Sunday, so there should be signs that this was ready even if the maker wasn't around.

There was a large saucepan of mixed vegetable soup simmering on the range, a tray of homemade rolls waiting to go in the oven, the dishes and cutlery ready to be taken into the dining room so Lily couldn't be far away.

She put the rolls in to bake and decided it made sense for the two of them and the baby to eat in the kitchen as it was warmer than the dining room. She was just laying the table when the back door banged and Lily rushed in.

The soup spoon clattered on the table and she rushed over to

Lily. 'What's wrong? I was worried when I arrived and you were missing.'

'I'm sorry, I had to rush home as my neighbour came to tell me there was someone from the Ministry of Agriculture banging on my door. How on earth they knew about my chickens I don't know.'

'Goodness, are you in trouble?'

'No, he wasn't there to make a fuss but to get me signed up so I can get grain and so on for the chickens more easily. We can't have the eggs that we're allowed on the ration now I've got chickens, but I don't have to sell any to them unless I've got a surplus.'

'Thank goodness for that. It makes sense to encourage people to keep chickens as well as dig for victory – if you're giving eggs to your neighbours and using them yourself then there are more for those who don't have them.'

'Thank you for laying the table in here,' Lily said. 'But you've put three places and it's only two of you and the highchair.'

'You eat with us when we're in here, it's only when we're in the dining room you don't join us.'

* * *

Lucinda retired immediately after lunch, hoping to be able to sleep as she was going to be out all night patrolling the streets. There was a tap on the door far too soon and groggily she pushed herself onto her elbows and answered.

'I'm coming, I'll be down in a minute, thank you for waking me, whoever it is.'

'It's Emily, I just wanted to tell you that it's snowing. I should put several layers on as it's going to be perishing outside tonight. Our backsides froze to the seat on the ferry when we came back across the river an hour ago.'

'My breath's steaming in front of me in here. Maybe we're going to have a white Christmas this year.'

'It certainly seems like it. I have your tea waiting.'

Jonathan was just coming in as Lucinda arrived in the kitchen. 'I don't envy you your patrol this evening, Lucinda, the snow's heavier.'

'I hope that means the Luftwaffe will stay in France and Belgium and not be bombing us tonight.'

The boys were slurping down tea and munching broken biscuits – one would have thought they had hollow legs the amount of food they consumed without putting on an ounce. Their cooked meal was after the baby went to bed but they couldn't survive, according to them, until six o'clock without something to fill the gap.

'The bombers and the fighters can't fly if it's below freezing because the wings ice up,' George said.

'Anyway, they won't be able to see anything through the snow, it's a blizzard out there now,' Sammy added.

'Does that mean I don't have to do my patrol?'

'Why don't you pop round to Mr Hatch and ask him?' Lily suggested as she bustled around the kitchen, putting the final touches to the evening meal before she left.

'I'll do that, good idea, thank you. Elizabeth, why don't we abandon the dining room until the weather improves and eat in here?'

'I was about to suggest the same thing, my dear, we did that last winter too. Christmas Day we'll light the fire and dress the table. Now we've got a lovely plump cockerel from Lily and Mr Turner for lunch it's going to be a splendid meal.'

* * *

Lucinda skidded on the ice as she approached Mr Hatch's front door and instead of knocking politely she crashed headfirst into it. Moments later, Mrs Hatch opened it.

'Goodness me, Miss Somiton, we thought the Nazis had come. Are you all right?'

'Yes, it's lethal out there. Could I have a quick word with Mr Hatch?'

'If you're going to ask him whether you should patrol tonight, he said to tell you if you came round that you don't have to. No bombers on a night like this.'

'That's the best news I've had all day. Thank you, I wasn't looking forward to spending the night out in this snowstorm. There's already a couple of inches underfoot and it's now covering the ice from yesterday.'

'I reckon no one will be out, only three more days until Christmas so let's hope the blooming Germans stay at home until the New Year and give the poor souls in London and other cities time to enjoy our Lord's birthday.' Mrs Hatch spoke in a rush with not even a pause for breath.

'Amen to that. Good night, Mrs Hatch. Be very careful when you come out tomorrow, it's going to be even worse than it is now.'

Lucinda skidded and slid home, unsurprised that there were no other pedestrians about in the freezing darkness. It was a miracle she didn't end up on her derrière as it almost happened twice.

The welcome warmth of the boot room greeted her as she stepped in through the back door of Harbour House. She paused for a few minutes, inhaling the familiar aroma, understanding that for the first time in her life she had a home, was living with people who loved her, wanted her to be there.

If Mrs Castleton hadn't contacted the gossip columnists, then

Lucinda wouldn't be here. That woman had done her a huge favour and if she ever met Mrs Castleton then instead of being angry, she'd thank her.

* * *

Emily and her brothers had helped Penny and the twins decorate their ramshackle house. It had taken all day, the twins were covered in flour and water paste by the end of it, but the tree and the sitting room, as well as the entrance hall and passageway, were now festooned with paper chains and bits and bobs and looked really festive.

Mummy was putting Grace to bed, Lucinda had just got back from seeing Mr Hatch and discovering that she didn't have to patrol tonight, and the boys were putting the finishing touch to the kitchen table so they could eat.

'Daddy, was that telephone call you just took from Grandma?'

He nodded. 'It was, she was just telling me that your grandfather has perked up, knowing that we're coming to see them in a few days. She said they're going to pretend it won't be Christmas until we get there.'

'Lucky boys, if they're going to get two Christmas lunches. Have you heard when the car's coming?'

'Actually, I got a call at work earlier today. Someone's driving down with it on the 27th, which means we'll be leaving the day after Boxing Day.'

'Golly, so soon. Friday's only four days away. We go back to school on 6 January – will you be back by then?'

'Another phone call that I received was to say that the boys' school took a direct hit from an incendiary and there's been extensive fire damage. Nobody was hurt, but it's unlikely the Royal Grammar will open on time even if your school does.'

'I'm surprised that George and Sammy haven't heard about it. The schools have returned from their relocation because the powers that be decided Colchester isn't dangerous, and the very weekend they return the school goes up in flames.'

'Hardly that, sweetheart, but I see the irony.'

* * *

Over supper, the conversation was lively and mostly about the incendiary damage to the boys' school. Emily preferred eating in the kitchen, there was ample room around the large table and it was much warmer and less formal than the dining room.

'Do we need to start packing for Kent before Christmas, Mummy?' George asked as Lucinda and Emily cleared the dinner plates and went to fetch the jam roly-poly and custard for dessert.

'Goodness me, young man, you're not going on a six-month sea voyage, just to see your grandparents for a few days. There's no need to even think about packing anything until Boxing Day and that's four days away.'

'When I was evacuated we were only allowed to bring a change of clothes, one toy, and our pyjamas,' Sammy said. 'The War Office must have thought the families taking us in would give us what we didn't have.'

'I don't suppose many of the children coming from the East End like you did, Sammy, had more than that to bring,' George said.

Emily glared at him, hoping to stop him before he made things worse. She needn't have worried.

'I'm so glad you came to us, Sammy, imagine if you hadn't, you'd probably be back in London now and not my brother. This family wouldn't be the same without you.'

'It certainly wouldn't, well said, George, we're fortunate to have been able to adopt you, Sammy,' Daddy said.

'I'm the lucky one; I'm like a pig in clover living here. One day when I'm a bloke in a smart suit, driving a big black car, I'll go back to where I came from just to show them how well I've done.'

George grinned. 'I'm going to have a green MG sports car; I'll also have an apartment in Kensington.'

Mummy looked at Emily. 'What about you, darling girl, where do you see yourself in ten years?'

'I'll just be leaving university. I want to be an engineer but I don't suppose a woman will be allowed to do that when the war's over as the men will want those sorts of jobs so perhaps I'll be an architect instead.'

Lucinda reached across and squeezed her hand. 'You can be anything you want to be, Emily, things have already changed for women. Do you want to be a civil engineer or a mechanical?'

'Civil. I'd love to design big structures, roads, bridges, office buildings but probably being an architect might be more use as we're going to need houses for those who have been bombed out.'

George sniggered. 'Crikey, in ten years' time I hope the war will have been over for years and everybody will have a home. I'm going to be flying for a commercial airline when I'm grown up, what about you, Sammy?'

'My best subject's maths, Mr Ponsonby said I could be a chartered accountant. I'm not sure what that is but if it involves maths, I'll give it a go. As long as it means I can have a big car and a smart suit then that's what I'll do.'

Emily was sitting next to Lucinda and looked at her, eager to hear what she had in mind. She was already an adult, even if she wasn't considered to be one until she was twenty-one.

'I can't really think any further than what I'm going to do next

year. I'm hoping I'll be called for a test flight to join the ATA but
failing that I expect I'll get an interview for the WAAF. I'm eager
to be more involved than just patrolling lower Wivenhoe every
night. I hate to say this, but I can't see this beastly war being over
for ages yet. I think whatever I'm doing in a couple of months is
what I'll be doing for the next few years.'

13

Ralph did everything expected of him over the next few days. He attended church on Christmas Day itself, built snowmen with his girls and made love to his wife every night.

However, keeping up the pretence that he was a loving husband and father began to pall and he was relieved when he got a telephone call from the War Office asking him to come in.

'I'm sorry, darling, I've had far longer at home than I expected. It's been the most wonderful Christmas, but duty calls.'

Leone's smile was blinding and he felt a flicker of remorse that he was basically lying to her. Then he pushed this guilt aside, as it didn't really matter that his feelings for her and the two girls weren't genuine as long as they thought they were.

Hugh and Beatrice and their two plain daughters had welcomed them into the ancestral home for Christmas lunch itself. Ralph had enjoyed this – there was nothing he liked better than to be waited on by footmen and a butler in a house three times the size of his own.

'Come home when you can.'

'I'll come when I have permission to leave. I promise I'll be working and staying at the flat on my own if I'm not at home with you.'

'I believe you. I think you've learned your lesson, realised what you almost lost, and now we can be happy, especially if we have a boy next time.'

'Next time? Are you so sure that we'll have another child?'

'I am, it might not be this month, but I have a good feeling about it.'

He embraced her and kissed her fondly. Why had he been wasting his time chasing after other women when he had such a treasure at home? Maybe being a family man wouldn't be quite as bad as he imagined.

There'd been no massive raids over Christmas, just sporadic bombing, so at least the bad weather was beneficial in some ways. As he trudged through the snow to his underground office, his thoughts turned to the havoc he was going to wreak on the Somiton girl.

Knowing how slowly things were likely to be dealt with after the Christmas break – even though few people actually had the time off since the war started – it was unlikely that her application would be dealt with until the New Year. This meant he'd got plenty of time to set things in motion.

* * *

Emily had helped her brothers pack and had been there to wave them off when they'd left yesterday. Lily had been given the next few days free as there was absolutely no necessity to have a cook–housekeeper when there were only two people in the house.

Lucinda would be asleep until mid-afternoon so as long as Emily was home to wake her she could do as she pleased. She decided to take a train into Colchester and visit Nancy. She was expecting a baby in a couple of months, and if her husband, captain of a Thames barge, was away, there'd be nobody to walk the dog.

Even with two pairs of socks inside her rubber boots, thick scarf, woolly hat and gloves plus several layers underneath, Emily's toes were frozen by the time she trudged around to the yard of Nancy's haberdashery shop in Head Street.

Fortunately, the back gate was unlocked and she slithered her way to the door. Boyd saw her through the kitchen window and began to bark. There was no need to knock as the door was opened by Mr Brooks.

'Crikey, what are you doing here? No sensible person is out in this weather.'

Emily smiled. 'I'll tell you if you let me in. How are Nancy and Annie?'

'I'm absolutely tickety-boo, thanks, love, and so is Annie as her Richard's got leave for a few days as his ship was damaged and is in dock for a while,' Nancy called from a chair at the kitchen table.

'I came to take the dogs out, I didn't want you staggering about in your condition in this weather.'

'That's kind of you, love, but Dan's already taken him. Get your things off and I'll make you a nice cup of cocoa, I've got some lovely buns we can toast and have with jam.'

'You stop where you are, Nancy, I'll make the cocoa. You don't want to overdo it, that's what the midwife said when she came the other day.'

'I'm having a baby, not ill, and the shop will be open on Saturday as usual.'

'In which case, love, it'll be me serving the ladies with knicker elastic. See how that goes down.'

Emily giggled. She loved hearing the two of them talking. She didn't want to get married as young as Nancy had but when she did she hoped it would be to someone she could love and laugh with like they did.

'My family, apart from me and Lucinda, have gone to Kent. Daddy's got a car from London so they're driving. Grandpa's fading away, they want to visit him for the last time.'

'That's sad, but he's ever so old, let's hope they get there and back in one piece, it's not the weather for driving,' Nancy said. Then she frowned. 'You told me last time you came that Miss Somiton's out all night – does that mean you're going to be on your own?'

Emily stared at her. 'Golly, I don't think any of us considered that. I don't suppose it matters as I'll be asleep most of the time and I've got Ginger to protect me.' She nodded. 'Anyway, it's already been one night and I didn't even notice and then tomorrow's Sunday and she doesn't work at the weekend.'

'It's not right, you might look older but you're only twelve, you should have a grown-up there,' Nancy said.

'I've got a telephone, Mrs Cousins and the doctor live next door and if I opened the window and shouted, I think half a dozen people would hear and come running to help.'

'Don't fret, love, Mr Roby wouldn't have gone if he thought Emily couldn't manage. You could always go out on patrol with Miss Somiton. There's no school for Emily until next week so she could sleep all day same as she does,' Mr Brooks said.

'Don't be daft, Dan, she doesn't want to be tramping about in the snow in the middle of the night if she doesn't have to.'

'You're both right, I don't have to be on my own if I don't want to be. But on balance, I'd rather be alone in a warm bed than with Lucinda in the middle of the night in the snow.'

* * *

Emily spent a happy hour with her friends and then volunteered to do some shopping before she returned home. She was known to the shopkeepers in Head Street so there was no problem buying what was needed using Nancy's ration book.

As she unlocked the back door of Harbour House, she heard the telephone jangling outside the sitting room and raced down the passageway to answer it without removing her boots. She didn't want Lucinda to have to get up to answer it.

'Harbour House, Miss Roby speaking, how can I help you?'

'Emily, I thought I'd telephone and let you know how things are here. Your grandfather is overjoyed to see us and there isn't nearly as much snow in Kent as there is in Essex.'

'Daddy, how lovely to hear from you. I just went into Colchester to see if I could help Nancy by taking the dogs out, but I wasn't needed. I just did some shopping instead.'

'Good girl, we won't be staying for more than a couple of nights. If Lucinda's back on duty then you'll be on your own—'

'Goodness, I'll be asleep, there's no need for you to worry about me. Mr Brooks suggested that I could go out with Lucinda if I was worried about being on my own, but I'd much rather be in my warm bed.'

'I don't know how we didn't consider this before we left. I'm still not entirely happy about the situation, but if you change your mind then we'll come back at once.'

'George and Sammy would never forgive me. No, Daddy, you need to spend as much time as you can with Grandpa. Don't worry about me.'

'Your mother suggested that you could invite Doris to stay with you – she's a year older than you. It means you would have to brave the elements and catch the ferry across the river, but it might be worth it if you think your friend would come.'

'Thank you, I'm sure she'd love to. It's too late to go today as it'll be dark soon and I've got to get Lucinda up. I'll go tomorrow morning when the shipyard workers are using the ferry as then I'll be certain it's running. Give everyone my love. Goodbye.'

She was smiling as she replaced the receiver in the cradle. Doris would be absolutely perfect as a companion – she was more practical than either Penny or herself and it would be super fun being able to stay up late listening to the wireless like grown-ups every evening.

* * *

Doris was thrilled to be invited to come and stay for a few nights and her grandparents were happy to give their permission.

'You mind your Ps and Qs, don't take no liberties, behave yourself,' her nan said as they were about to leave.

'Don't worry, I know what's what, I'm tickled pink to be asked. I've never been away from home before and it'll be like a holiday.'

On the way down the hill to catch the ferry, they both fell over twice but it didn't matter, it was all part of the fun. They ran the short distance from the river to Harbour House and Emily's hands were so cold it took several minutes to unlock the back door so they could get into the warm.

'Crikey, I'm glad to be inside, my feet are like blocks of ice,' Doris said as she hooked off her boots.

'The slippers you use are right there waiting for you. We're going to sleep in the boys' room as it's got two beds. We're also going to light the fire – it'll be such fun.'

* * *

Lucinda was woken with an actual mug of tea, not just the usual knock on the door. Emily handed it to her.

'Doris is staying here until everyone comes back. That means I won't be on my own at night – not that I minded – but it's much more fun having one of my best friends here.'

Lucinda was surprised Emily had struck up such a strong friendship with someone so different from her. It just showed what a special girl she was.

'Has it snowed any more?'

'No, unfortunately the skies are fairly clear, not quite a bomber's moon but almost as bad. I'm hoping it's so many degrees below zero that the Luftwaffe can't fly because of the ice – I think it forms on the wings, but I might be wrong.'

'People are a bit on edge now after the incendiaries last week in Colchester. Have you checked that the shelter under the house is usable? Its previous life was just as a vegetable cellar, after all.'

'We haven't, and we're certainly not going down there now as it's far too cold. We'll have a look tomorrow. I think there's a paraffin stove and Doris will know how to light that safely as they've got one in their outhouse.'

'Good show, thanks for the tea. I'll be down for my sandwiches in ten minutes.'

'Golly, I'd forgotten all about those. Don't worry, they'll be ready when you come.'

* * *

Emily had been right and, half an hour after Lucinda had begun patrolling, the dreaded sound of German bombers approaching meant that London was going to get bombed again. She watched, her heart sinking, as wave after wave flew past. This was going to be a massive raid. Then they were surrounded by a squadron of fighters, the sky was ripped apart by machine-gun bullets. She was delighted to see two of the German planes had fire coming from various parts of their fuselage as they spiralled away into the darkness, hopefully to crash somewhere away from houses.

Lucinda jumped up and down cheering and she saw a couple of curtains twitch in the nearby houses. The siren didn't wail so whoever was in charge, no doubt somewhere in a headquarters underground, didn't believe any bombs were going to be dropped in this area.

As she passed the Black Buoy, someone opened the door and light flooded out onto the snow. 'Shut that blooming door. Can't you hear the bombers going over? Do you want a bomb dropped on your head?'

A cheerful voice replied, 'Sorry, love, tripped over the bleeding thing and it came down on me head.'

The door had been slammed shut, leaving the speaker outside. She shone her torch in his direction and laughed. He was completely entangled in the blackout curtain, his arms and legs making bumps in the material but not emerging.

'Stand still, I'll extricate you before you break your neck. You're standing on the hem, keep still and I'll sort you out.'

'Righto, ta, love, can't tell me arse from me elbow.'

A few minutes later, a tousle-haired, friendly young man emerged, grinning. 'We can't go in that way as there's no blackout, I'm holding it.'

'Go around to the back door and up the stairs. This needs to be put back before anyone else comes out. Good night, if I see any light here again tell the landlord he'll be fined.'

This small incident made her smile but it hadn't made her any warmer. She could hear the ack-ack guns firing at Harwich, they would be protecting any naval ships docked there. The search lights arced through the blackness, searching for a target, but the Luftwaffe were gone, at least for the moment.

Experience told her the first bombers wouldn't linger in London as the longer they stayed the more likely they were to be shot down – not by the big guns, as they rarely hit anything, but by the fighters.

She wouldn't be able to see the fire glow from here but she could imagine the horror, the devastation in London at the moment, and sent up a quick prayer for those on the receiving end of this raid. One thing she was certain of was that no Londoner would panic – they'd just get on with it as they had been doing for the past three months. Hitler wasn't going to demoralise Britain, however many bombs he dropped.

* * *

Weary, fed up and frozen solid, Lucinda pushed her way into the house at five o'clock. Why were the lights on? Her pulse jumped. Had there been an emergency in her absence?

'Lucinda, you must have had a dreadful night. We heard the bombers and listened to the wireless and it's been shockingly bad night for them. Thousands of incendiaries, half the city is in flames. We found it hard to sleep knowing that so got up to make you a proper breakfast,' Emily said and rushed forward and hugged her, despite the fact that she was still wearing her ice-encrusted outer garments.

'I appreciate it, I was feeling a bit low as you might imagine. A large mug of tea is exactly what I want after I've taken off my coat and things.'

She munched her way through a delicious plate of fried bread and baked beans, closely followed by several slices of toast and Marmite.

'That was scrumptious, thank you so much both of you. It's going to be at least another two hours before it's fully light so why don't you both go back to bed?'

'It's Saturday today – you don't have to work. Have you got any plans for the weekend?'

'I think I'll spend it with you and Doris, if that's all right. Don't forget, we're going to investigate your air-raid shelter to make sure it's fully functioning. Why don't we get fish and chips for tea?'

The girls were delighted with her suggestion and an hour after arriving home Lucinda was snuggled up with her hot water bottle and her extremities were finally thawing out.

She was woken by the two girls moving about next door. They weren't noisy but Lucinda was eager to get up.

Six months ago, the thought of spending even an hour with two girls of their age would have filled her with horror, now she couldn't wait. She emerged from her room fully clothed about the same time as they did.

They had a second breakfast, or a very early lunch, and the three of them were ready to venture down the steps to the shelter which so far hadn't been used.

'Golly, we forgot to bring in the milk, it's frozen,' Emily said. 'Look, there's ice poking out of the top.'

Doris grabbed the small metal crate that the milk was in and grinned. 'It'll taste the same once it's defrosted.' The five pint bottles rattled as she carried them into the scullery.

The wooden door of the shelter was iced shut and it took the combined efforts of the three of them to prise it open. Lucinda sniffed and was reassured.

'It doesn't smell awful, not damp as I expected. It seems you're a dab hand at lighting lamps and paraffin stoves, Doris, so if we shine our torches in the right direction can you do that for us?'

'My pleasure, I do it all the time at home, we ain't got no electric nor gas in our cottage.'

No wonder Doris was so happy to come to Harbour House, which was positively luxurious compared to her house. Not what Lucinda was accustomed to, but nevertheless this was her home, and she loved it, even if it didn't have a proper bathroom and no garden to speak of.

14

Emily enjoyed sprucing up the underground shelter with Lucinda and Doris. 'It's cosy down here even if it does smell of paraffin,' she said. 'I bet the boys will want to make it their den when they get back.'

'I don't reckon it'd be safe down here with those two racketing about,' Doris said. 'What with oil lamps and paraffin stoves and everything.'

'Yes, you're right. We won't mention it to them – it'll be all right in the summer when they don't need the paraffin stove. I think they'd be safe enough with an oil lamp.'

'Only three days and we're back to school. I leave at Easter and am going to work in munitions on Hythe Hill,' Doris said.

'Don't do that, it's so dangerous. Surely you can find something safer and more enjoyable?'

There'd been some dreadful accidents in these dangerous places and she didn't want her dear friend to be killed by exploding bombs or bullets.

'I ain't lucky like you, Emily, I can't please myself. I need to get the job which pays the best money. Me nan and grandad are relying on me. Penny's mum has put in a word for me and there's a job if I want it where she works.'

Emily thought of a way to keep Doris safe and blurted out her idea without really considering how Doris might react.

'I've just had an idea – if Lily leaves then why don't you be our housekeeper? You could get here easily enough on the ferry every day. I know she gets a good wage.'

Instead of looking pleased by her suggestion, Doris scowled. 'So you think of me as a skivvy then? I thought I was your friend.'

'I've only got two friends: you and Penny. Nancy's an older friend, and she used to work for us, and I count Annie as a friend and she worked here too. It doesn't matter what you do for a living, it's who you are that counts. I'd love to have you here all the time, you'd still be my best friend, but I can see why you might find it a bit tricky.'

'Well, that's all right then. Why do you think that Lily's going to leave? She seems happy here, like one of the family.'

Emily grinned and affectionately pressed Doris's shoulder. 'There, you understand what I was saying. I heard Lily talking to her daughter and I think there might be a baby sometime in the future.'

'Crikey, Daphne's not even married yet.'

'No, not Daphne, Lily. She and Mr Turner want another baby. She's about the same age as my mother was when she had Grace so it's perfectly possible.'

'Good luck to them, I say, I wouldn't want to bring a nipper into the world right now, but I suppose at their age they can't afford to wait.'

Emily regretted upsetting Doris but hoped she'd smoothed things over. She was so lucky that she could remain at school until she was eighteen when Doris had no option but to leave and start working.

* * *

The next three days were equally enjoyable, even going to church where their breath steamed in front of them and the congregation shivered. It was colder in the old building than in the churchyard.

Daddy had telephoned to say they would be home on Thursday. This meant the boys would miss the first day of term, if the school even opened then, but nothing much happened the first day so it wouldn't really matter academically.

Saying goodbye to Doris was going to be difficult as they'd had such a jolly time pretending to be grown-ups. The evenings had been especially good after Lucinda had gone to work as they relaxed in the sitting room listening to the wireless and even drank their night-time cocoa in there. Having the Christmas tree lights made the room magical and the evenings even better.

On Wednesday, as she was waiting with Doris for the ferry to come back from the other side of the river, Doris asked a question that had also been bothering Emily.

'Why didn't Penny come over? You put a note through her door saying she was very welcome even if only for a day. I'm going straight there when I get back, if there's anything going on then I'll go to the telephone box and give you a ring to let you know.'

'We should have gone to see her. I feel a bit guilty about that, but we were having such a good time and the weather's been so frightful, I didn't suggest it. Here, I've got some pennies, you take them in case you have to make that telephone call. It's not fair if you have to pay.'

Doris didn't argue and dropped the pennies into her pocket. 'I'll give them back to you if I don't use them. You'll be coming across to mine on Saturday, won't you?'

'I suppose we could wait until Penny comes into school tomorrow, but I don't want her to think that we forgot about her completely.'

'Even if we did? We could easily have nipped across, she must think we're rotten friends.'

'I'm coming with you. It's not even two o'clock so I can easily be back before dark,' Emily said.

'That's the ticket. I never liked to suggest it but I wasn't keen to go on me own.'

'I'm sorry, I'll have to have two of the pennies back as I only had those coppers with me,' Emily said. It cost 1d each way.

The water was high, the crossing choppy but fortunately Emily was sitting in the centre of the seat so it wasn't her that got a wet backside.

She usually ignored the youth who helped people disembark but this time she was grateful for his strong hand to guide her from the rocking ferry.

'Blimey, my bum's soaked. I'll be frozen by the time I get home,' Doris said with a grimace. 'It's blooming well gone right through my coat.'

'Why don't you go home and change and then join me over the lane at Penny's house?'

'I ain't got another coat so might as well stay as I am. Imagine what it must be like rowing that blooming ferry backwards and forwards all day in this weather.'

'I think there are two ferrymen, one from Rowhedge and one from Wivenhoe and they do half a day each.'

It would have been better if they'd been able to run up the hill but it was too slippery as the snow underneath had frozen and then fresh snow had fallen overnight. Emily was concerned about her family coming home in a car tomorrow as the roads would be absolutely lethal.

'Do you think the army clears the main roads so their lorries can get through?'

'I reckon so, there's thousands and thousands of squaddies hanging around idle since they was brought back from Dunkirk. The blighters have got to do something to keep fit and make themselves useful.'

'Of course, how silly of me. I was just thinking about my family coming home if the roads hadn't been cleared.'

They'd now slithered their way up the hill and were outside the house where Penny lived.

'Shall we go round the back, Doris? That will save someone having to walk through the house from the kitchen. That's where they'll be as it's warmer than anywhere else.'

They didn't look at the front of the house on the way to the back gate as they were too busy trying not to slip.

The gate was bolted on the inside but Doris was tall enough to reach over and slide it back. The twins couldn't reach it without standing on something.

The path hadn't been cleared and there were no fresh foot-prints in the snow. Emily was now seriously concerned for her friend and her family.

She pointed to the un-blemished snow in front of the back door and Doris nodded.

'Something's not right. The blackouts are still down.'

Emily felt a rush of relief. 'The only reason for that is because they're not there. They must have gone away for Christmas.'

'I hope so, otherwise we'll find a row of dead bodies inside.'

Emily snorted. 'Don't be so melodramatic, Doris, the obvious answer's usually the correct one.'

After hammering on the door for several minutes and getting no response they were both convinced the house was empty.

'I reckon me nan will know what's what. We should have gone there first.'

* * *

Doris was right and Nan told them that Penny and her family had got a travel warrant to go and see Captain Simmons, who was with his regiment somewhere in Kent. Emily was relieved and happy that her friend had managed to see her father, after being apart from him for so many months.

She hugged Doris and then trudged down to the ferry, wishing she'd thought of this explanation before making such an unpleasant excursion.

* * *

Lucinda was looking forward to seeing the house full again when the remainder of the family returned from Kent today. Emily was back at school; Lily had the house sparkling and, in honour of the occasion, all the fires were being lit.

London had been hit again by a massive raid, as had other cities throughout the country. The RAF were doing retaliation bombing but she'd not heard that they were being particularly successful. It was the fighters, the Hurricanes and Spitfires, that were key to keeping up British morale.

She'd managed to buy an alarm clock from Mr Chaney on the corner of Queen's Road so didn't have to rely on someone waking her up to go on patrol. Doing her duty was all very well, but there was really no necessity for anybody to be wandering around the streets in the middle of the night as there'd been no further incidents of any sort. Even issuing a fine for showing a light would make her life more interesting.

'Did you have a good sleep, Miss Somiton? There're three letters for you, I put them in the box by the telephone,' Lily said.

'Thank you, I'll read them whilst I drink my tea. Goodness, have I got actual cheese on toast today? How did you manage that?'

'My chickens are still laying the occasional egg and I swapped half a dozen for a nice piece of cheese. It's too dry to eat in a sandwich but it'll be lovely toasted.'

Lucinda collected her letters and saw that one was postmarked Hatfield. Did she dare open it? So much depended on at least getting a chance to show her skills as a pilot.

She carefully slid her finger under the flap on the envelope and pulled out a single sheet. She had to read it twice. Lily came in with her tea on a tray and Lucinda looked at her, her eyes brimming.

'I've got an interview to be an ATA pilot. I can't believe it, I'm so excited.'

'When is it?'

'Golly, I didn't take that in. Let me see – it's next Wednesday, it says to come regardless of the weather and be prepared to stay until it's safe to fly.'

'Where's Hatfield when it's at home?'

'I think it's about twenty miles from London. I'll catch the train from Paddington and then hope to cadge a lift to the airfield.'

'What time do you have to be there?'

'Good grief, it says by nine o'clock. That means I'll have to leave Wivenhoe on the first train to make sure I've got enough time to walk the two miles if I have to.'

'There's one at five thirty – it wakes us up every morning. You might be a bit late if you have to walk but with any luck you'll get a lift and arrive spot on.'

Lucinda didn't want her delicious cheese on toast to get cold so left the other letter until she'd finished. It was already dark and she'd expected the family to be home by now. Driving with barely any headlights, just a narrow pinpoint, in the blackout was something she thought Jonathan would have avoided.

The thought of them driving in the dark made her worry and what had seemed delicious a few moments ago now no longer appealed. Ginger meowed and purred around her feet, looking hopeful.

'All right, you can have it. Don't tell Lily, she'll be very upset I gave the precious cheese to you.'

Despite being a veteran hunter, bringing home rabbits regularly whilst the bunnies were still to be seen out of their burrows, the huge cat had never stolen anything from someone's plate. He had taken things left lying around in the pantry – but that was different.

He'd just wolfed down the last crumb when Lucinda heard a car pulling up outside. Her heart skipped. She ran to the front door, slipped behind the blackout curtain and opened it.

'Home at last, I was getting worried as I thought you'd be here earlier,' Lucinda called loudly from the doorstep. She was wearing her slippers so couldn't go down to meet them.

Jonathan yelled back and she heard Elizabeth tutting and telling him to be quiet and the boys were laughing.

'Had to do several detours because of the bombs last night in London. Grace's asleep so Elizabeth will put her straight to bed.'

The boys tore up the path and she hugged them both. 'There's cheese on toast for tea, Lily's just been waiting for you to get back. We've missed you so much. Did you enjoy yourselves?'

'We did, it was super fun, we played with the dogs, skated on the lake, made snowmen and have got loads of smashing things that used to be Daddy's when he was a boy. Is Emily back from school yet, we've got something for her too?'

'No, but she'll be on the next train. Take your shoes off before you go into the kitchen – I've left your slippers there as I thought you would go in through the back door.'

Elizabeth arrived next cradling the baby and Lucinda held back the curtain to allow her free entry. 'Jonathan's going to put the luggage by the gate and then park the car in Little Wick, Dr Cousins said we could do that as long as we don't box him in.'

Lucinda closed the door and hurried back to the kitchen where she changed into her outdoor shoes and pulled on her coat. She'd bring in the luggage then Jonathan could come straight in.

The boys were rushing about the house, overexcited to be home and desperate to be able to show Emily what they'd brought with them.

Lucinda was on her third journey when Jonathan appeared. 'Thank you, you didn't have to do this. I just heard the train steam in so Emily will be home in a minute.'

She joined them at the table, even though she'd eaten her tea – or rather the cat had eaten most of it – and listened to the boys. George seemed like his old self, laughing and smiling, the trip had done him good. What bothered her was that none of them mentioned Major Roby and she rather thought that was because the news was too sad to talk about.

* * *

Over the Christmas break, Mr Hatch had managed to persuade some workmen to build a small wooden open-fronted shelter. This had been stocked with a Primus stove, a wooden chair and a thick blanket so now they could both take a much-needed break every couple of hours.

Tonight would be the first time Lucinda would be using it – the vicar's permission had been forthcoming, so it had been put by the gate in the churchyard.

Lily handed her the precious thermos flask filled with lovely hot tea. 'There you are, Miss Somiton, you can put this in your little hut and drink it later.'

The wind from the river was bitter, it was bad enough being an ARP warden in this weather, how was she going to manage flying in an open-cockpit Tiger Moth when she was finding doing this so unpleasant?

After drinking half the flask of tea, Lucinda felt more optimistic. Then she remembered she'd not opened the other two letters and she'd left them in her room on her bureau. The important one had been the invitation to try out for the ATA; she thought that one of them must be from the bank about the trust fund and possibly the third could be from someone in the WAAF or the WRNS telling her to attend somewhere for their interview.

When she'd learned to fly – also in a Tiger Moth – she and the other three girls who'd been fortunate enough to have that opportunity had shared the necessary clothing. How she wished that she'd been the one to keep the goggles, leather helmet and leather gloves and not one of the other girls.

What she'd need were thick trousers and her jodhpurs would be perfect. She'd also got jodhpur boots, a thick hacking jacket and a variety of other suitable things in the flat in Knightsbridge.

Somehow, she'd have to collect them between now and next week. She wasn't altogether sure that returning to the scene of her disgrace was a good idea but she'd no option. If she wanted to become an ATA pilot, then she had to put all that behind her.

Ralph wasn't the man she'd thought him to be. During their

three months together she thought that she'd got to know him well. His threats would have been merely bluster. He'd almost lost his job, his marriage, and she was sure he wouldn't do anything to risk that a second time.

Tramping about the sleeping village gave Lucinda plenty of time to think. She'd go to London on Tuesday – risk being bombed overnight – and collect what she needed. Then she'd have ample time to get to Hatfield the next morning.

The family would be pleased for her, but Mr Hatch wouldn't be as he'd have to find somebody else to patrol Tuesday and Wednesday, and possibly Thursday as well.

15

Emily had been relieved the news about Grandpa wasn't as bad as she'd expected. By the end of the week that her family had been there he was up and about and almost his old self. Lucinda's news that she was going to Hatfield to try out as a pilot was so exciting and she couldn't wait to get to school on Friday and tell Penny about it. Her friend hadn't been at school yesterday but hopefully would be back today.

Being at school was a waste of time as so far all that had happened was that the girls had been reorganised, but no lessons had been taught. She and Penny and the rest of the upper fourth scholarship girls were now in a new classroom on the first floor, down the passageway from the medical room. The girls who'd returned from relocation had thrown Greyfriars into chaos. Even the teachers didn't seem to know what was going on.

After lunch, she and Penny found a quiet corner in the cloakroom so they were hidden by the coats. It was also warmer there than most other places.

'This is the first chance we've had to catch up – I've really missed you. Did you have a good time in Kent for Christmas?'

'We stayed in a really nice hotel close to the barracks, the food was good, the place was warmer than home and Toby and Thomas entertained the other residents.'

'That sounds all right. It occurred to me that as there's not much going on with the army that your father should be able to get leave. I thought he was something in the city, not a regular soldier, so how come he was conscripted at his age?'

'He spent every spare minute in the Territorials, the reservists, so as an experienced training officer they needed him. Because of his age he didn't go with the BEF. He wanted to see us because his regiment's preparing to be sent overseas somewhere. This time he'll have to go.'

'Golly, that's horrible for you all. Your mother must be very upset.'

Penny shrugged. 'To be honest, I don't think there's much affection between them. We only went so the twins could see him as they'd forgotten what he looked like.'

'What about you? Don't you like him either?'

'He's never been interested in me. He wanted a boy and was overjoyed when my brothers arrived but they were too much for him. Mum told me he could have refused to go to Kent as he wasn't a regular, but he couldn't get away fast enough.'

'That's sad. Were your brothers pleased to see him? Did he make a fuss of them?'

'Not really, although they were very well behaved, at least they were for them. They loved seeing the soldiers, watching them drill and so on. I'd much rather have come and stayed with you, but I couldn't let Mum travel with the boys on her own,' Penny said.

'Well, I'm glad you're back. Did you get the twins to school all right this morning?'

'Yes, they actually enjoyed it yesterday. I'm not sure the

teacher felt the same way as she looked exhausted when I collected them. That's why I didn't come in, just in case I had to collect them because they were being so difficult. It's going to make life so much easier as now Mum can do regular hours and our finances will improve.'

'You have to leave them early at school and collect them late – I'm surprised the school agreed,' Emily said.

'Someone from Paxman's wrote to the headmaster so they had no choice. Any road up, we'd better go as the bell will be going soon.'

'I've never heard that phrase – what does it mean?' Emily asked as they headed upstairs.

'The boys learnt it from one of the sergeants who comes from somewhere in the north of England. It just means anyway, but I think it's fun.'

* * *

George and Sammy didn't ask to come with Emily the next morning. They were still engrossed in their new-old toys. They'd brought back a suitcase full of treasures. Several jigsaws, some strange board games, a few lead soldiers but the best was a clock-work train set.

Penny didn't have to take care of her brothers at the weekend any more which meant every Saturday was now theirs to do as they pleased. She'd told Penny not to track down to the ferry as the weather was so awful and asked her to say the same to Doris.

They were spending today in the little cottage. Mr and Mrs Smith, better known as Nan and Grandad even to Emily and Penny, had asked the girls to clear out the loft for them. In return they'd get lunch and tea provided.

Halfway through the morning, they had an unexpected extra helper.

'I found that little Jimmy sitting on the doorstep. I didn't have the heart to send him home so I'm sending him up to you. I'm too old to deal with tiddlers,' Nan called up the stairs.

Penny was closest to the steep steps to the loft so she turned so her back was against the almost-ladder and slid down.

'Well, Jimmy, what are you doing here? You should be at home in the warm.'

'I ain't had no breakfast nor any tea last night. The big ones locked me in the cupboard and never let me out until it were dark.'

'Goodness, that wasn't very kind of them. You stay here with Doris and Emily and I'll see if I can find you something.'

Emily slid down the same way that Penny had and Jimmy laughed. 'Blimey, can I have a go at that? See, got me nice clothes on. I'd not let no one take them away.'

Doris poked her head out. 'Let's see if you can climb up without falling off. I'll be at the top and Emily will be behind in case you slip.'

The little boy was in his socks and shot up as if he'd been climbing steep ladder-stairs all his life. Without waiting for permission, he deftly turned on the top step and prepared to slide down. What he neglected to do was hold on and if Emily hadn't been standing at the bottom he'd have disappeared down the main staircase.

As he flew forward, Emily braced herself and caught him easily. He scarcely weighed more than Grace and this worried her.

Jimmy was beaming. 'Can I do it again?'

Doris joined them on the top landing – there was scarcely enough room for all of them to stand together.

'You ain't doing that again, young man, if our Emily hadn't caught you, you'd have broken your neck. You were supposed to hold on the sides like what we did.'

'I never knew that, you never told me. I like being caught by Emily. She's soft and nice.'

Emily swallowed the lump in her throat. 'Did your mum come back yet?'

He shook his head. 'Good riddance to bad rubbish, if I got me dinner and that I'd be happy there. No bombs and I started school with Thomas and Toby. They treated me nice.'

Doris sat on the top step of the narrow staircase that led to the lower floor. The door at the bottom had been propped open to allow some light in as there was no electricity in this cottage.

'Do those horrible big children lock you in a cupboard all the time?'

'Only if they can catch me, I know where to hide. I found myself a lovely little cubbyhole, snug and warm at night. The rest of them sleep in the room next to the kitchen but I ain't going back in there, not for no one.'

Penny poked her head into the stairwell. 'Nan says to come down as she's got cake and tea for us and porridge and toast for Jimmy.'

Emily had expected him to rush off to get his food but he was still holding her hand. 'Can I have cake and tea as well after eating me porridge and toast?'

'I'm sure you can, sweetheart, if you haven't eaten since yesterday lunchtime you must be starving.'

Going down the narrow stairs with him holding onto her was going to be impossible so she picked him up and he put his arms around her neck and his legs around her waist and clung on as if he was drowning. She thought he probably hadn't had much love or affection in his short life and it just wasn't fair.

Grandad was in his rocking chair by the range with the ancient black-and-white cat in his lap. He nodded and smiled – he rarely spoke but seemed happy enough to see them all crowding into the kitchen.

Nan, a sprightly old lady with her grey hair pinned up neatly in a bun, pointed to the communicating door that led to the front room. 'You lot go in there, too much fuss with all of you in my kitchen for Grandad.'

There was an oval gate-leg table that had seen better days but was still highly polished and already opened up to its full size. A mismatch of wooden chairs stood around it and one of them had an old cushion on the seat.

'Cor, me own chair. Ta ever so, Doris, your nan's doing me proud.' Jimmy scrambled up and somehow he knew he had to wait till everyone else was seated before he started on his porridge.

'Eat up, there's plenty more in the pot if you want it. Not much sugar, but you can have a teaspoon and a bit of top of the milk from that jug,' Nan told him.

Emily watched the little boy scrupulously take exactly what he'd been told he could have and then tip a little of the thin cream onto his steaming porridge.

There had to be something they could do for this little boy and she and her friends would have to come up with a way to make his life bearable or there'd be no option but to inform the authorities and then he'd be put into an orphanage or foster care.

* * *

Ralph had returned home for a couple of nights and renewed his charm offensive. Leone was a poor substitute for Lucinda, but she'd do. If he couldn't have the woman he still fantasised about then he was damn well going to have wealth and status.

Spending time outside with his daughters wasn't as tedious as it might have been and his attention to them certainly pleased his wife. As he was leaving on the Monday morning, she followed him to the front door.

'I'm almost certain that I'm pregnant, Ralph, I'm only two days late but I'm always on time. I know the doctor can't confirm it until after I've missed my second one but I'm hopeful there'll be another Castleton in August.'

He hugged her. 'I'm not sure when I'll be able to come home again, there's a lot going on at the moment.' He gestured to the waiting car which was only sent to collect him in an emergency. 'If your symptoms are the same as before then I don't think we need a doctor to confirm it. I seem to remember that you were nauseous almost immediately – let me know if that happens as then we can start to plan.'

'Before you go, darling, I can't find my diamond bracelet, the one that my grandfather gave me. Do you remember you took it to have the catch mended? Do you think it might still be in London?'

Ralph knew exactly where it was, or where it used to be. He'd given it to Lucinda. He'd hoped that Leone had forgotten about it as she had so many expensive pieces of jewellery. He remembered that it had been put with the other things he'd given Lucinda and he prayed that she'd not taken them with her after the debacle a few weeks ago.

'I definitely picked it up from the jewellers, I thought I'd brought it home but possibly it's in the pocket of a different jacket. I'll search for it, if you haven't got it in your jewellery box then it must be there. I'm really sorry.'

'I'm not cross, but I would like it back. My parents are visiting as soon as the weather improves and they always expect me to wear it.'

He kissed her and then made a dash for the waiting car. His superior, a bad-tempered colonel, had sent it along with a short note insisting he returned to the office immediately.

The drive was more hazardous than usual, not just the appalling road conditions as the worst of the snow had been cleared, but because of the recent bomb damage. His driver had to make several lengthy and slow detours in order to get him to Horse Guards where his underground office was situated.

Ralph still had a key to Lucinda's apartment and after he'd finished work for the day he took the underground from West-minster station and emerged into the blackout a few stops later. The miserly beam on his torch was enough to stop him breaking his neck but if he hadn't known exactly where he was going then he doubted he'd have got there.

He wanted to collect the bracelet, and the other gifts if they were there, and get back to his own residence. He didn't want to be caught out in the streets when the bombing started as public shelters were notoriously insanitary and overcrowded. Being crushed with the hoi polloi didn't appeal. The one beneath his block would at least only be occupied by people like him.

If he used the front door, the concierge would see him and that would be a disaster. Lucinda must never know he'd been back. He smiled in the darkness, revelling in the knowledge that whatever she wanted to do after her initial training in the WRNS or the WAAF she'd find herself in the laundry or the kitchen. He made his way around to a little-used side door which was unlocked until around eight o'clock. It was now a little after six and he should be in and out in less than a quarter of an hour and safely away before the concierge came to lock the door.

* * *

Lucinda had loved the spacious, elegant, expensively furnished two-bedroom flat on the first floor of the Georgian house in Cadogan Square. Now, as she approached the entrance she felt sick. She didn't want to go in as everybody there knew what had happened. A well brought up young lady didn't have an affair with a married man and if she did, according to the circle she moved in, what happened next was entirely her fault. Nobody ever blamed the man.

Jonathan had wanted her to travel before the blackout as moving around in the city in the dark would be far harder than wandering about in Wivenhoe but she'd missed the train and it was now after six. It was too dark to see where one was going but as she was familiar with the route she had no trouble arriving safely.

She straightened her shoulders, put her head up and pushed open the heavy glass door that led to the luxurious entrance hall. The blackout curtain had been hung on a semicircular rail which meant negotiating it was simple.

There were no lights on at the front of the vestibule but there was a small lamp on the concierge's desk which threw a golden circle onto the polished surface.

'Good evening, Miss Somiton, I have your correspondence here. You didn't leave a forwarding address or I would have posted it on to you.'

'Thank you, Cyril, as you know I left in rather a hurry and a forwarding address was the last thing on my mind.'

'Nobody thinks badly of you, Miss Somiton, you were duped and what happened wasn't fair.'

'Never mind, I've moved on. I'll be staying in the flat tonight but leaving early tomorrow morning. I'm trying out to be a pilot with the ATA and have come to collect things that I'm going to need if I'm not to freeze to death.'

Knowing that her neighbours didn't think badly of her was a relief, it meant that maybe she could really start again and put the affair behind her.

'Good for you, you look well, I'm glad you've landed on your feet. I've read several articles in the newspapers about these ATA girls – they seem to be top drawer – you'll fit in perfectly.'

Lucinda had always got on with Cyril and was happy to tell him her good news. He listened avidly.

'My word, that's something. Good luck tomorrow, I hope you get in.'

As she approached the door to her flat, her erstwhile neighbour, an elderly gentleman who'd been something in the Foreign Office many years ago, opened his door.

'I heard the lift stop and as there's someone moving about already in your place, young lady, I wanted to see who it was as there's nobody else lives on this floor.'

Lucinda froze in shock. 'I know who it is. It's Castleton, he's no right to be in there, I'd forgotten that he still had a key.'

Mr Reynolds gripped her elbow and more or less pulled her into his flat. 'Don't attempt to go in. I'll dial 999 – I don't know anyone who's called that number and I'm excited to do so.'

Lucinda was about to stop him but changed her mind. It would serve Ralph right to be arrested for burglary. She didn't know a lot about this new system for calling the police, ambulance or fire engine, but did know it only worked if you lived within twelve miles of Mayfair. They were probably only about three miles away so it should be all right.

'How long has he been in there?'

'He arrived only five minutes ago. Be quiet, young lady, I'm getting connected.'

She listened to him telling the operator who he was, where he lived and why he'd called. He replaced the receiver with a bang. 'They are taking the matter seriously but there's been a major incident somewhere and nobody can come for half an hour.'

'Then ring down to Cyril, if he comes up with the caretaker that should be enough to give Castleton a nasty surprise.'

'Not as good as having him accosted by the constabulary, but this new strategy will serve the blighter right. He probably wouldn't have been charged by the police anyway as he's got a key, but he'll be seriously embarrassed to be found skulking about uninvited in your flat. What will he be looking for?'

'I can think of only one thing and that will be the expensive jewellery he gave me. He won't find it as I pawned it. I needed the money.'

The old man chuckled. 'Even better. Are you going to witness his humiliation or remain out of sight?'

'As I came in through the front door and spoke to Cyril, he knows I'm on the premises. I think it would be best if I spoke to him. Would you mind?'

The concierge picked up immediately and she explained what she thought was happening.

'Right, you stop with Mr Reynolds, Miss Somiton, Frank and I will deal with this. Don't worry, I'll not mention that you're here.'

'Thank you, as he doesn't have my permission to be in there he's definitely trespassing. Do you think that you could detain him for half an hour until the actual police arrive?'

'If Frank and I can cause this particular gentleman a deal of embarrassment then it'll be our pleasure, Miss Somiton. Leave it with us.'

Whilst she waited for them to arrive, she wondered if she'd made a serious error of judgement. Wouldn't it have been better to let Ralph go rather than involve someone else? He'd already threatened her, even though at the time she'd dismissed his threats as bluff. She'd a nasty suspicion that he'd blame her, whatever the outcome.

16

Ralph was engrossed in his task, cursing under his breath that the jewellery he was looking for wasn't where he'd expected. Now he'd have to search the flat and this meant he'd be far longer than was sensible. The interfering old neighbour might hear him and come to investigate. Then he smiled. The old fool would just think it was Lucinda, he'd not suspect for a moment it could be him.

There was a large walk-in closet in the main bedroom which not only had a rail for hanging clothes but also shelving for folded items and a narrow chest of drawers that ran from floor to ceiling. This was where he'd start his search. Rummaging through Lucinda's personal possessions didn't bother him, he wasn't going to take anything apart from what belonged to him.

He was surprised that she'd left so many of her things behind. Although clothes rationing had yet to start, items like this would already be in short supply. Everything was of the best quality, cashmere jumpers, silk underwear, haute couture ensembles. He was elbow deep in flimsies in one of the drawers when he stiffened. Somebody was coming.

'Sir, might I enquire what you're doing here fondling Miss Somiton's personal items of clothing?'

The concierge – he couldn't remember his name – wasn't alone as standing beside him was a man in overalls holding what looked like a large spanner.

'I have a key,' Ralph blurted, unable to think of anything more sensible.

'Do you have Miss Somiton's permission to be in here?'

'I'm just looking for property that belongs to me. It's none of your damn business.'

He slammed the drawer closed and surged forward, expecting the two men to move aside. He was a gentleman, an aristocrat, they were lower classes and would know their place.

To his horror, the two of them moved forward, forcing him to take a step backward. 'Get out of my way, how dare you impede my progress? I'll have you dismissed from your position.'

'You're here without permission from the owner of this property. You are trespassing at the very least and that's a criminal offence. Frank and I intend to make a citizen's arrest. Police have been informed and will be here soon. You can make your complaints to them.'

Before Ralph could react, attempt to bluster or bribe his way out of this disastrous situation, the two men reversed and slammed the door. He heard a chair being pushed under the handle.

He was trapped. The only way out was through that door. He slumped against the wall, his brain racing. He was a spook, an intelligence officer, had been recruited for his quick thinking and superior intellect. He had possibly fifteen minutes to come up with an explanation that would satisfy the police.

If news of this debacle surfaced anywhere then he'd be dismissed from his position, be forced to join one of the services instead. Ralph had been told by his colonel that if he brought any more disgrace to the intelligence service he'd be gone.

Even worse, if Leone got to hear about it, she'd not forgive him this time.

* * *

Lucinda hovered near the front door of Mr Reynolds's flat, anxious to know what was happening next door. Cyril had a master key so he could enter any of the flats in an emergency, usually a lost key or a resident being locked out, but this was different.

'Can you please go and investigate, Mr Reynolds? I'd be upset if he hurt either Cyril or Frank.'

'As you like, my dear girl. Are you coming with me?'

'No, I'll stand just inside the open door and listen.'

For an elderly gentleman, he was very sprightly and vanished into her flat in seconds. He returned moments later.

'They've got him cornered, locked in the closet. They're incensed that he was going through your personal items of clothing.'

'Horrid man, I can't understand how I was fooled by him. He ruined my good name and caused my family a lot of embarrassment.'

'You are a decade younger than him, an innocent girl who'd just left boarding school, small wonder you were taken in. He's a handsome man, rich and charming. He's entirely to blame for what happened.'

'I thought we were going to get married. His poor wife, it must have been even worse for her. I wonder why she took him back?'

Mr Reynolds stared at the lift door. 'I think the police are here. Do you want to speak to them?'

'Not unless I have to. Perhaps you could wait with Cyril and Frank, then you can tell me what happens and fetch me if you think it's necessary.'

'I'd be delighted to. Not had so much fun since my time in India.'

Lucinda listened from the hall through the half-open door. She'd expected to see a couple of uniformed constables in navy-blue uniforms and tall hats go past but instead two plainclothes detectives had come to investigate.

Mr Reynolds briefly explained his involvement but didn't inform the police that he was aware of the identity of the intruder. 'I informed the concierge and I believe that he and the caretaker have shut the trespasser in a cupboard and are awaiting your arrival.'

'Thank you, Mr Reynolds, kindly return to your flat and leave us to investigate. If we wish to speak to you again then we know where you are,' the older of the two men said.

Lucinda shrank back against the wall, wondering why Scotland Yard had decided to send these men and not a couple of ordinary constables. Ralph was going to be so angry and as he couldn't direct his fury at these detectives he would turn it towards Mr Reynolds, the concierge and the caretaker. She couldn't allow this to happen. If he was going to take it out on someone then it should be her, she wasn't going to have anyone else suffer on her behalf.

'I think I'd better go in there, I don't want anyone else involved. This wouldn't have happened if it wasn't for my foolishness and I don't suppose he's doing any harm really,' she told Mr Reynolds.

'As you wish, my dear. Those senior policemen won't be

happy they've been called out expecting to find a spy, only to discover it's someone that you know rather well.'

Despite the awful circumstances, Lucinda giggled. 'I suppose I shouldn't tell you this, Mr Reynolds, but Castleton is a spy, but for us, not for the Germans. At least he works in intelligence, which I think makes him one.'

He chuckled and patted her arm. 'Then they won't be disappointed. A man in his position shouldn't have trespassed. I'm sure his superiors won't be impressed when they hear about it.'

She smiled her thanks and hurried to her own door which had been left open. She could hear Ralph snarling at someone and she almost lost her nerve.

She stepped in and called brightly. 'Hello, what's going on in here? I've come to collect some items that I left a few weeks ago and really didn't expect to find my flat occupied by five gentlemen.'

Ralph turned to her and smiled as if he was pleased to see her, as if she'd arrived to explain his presence. 'I'm sorry, I arrived early and let myself in. I really didn't expect to be arrested.'

This was her opportunity to step up and smooth things over. His smile was winning but his eyes said something quite different. They were warning her – if she didn't do as he wanted she'd regret it.

'Mr Castleton, you should have returned the key when your wife revealed the fact that you were having an adulterous relationship with me. I told you last time we met that things were over between us. You have absolutely no right to be here. You are trespassing – or perhaps you knew I was coming and intended to do me harm as you threatened to do.'

His skin paled, her unexpected attack had left him at a loss to know what to say to his advantage.

'Miss Somiton,' the senior policeman said to her, 'let me get this straight. This man is your erstwhile lover, he threatened you with physical harm and is here without your consent.'

Her heart was thudding so loudly she could scarcely make sense of what he'd said.

'Yes, that's right,' she managed to whisper.

'Then the matter's clear. Castleton, you are under arrest for trespassing, which is a criminal offence.'

Ralph recovered his composure and his voice. 'You will address me with respect, my brother is Sir Hugh Castleton, and I am a senior member of the intelligence service.'

To her astonishment, the policeman laughed. 'So, Sergeant Jessop, it seems we've caught a spy after all, just not a German one.'

'Excuse me, Detective Inspector, but I don't want to press charges. I just wish this man to be removed from my London flat and to have his assurance that he won't return and that neither will he attempt to contact me in future.'

'Miss Somiton, an offence has been committed. We were called away from something important to deal with it. Mr Castleton will have to accompany us to Scotland Yard where he will be issued with a caution and his employers will be informed.'

'I came to collect items that belong to me, Miss Somiton. Where's my jewellery?'

'You gave those things to me; they were mine to dispose of as I wished. I pawned them and threw away the ticket.' The bit about the ticket wasn't true as she knew exactly where it was – at Harbour House in her stationery wallet.

If looks could be fatal, she would be lying dead on the parquet flooring. At least they didn't take him away in handcuffs, which must have been a small consolation to him.

'Well, serves him right, Miss Somiton, nasty bit of work, I'd have been happy to knock him out with me spanner if I'd had to,' the caretaker said.

'Thank you both for coming up. I regret now that I involved anyone. It would have been better for me to have dealt with it myself.'

Cyril shook his head. 'He could have hurt you, Miss Somiton, I don't think he makes threats idly. You look out for yourself, especially now he knows where you live in the country.'

Lucinda shook hands with the concierge and the caretaker and then thanked her neighbour. 'I'm sorry that you three were involved in my unpleasant business. What an awful coincidence that I chose to return here at exactly the same time as that man.'

Cyril and Frank hurried off as they'd been away from their posts for too long already. Mr Reynolds followed her into the flat which she thought unnecessary.

'Thank you, but I can manage from here. There won't be any other trespassers waiting to pounce on me.'

'I beg your pardon, my dear, I'm afraid my curiosity overcame my good manners. I'm just curious to see if there are any differences between your abode and mine.'

'I'm sorry, I'm a little on edge still. Please, do come in and look around. As far as I know they're identical in size, but things are slightly differently arranged.'

This proved to be the case and whilst she escorted the old man around she explained why she'd returned.

'Good for you, my dear, I might be old and cantankerous but I don't fall into that camp of old buffers who think young women should remain at home warming slippers and cooking meals.'

'That's good to know. I really want the ATA to take me on. I expect that I'll have to do a bit more training but my instructor, when I learnt to fly, said I was a natural.'

'I think I've got something for you that might be useful. Why don't you stay with me? Your flat's cold and unwelcoming, your cupboards are empty, I'm a dab hand in the kitchen and would be honoured to cook for you tonight.'

'How kind of you, yes, I'd much rather stay anywhere but in here. I've only unpleasant memories and I used to love it, but I think I'll find a tenant as I'll never live here again myself.'

His eyes lit up. 'Collect what you want, my dear, and come next door. We need to talk.'

Lucinda hastily collected her jodhs, boots, hacking jacket and thick jumpers and stuffed them in a leather suitcase. Her overnight bag was too small to take these extra items.

She wished she'd got to know Mr Reynolds better when she'd been living here, but she'd only been in London for two or three weeks before Ralph had swept her off her feet. She now had a proper family in the Robys, but she thought she'd consider Mr Reynolds as a substitute grandfather. Obviously, her grandparents were long gone and she'd never known any of them.

As she left the apartment for what she thought might be the last time, she noticed the key Ralph had retained was now on the hall table. She snatched it up and dropped it into her handbag.

* * *

She was served a delicious pie with tasty gravy and perfectly cooked vegetables. Apart from Jonathan, she'd never met another man who could cook.

'Do you have a family, Mr Reynolds?'

'I don't, I was never married. I was an only child, as were my parents, so I've no cousins, aunts or uncles either.'

'How sad, but I'm sure you have lots of good friends. Someone as nice as you must have good friends.'

'I do have a particular friend, Reginald Bairstow, we've been friends since university.' He looked at her and she understood.

'I'm glad you have someone. I think it's very unfair the way things are arranged for people with particular friends like yours.' Then the penny dropped. 'Do you think Mr Bairstow might like to rent my flat?'

His smile was all the answer she needed. 'He'd be delighted and so would I. It's hard for us to meet safely when the weather's so bad. As I know we're now on the same page – I can talk freely. Did you know at the Ritz there's a bar in the cellar where people with friends like mine can meet freely?'

'I didn't, I don't go there very often, I prefer the Savoy.'

'Would you excuse me for a moment, my dear, whilst I give the good news to my friend? Do you know how much rent you might wish to charge?'

'Whatever Mr Bairstow thinks is fair will be fine for me. I have a bank account – I'll give you the details to give to him.'

Her host was gone for less than five minutes and returned rejuvenated. He also had a gift for her. 'I was given these many years ago by another good friend as I used to ride a motorbike. They came in very useful. As you might imagine, I no longer use them, so I'd like you to have them.'

He handed over a supple leather flying helmet, goggles and long leather gauntlets. Lucinda stared at them. They were absolutely perfect and exactly what she needed.

'Are you quite sure?' He nodded. 'Then, thank you so very much, Mr Reynolds.'

'My name's Harold. I rather think we're friends now and formality's no longer essential between us.'

'If you don't mind, could I call you Uncle Harold? I don't have any uncles and I'd just love to adopt you as mine, and your friend could become Uncle Reginald if he agrees. I'm sure you know my name's Lucinda – I'd be delighted if you stopped calling me Miss Somiton.'

His eyes were moist, as were hers. Things had worked out so perfectly tonight that she thought tomorrow would go just as well, that she would be able to do the circuits and bumps successfully and be able to join the other twenty or so women.

'I really don't want to come back here if I can possibly help it. If I pay for the boxes and the transport, do you think you and your friend would be kind enough to pack up all my personal items? Then they need to be sent to Harbour House, High Street, Wivenhoe, Essex. Mr and Mrs Roby will take care of everything for me.'

'We'd be delighted to do that. What about the furniture, bedding and so on?'

'That comes as part of the rent. I'm sure you and your friend will find things much easier once you're living side by side.'

'You've made two old men very happy indeed, my dear girl. God bless you, and if ever you come to London, call in and see us.'

They hugged – Lucinda usually avoided any sort of physical contact apart from with close family but for some reason she felt a real connection to Uncle Harold.

* * *

Lucinda caught the first train from Paddington and because she'd purchased a first-class ticket she found a seat. It was a short journey, with fewer stops than she'd anticipated, and she arrived at Hatfield station in far less than an hour.

A lady in a green overall, a member of the WRVS, handed her an enamel mug of tea from the canteen trolley as she passed it.

She drank it gratefully as she'd left Uncle Harold's flat long before he'd got up.

It was barely light, the temperature seemed to have dropped by several degrees, but the sky was clear with no sign of further snow falling. There were no taxis, no RAF transport vehicles, in fact nobody she could even ask for directions from.

She walked back into the station and found a guard. 'I have to get to Hatfield airbase – could you please tell me how to get there on foot?'

'It's a long walk, but you look fit enough. No more than two miles, stay on this road until you leave the town. You'll come to a crossroads, take the first left and Bob's your uncle. With any luck you'll get a lift, there's plenty of traffic goes up and down that road to the airfield, taking things to the de Havilland factory and that.'

'Thank you, I've got to be there by nine o'clock. Even in this weather I'm certain I can walk that distance and be there in plenty of time.'

She'd not been walking for long when a lorry pulled up beside her. A friendly young officer in RAF blue wound down the window and leaned out.

'Do you want a lift, miss?'

'I do, if that's not too much trouble. I need to get to Hatfield airfield.'

'Then hop in the back, there's a couple of WAAF already in there. Are you a secretary?'

'No, I'm hoping to join the ATA. Thank you so much. I really don't want to be late.'

He looked less friendly. 'You won't be flying today, miss, too cold.'

He didn't offer to come round and let down the back of the vehicle which she thought rather rude, but she was tall enough to be able to do it for herself. She was looking forward to meeting some other young women doing their bit for the war.

She hurried around to the rear and the two WAAF were waiting for her. 'Chuck up your cases, then Jill and I will heave you in to join us.'

* * *

Ralph was incandescent to be escorted from Lucinda's flat like a common criminal but thought antagonising these detectives would just exacerbate the situation. If that girl had spoken up for him then he wouldn't be in this position. If these plods did as they threatened and informed the colonel he might well lose his position and be forced to join the army and put his life on the line. He thanked God it was the blackout and no one would have seen his disgrace.

The sergeant drove, the inspector sat beside him, and he was on the back seat. Thank God he hadn't been handcuffed. The Luftwaffe were on their way – the huge lights were arcing the sky, searching for targets. The balloons had been wound up and no doubt the fighters were screaming towards the incoming bombers.

The sirens began their distinctive rise and fall. The car stopped abruptly, shooting him forward so he banged his knees painfully on the back of the seat.

Without turning round, the inspector spoke to him. 'Get out, Castleton, think yourself lucky, I've got better things to do than take you to the yard.'

Ralph had never got out of a car so fast. He watched it speed away, his fists clenched, his pulse rapid. That was a narrow escape – he'd been lucky. But God knows what he was going to tell Leone about her missing bracelet.

An ARP warden saw him standing on the pavement and blew his whistle. 'Down the underground, it's nearer than the shelter, you don't want to stand about out here. We're in for a pasting tonight.'

Ralph raised his hand, showing he'd heard and understood. He was only a few yards from Sloane Square underground and ran down the steps behind a dozen or so others. He doubted there'd be as many sheltering in this area as the big houses and wealthy residents would have their own arrangements.

He was astonished at how many people were down there and even more surprised when he heard the distinctive rumble of a train approaching. His luck was certainly holding tonight as he could catch this train and get off at Charing Cross and from there it would be easy to get back to Westminster.

He barely managed to squeeze in the packed underground train. This surprised him as most people would be travelling in the opposite direction, not towards the centre of London in the middle of an air raid.

* * *

The following morning, he arrived early and was at his desk dealing with some urgent paperwork when a secretary called him on the telephone to say that the colonel wanted to see him. This wasn't a good sign.

'I told you that you were on thin ice, Castleton, and last night you fell through it. I just received a telephone call from Scotland Yard. You can imagine my reaction to the news that one of my senior intelligence officers had been cautioned for trespass and attempted burglary.'

'I wasn't cautioned, sir, I returned home and didn't go to the Yard.'

'I don't give a rat's arse whether you were officially cautioned or not. Your position here is terminated. You will report to Major Branston upstairs immediately. You were an officer cadet, you're now a junior lieutenant in the army. The major will give you the details of your new position.'

Ralph nodded and walked out. His life was ruined. He could be posted to some godforsaken place in a desert or a jungle. His wasn't the only life that was about to be upended – Lucinda Somiton would suffer for her interference. Being stuck in the laundry wasn't punishment enough, he'd think of something more destructive, life changing, totally ruin her smug little life.

Emily had told her parents about Jimmy Smith and her concerns that he was being neglected.

'Doris says that if we involve the authorities then it's likely he'll be taken to a children's home or orphanage. Also, the other children living there might be in danger of being removed as well.'

'I'm quite certain that with so many orphans, abandoned children and homeless families no one's going to do anything about the other children. It's just this little boy who's the problem,' Daddy said.

'My friends are going to keep an eye on him. He's getting lunch at school – I'm not altogether sure how they manage that, but he said he got things like mince and potatoes, steamed pudding, bubble and squeak – that sort of thing. It's good to know that during the week he's being fed.'

'I expect the teacher knows his circumstances and is keeping an eye on him. He's not our responsibility, Emily, but I'm proud of you and your friends for caring so much,' Mummy said.

'Are the boys able to go back on Monday? Has the fire damage at their school been repaired?' Emily asked.

'No, the winter holiday has been extended for a further week. They'll be back on the 15th. I haven't dared tell them that they're going to miss their half-term break in order to catch up on some of the missed time,' Daddy said.

* * *

Lucinda had left for London on Tuesday afternoon and since then the weather had deteriorated. The only good thing about this was it was probably too heavy for the Luftwaffe to come. Emily didn't think that Knightsbridge, where Lucinda was going, had been bombed so far as most of them had been dropped on the docks and in the East End.

Things had settled down at school and normal lessons had resumed. Things would have been tickety-boo if it wasn't for the fact that the girls who'd joined them immediately formed an anti-scholarship group and were doing everything they could to make life difficult.

Obviously, the nine of them got together and tried to look out for each other. They ate together, spent break time together and now sat during lessons as far away from the other group as they could. The class had divided into two cliques, and it was inevitable that things would escalate and one of their teachers would notice.

This happened on the Wednesday when the ringleader of the others instigated a confrontation. Emily, Penny, and the girls with whom she'd now become more friendly went to collect their coats and change out of their indoor shoes as today had been deemed clement enough to spend at least half the lunch break outside in the snow.

'My boots and coat have gone from my peg,' Sarah said, 'I know I put them in the right place when I arrived this morning.'

This was then they discovered all their things had been taken. They couldn't go out as they were and would be punished if they were found inside when it was an outside break time.

'We can't take theirs as they've already gone outside,' Penny said, 'but we can take their indoor shoes.'

'I don't think that's a good idea,' Emily said. 'At the moment they're in the wrong but if we retaliate then we'll be in trouble too.'

Her comment was disregarded, even by Penny. 'I hope you're not going to tell tales, Emily Roby,' one of them said in a decidedly unfriendly way.

'No, but I'm not going to participate in whatever you plan to do. I've a sudden desperate need to visit the WC.'

If she didn't see what they did then she couldn't be asked difficult questions and be forced to lie. She was surprised that Penny had sided with the others – maybe she wasn't such a good friend after all. Then the outer door to the loos banged and she was joined by two others.

'Sorry,' Penny said with a sheepish smile. 'I don't know why I sided with them and not you. I really don't want to get into any trouble and I don't think retaliating is going to help matters.'

Joyce, the frizzy-redheaded girl from Great Horkesley, grinned. 'We can't lurk in here for long without the prefects turfing us out. Why don't we go to the art room?'

They took the back stairs which meant they avoided the cloakrooms and therefore wouldn't see what was going on and arrived in a rush to find the art mistress, Mrs Brown, in the process of putting up a wall display of drawings and paintings done by the girls who'd been relocated.

'Excellent, I was hoping some of my favourite girls would

wander up here rather than go outside. I need to get this done before the bell goes and with your help that should be easily accomplished.'

They spent the remainder of the lunch break covering the walls with the watercolours and pencil drawings. Mrs Brown thanked them and reminded them that they were welcome to spend time in her room whenever they wanted.

On the way back to the form room a few minutes before the bell was due to ring, Penny said what Emily was thinking. 'They weren't very good, were they? I suppose that's why the display will remain in the art room and not be downstairs where everyone can see them.'

They were halfway down the stairs when the siren began to wail. Emily frowned. 'Now we're in trouble, we're going to have to go to the shelter as we are and there's going to be a dreadful fuss.'

The rule was to exit by the nearest door and this was at the bottom of the staircase they were on. 'Maybe we'll be all right,' Joyce said, 'as we've been in the art room we couldn't go to the cloakroom to change anyway.'

'Good point. For all we know they've put everything back. Come on, I'm not going to be late. There must be others in a similar situation, as not everybody would have been outside.'

They were frozen, their indoor shoes sopping wet, by the time they reached the shelter on the other side of the school playground. Emily was pleased to see they weren't the only ones who'd been obliged to troop out in indoor things.

There were two shelters – the babies and the prep school girls plus the lower fourth went in one and the upper fourth and lower fifth in the other. Their shelter was half-full already and it was too gloomy to see if the other scholarship girls had found their boots and coats before coming out.

There was a hum of conversation until Miss King, the headmistress, arrived and closed the door. Then it was deathly quiet, breath steaming in front of them, everybody shivering.

'Girls, as you know the boys' school was damaged by incendiary bombs and will not be open for another week. If school had been open and the building occupied there might have been fatalities and injuries. Therefore, we shall be taking the warning siren more seriously in future.'

There was a chorus of 'Yes, Miss King,' and a general shuffling of bottoms on the benches.

'Settle down, girls, I know it's cold in here and some of you didn't have the opportunity to put on your outdoor clothes. Being cold won't kill you, having a bomb dropped on you certainly would.'

Usually, one of the teachers would instigate a lively game of 'I packed my bag' but today this didn't happen. Slowly the girls began to talk amongst themselves, everybody on edge, ready to be silent if told.

Slowly Emily's eyes adjusted to the darkness, there was just one oil lamp at the exit and one at the other end so whoever was unfortunate enough to have to use the chemical toilet behind the curtain could see what they were doing.

Sitting opposite was the ringleader of the other group, on either side of her were the rest of the clique. Emily couldn't see the other scholarship girls and this bothered her.

'Penny, Joyce, can you see the others? I'm worried they might be inside.'

The three of them swivelled in their seats. Joyce bravely pretended she needed the primitive WC so she could walk to that end. Emily walked the other way, where the teachers were, her mind racing, trying to think of something to say that would seem like a valid reason to be out of her seat.

'Excuse me, Mrs Brown, my feet are soaking wet, I've already got chilblains, would it be better to take my socks off or stay as I am?' She'd deliberately chosen the art teacher as she was less likely to get her head bitten off for impertinence or disobedience.

'Take your socks off, Emily, tell the other girls in a similar situation to do the same. I was told that if your clothes are wet when the temperature is below zero you're better off naked rather than keeping them on.'

This was such an unexpected reply, even Miss King laughed. 'Good heavens, Mrs Brown, don't give the girls ideas. I think having bare feet is enough excitement for today.'

Emily squelched back to her place on the bench and then the three of them removed their socks and put their feet back into their wet indoor shoes.

'We're really sorry for playing that prank, Emily, we didn't intend that any of you would have to come outside without your things. We only kept them for a little while, we just wanted to see your reaction, then we put them back.'

'That's all very well, Cynthia, but five of my friends are still inside because of what you did. If a bomb drops on the school and they die, then it'll be your fault.'

Emily immediately regretted her words to the girl sitting opposite her in the shelter. 'I'm sorry, I shouldn't have said that, if my friends remained inside then that's their decision. There are several of us in here who came out in our indoor things – they could have done the same thing.'

'Thank you for saying that, Emily, all this is my fault. It was supposed to be a prank, but it turned into something much worse. I don't know why we've got to this point, but I'd like us to at least be civil to each other in future.'

'I've never been anything but civil to you, the unpleasantness has come entirely from your side of the classroom. However, as far as I'm concerned the matter's closed. I can't speak for those that aren't here.'

Miss King spoke from the door. 'The all-clear has just sounded, thank goodness. Will those in their indoor shoes and no coats come forward first. Go at once to your cloakroom and put on your outside garments and shoes and then go to the dining hall. I shall arrange for a hot drink to be brought out to you.'

There were three girls in front of Emily and several behind her and they made a concerted dash for the exit. The all-clear was a continuous sound and a very welcome one. With her wet socks rolled up in a ball in her hand, she crunched over the snow and back in the way she'd exited, her two friends were close behind her.

'I wonder where the others are? I don't think anybody took a name call,' Penny said through chattering teeth.

'I don't care. It was their decision. If they get into trouble, it's nothing to do with us,' Emily replied.

As promised, the missing garments and shoes were back where they should have been in the first place. Like most of the girls, Emily wore two pairs of socks in her boots and perched on the narrow bench beneath the coat pegs to pull the second pair on her icy feet. Her boots followed and then she stood up and grabbed her coat. It was easier to put that on out of the narrow confines of the cloakroom area.

Penny and Joyce did the same. Then the eight shivering girls hurried down the corridor to the dining hall.

'Goodness, the others are in here. And from the sound of it, the kitchen staff didn't bother to go out to the shelter. I wonder if Miss King's aware of that?' Emily said.

After a mug of delicious sweetened cocoa, made with actual

milk and not water, plus a piece of Victoria sandwich, those that
had come in with her were warm and chatting freely.

'We'd better get to class,' Penny said, 'we've been here twenty
minutes already.'

'I don't think Miss Hodgkins will appreciate us trooping in
halfway through a maths lesson. I'm going to stay here until the
bell goes,' Joyce said.

The scholarship girls had left as soon as they'd heard other
girls in the corridor returning to their form rooms, hoping to
mingle with them and that their absence hadn't been noted.

Those that had permission to be in the dining hall agreed
with Joyce and remained where they were until the end-of-lesson
bell was rung. The final double period today was history and, as
the teacher came to them, they would be in their form room on
the first floor.

For the first time since classes had been reorganised at the
start of the January term, the atmosphere was less fraught.
Instead of the scholarship girls sitting isolated on the far side of
the classroom, they sat where there were empty seats. Cynthia
had ended the unnecessary quarrel – thank goodness.

* * *

Emily collected the doctor's little girl, Claire, from the prep
school and hand in hand they skidded and slipped down Queen's
Street to the station.

'When are George and Sammy coming back to school?'

'Next week, I wish we'd had an extra few days' holiday. It's
miserable getting to school in this weather.'

She delivered Claire to Little Wick and then hurried around
to the back of Harbour House, pleased that her brothers were in

the kitchen to greet her. She told them about the incident at school and waved her frozen socks at them.

'Crikey, that could have been dreadful,' Sammy said, 'but it turned out all right as you got cake and cocoa instead of maths.'

'Even better, the rift with the fee-paying girls appears to be over. I wonder how Lucinda will get on with her trial flight tomorrow. She told me she hasn't flown for more than a year.'

'I expect it's something you remember how to do. They must know and will make allowances,' George said, sounding very grown-up.

'Are we allowed to have a fire in your bedroom tonight?' Emily asked hopefully.

'We've had one all day, are you coming to do jigsaws or play Monopoly or something else until supper time?'

'I haven't got any homework tonight so I'd love to do any of those. My feet are still cold and so am I, I hope I don't get a nasty cold after my unpleasant experience today.'

Sammy looked at her closely. 'You do look a bit pasty, don't get the measles, a boy at school died from that last term.'

'I don't see why I should get measles from getting wet feet – you catch that from being with someone else who's got measles. I'm absolutely fine, let's do a jigsaw each and see who finishes first. The winner can pick what we do next.'

When Emily went up to bed with her hot water bottle, she was feeling rather unwell but hadn't bothered her parents with this piece of information. As far as she knew, there'd been no girls off school in her form with a contagious illness. Whatever it was she was going down with was probably no worse than a bad cold. Dr Cousins had told her that getting wet didn't cause a cold but if you're already getting one it could make it worse.

The following morning she felt awful, cold, shivery, aching all over and couldn't find the energy to get out of bed. Swallowing was painful, her head hurt so she just went back to sleep.

'Emily, can you open your eyes for me?'

Someone was talking to her but she wasn't sure who it was. It wasn't her daddy or mummy – she thought it might be the doctor.

With some difficulty, she prised her lids up and saw she was ringed by a trio of anxious adult faces. She wanted to tell them she just had a cold but she couldn't speak. She closed her eyes again as it was easier than trying to talk to anybody.

From a distance, she heard her parents and the doctor discussing her. Then one of them held her head and spooned in a little warm water. Swallowing was horrible and she closed her mouth, turned her head away and went back to sleep.

She was woken and made to swallow even though it was agony. She vaguely recalled being lifted onto some sort of receptacle to empty her bladder. Then, she wasn't exactly sure how long later, she woke up able to swallow without wanting to cry.

'My darling girl, your temperature's going down, Dr Cousins is happy with your progress. The worst is over.'

Blearily she looked across and saw Mummy sitting in a chair close to her. 'I need a drink,' she croaked. Talking was painful but at least she could now form words that made sense.

Emily swallowed a glass of warm water and then went back to sleep. The next time she woke up, it wasn't a drink she wanted but the WC. She pushed herself into a sitting position, expecting to see someone sitting in the chair, but it was empty.

The commode was behind a screen – never used and she'd not expected to ever have to do so – but now she had no option. Trying to get down two flights of stairs when her legs would barely hold her was a recipe for disaster.

She managed to stagger to the screen and then back to bed

without collapsing. There were two hot water bottles in her bed – what luxury – somebody must be doing without as there was only enough for one each.

Emily wasn't sure how long she'd been unwell. Had Lucinda returned from Hatfield? Was it still snowing? Had she passed whatever it was to her baby sister? A heavy weight settled on her chest – she might only be twelve years old, but she knew if the baby got what she'd had then the infant wouldn't survive.

Where was Mummy? Why was the house so quiet? She had to go downstairs and see for herself that nobody else had gone down with whatever it was she'd had that had made her so unwell.

It took her several attempts to put on her dressing gown, slippers were impossible. In bare feet she shuffled like an old woman to the door – which was open – and paused on the top step, trying to find the energy and courage to attempt the steep staircase that led from the attic to the first floor.

She was dangerously wobbly. If she sat down then she could descend on her bottom. That way, if she felt faint, she wouldn't fall headfirst and break her neck. She was halfway down when Lily appeared holding a tray.

'What are you doing? You shouldn't even be out of bed. Your mum will have my guts for garters if she finds out I let you get up. You've been ever so ill.'

'Grace, is she all right? Did anyone else catch this?'

'No, you've had a bad throat and a high temperature, I don't think it's all that catching. Can you reverse? Bump your way back to bed the way you've come down?'

'I think so. How long have I been ill?'

'It's Friday morning, so you've only missed Thursday. The boys were grumpy as they had to go back to school today. Miss

Somiton telephoned to say that she had her test yesterday as the weather was too bad for flying on the Wednesday.'

Emily nodded and concentrated on shuffling backwards. It took her longer to go up than it had to come down but eventually she succeeded. However, getting onto her feet proved impossible.

Lily gripped her elbows and got her back into bed. Then she returned to collect the tray and sat with Emily whilst she attempted to swallow as much as she could and enjoyed each mouthful she managed before abandoning the soup.

18

Lucinda hadn't expected the lorry that had stopped to give her a lift to be empty, but it was almost full of boxes, leaving barely enough room for the three of them to squash into the available space behind the tailgate.

'Good grief, this is a bit of a squeeze. I'm Lucinda Somiton, thanks for the heave in.'

'You're welcome,' Jill said. 'You're obviously not one of us, why are you going to Hatfield?'

'I've got a test flight and am here to try out for the ATA.'

This really impressed them.

'Crikey, they started with only eight last year and now there must be two dozen or more,' the other girl said.

'When I read in the newspaper that more women were going to be allowed to fly with the ATA I immediately sent in a letter to Miss Gower, not expecting to hear back so soon. I'm as astonished as you are to be here.'

'Well, good luck. I might be a WAAF, but I prefer to stay firmly on the ground,' Jill said as they hit a pothole and were bounced into the air and landed in a painful heap.

'Sorry, I should have jammed my suitcases in more securely. I hope they didn't hurt you,' Lucinda said.

'The driver's doing it on purpose. We're both drivers and are going to be stationed with them for a few months. You'd think that he'd be pleased he's not going to have to do so many boring jobs as they'll be given to us,' Jill said as she rubbed her bruised elbow.

Fortunately, it was a short drive and the lorry shuddered to a halt inside the gates of Hatfield base. This wasn't an active base, it was where some pilots first learnt to fly and experienced ones test-flew planes for de Havilland whose factory was here.

The driver revved the engine. The officer yelled that Lucinda should get out. She threw her suitcases over the tailgate and followed them. She was barely on her feet when the lorry shot off. If she'd been half-out then she'd have fallen and possibly been seriously injured.

Why were some men so obnoxious? They should be pleased women were being trained to take over the mundane jobs and not resent it and behave like spoilt brats.

The first thing she noticed as she approached the gate was that there were no planes in the air and she'd expected lots of them to be going round and round doing their circuits and bumps as this was an RAF pilot training ground as well as where the girls flew from.

There was a barrier, but she'd scrambled out of the lorry on the base side of it so was possibly in trouble. She had to bang on the guard's window to attract the attention of the man inside. He'd been smoking and reading the paper and didn't appreciate being dragged away. Hardly the behaviour of an efficient guard. He shoved the glass back noisily.

'What do you want? You shouldn't be hanging about here, no civilians allowed.'

Hardly encouraging. 'I'm here for a test flight; Miss Gower's expecting me.'

His feet slammed to the boards and his expression changed from disinterested to alarmed. 'I beg your pardon, miss, I never knew no one was coming today.' He pointed to a hangar on the far side of the airfield. 'The ladies are over there somewhere. You don't want to be taking your suitcases with you.'

'In fact I do as, if I'm flying, I need to change.'

He shrugged and slammed the window closed.

Lucinda tucked the small suitcase under her left arm and grabbed the handle of the larger one, leaving her right arm free in case she had to shake hands with someone she met. There were various vehicles zooming about, large and small, some open topped and others closed, but none of them stopped to offer her a ride.

She checked her wristwatch and was in good time, half an hour early, in fact. She'd been stared at, glared at, but no one had asked her what she was doing there with her suitcases and she found that odd. This was an RAF base, definitely not somewhere a civilian should be wandering about unescorted.

'Hey, you, what in God's name are you doing with those suitcases?' The speaker was male but Lucinda couldn't see where the voice was coming from – there were several buildings and aircraft close by.

'I'm carrying them,' she answered, risking being facetious.

It worked and he chuckled and a tousled blond-haired young man appeared from behind a Tiger Moth. 'I'll rephrase that. Why are you prowling around here?'

'I don't think I'm prowling, I'm just looking for Miss Gower as I've been called in to have a flight test to join the ATA.'

'Have you, by jingo? I'll take you to her. Nothing's up today, too bally cold, but you should be able to fly tomorrow.' He smiled and wiped his hands on his dungarees. 'I'm Sergeant Duncan Frobisher; I was just giving the old Moth the once over as it's what you'll be using.'

Without putting down her cases, Lucinda offered her right hand and they shook. 'I'm Lucinda Somiton, I think I'm pleased to meet you.'

'Here, dump those in that corner. They'll be safe there. I'll take you to Miss Gower. I heard that she's actively looking for new recruits and you must be the first of them.'

* * *

Miss Gower greeted her with enthusiasm. 'My dear girl, I can't tell you how pleased I am to have you here. Nothing doing today, I'm afraid, but you'll be first up when the temperature rises.'

'Am I being tested by an RAF instructor?'

'No, I've been running this section for over a year and am now considered quite experienced enough to conduct the test myself.'

'I hoped that would be the case.'

'I'll be sitting in the rear seat giving you directions. I'll get one of the girls to take you through everything whilst you're on the ground. You've got an impressive number of logged hours but it's more than a year since you were up.'

'If I pass the test, when would I be able to join you here?'

'If you're as good as you say you are then it should be a piece of cake. I expect you to go to London and order your uniform, then go home and say your farewells and return here.'

Lucinda had something else she had to ask. 'Miss Gower, I'm delighted to be here but surprised. I'm sure you've had dozens of eager young ladies with flying experience asking to join. Why did you invite me for a test flight so quickly?'

Her answer was unexpected and Lucinda was shocked.

'That Ralph Castleton is an absolute bounder. Leone Castleton used to be a good friend of mine, we were at school together, but I didn't approve of what she did to you. Quite unnecessary. That's why you're here, I thought you needed a new start and what could be better than to join this small band of ladies I've got together?' Miss Gower nodded. 'Also, I've just been given the go-ahead to recruit as many girls as I can find that are suitably qualified. There will be a string of them arriving over the next few weeks.'

'Golly, of all the reasons I'd considered that was certainly not one of them. Aren't you terribly shocked by my behaviour? Everybody else I know has cut me off completely, including my parents.'

'My mother's a friend of your family so when I got your letter I asked her what she knew about you, therefore I'm aware of your circumstances.'

'Circumstances?'

'My dear girl, I know your secret so there's no need to pretend with me. Your parents are actually your grandparents and you're the by-blow of your brother Alfie.'

Lucinda dropped the cases and staggered backwards. It had never once occurred to her that she wasn't who she thought she was but now she understood why her childhood had been so miserable, why her brother Alfie had always avoided her.

Miss Gower took her arm and guided her into a large wooden hut with several rooms that served as their headquarters. There were more than a dozen women sitting about, some knitting, some reading, some playing cards but all waiting for the weather to clear so they could get on with their jobs.

'A mug of tea for Lucinda, I've just given her an awful shock. Come along, my dear, we'll go into my office where we can be private.'

The tea was provided. Scarcely aware of her surroundings, with shaking hands Lucinda cupped it, trying not to spill it on the desk which was covered with important-looking documents and slips. After a couple of attempts she managed to swallow and the hot liquid did help.

'I don't know why I never considered they were my grandparents. I've always thought I was an embarrassment, that for someone in their fifties to have had a baby was unusual, but not that there might be another reason.' Lucinda drank a few more mouthfuls, trying to make sense of what she'd been told. 'I thought illegitimate children in families like mine were farmed out to tenant farmers to raise as their own.'

'Possibly, but to give them their due, they did the right thing. Your real father was married and had a child of his own and your natural mother sadly died when you were born. I think it was that that persuaded them to take you themselves.'

'Goodness me, if you know does that mean that the family I now belong to, the family I thought were some sort of distant cousins, also know?'

'Why would they? Only your actual father and your grandparents know the true circumstances,' Miss Gower said.

'And you, and your mother, and now everybody else who might have overheard us talking outside.'

'If anybody heard, which is unlikely as the door's closed, I can assure you it won't go any further.'

For some reason this mattered to her. 'I've never been happy, knew I wasn't wanted, and in a way I'm relieved to find the real reason behind this. I don't care if your friends know that I'm a bastard—'

'Don't say that, you're Lucinda Somiton. And I'm quite sure tomorrow or the next day you'll be one of us – an ATA girl.'

Lucinda finished her tea, her mind whirling, but pleased she knew the truth at last and even happier that it had been someone she admired so much who'd told her.

'Miss Gower, I've recovered from the shock. I can't tell you how excited I am to be here and can't wait to be dressed in that lovely smart uniform.'

'Call me Pauline, not Miss Gower. You must be coming up to twenty soon, there are three other pilots around your age; one of them, Rose, is in the other room. I'll introduce you to everybody.'

* * *

Lucinda spent the remainder of the day getting to know the women she'd be working with. Rose she took to immediately and when she was offered the spare room for the night, in Rose's little rented cottage a couple of miles away from the base, Lucinda accepted immediately. The room was small, cold, unwelcoming but she loved it. Being uncomfortable was something she had to get used to if she was going to survive in the ATA.

When she got up on Thursday morning, she dressed in the clothes she'd brought for flying. She was certain today she'd take her test. There was no ice on the inside of the window, she could hear the snow dripping from the roof, it was definitely flying weather.

Rose greeted her approvingly. 'You just need to get hold of an Irvine jacket. You can buy them at the same place you order your uniform. You can also get a Sidcot suit – Pauline is trying to get them issued to us free but at the moment we have to buy them.'

* * *

Emily wasn't going to be allowed to get out of bed for another boring twenty-four hours. The doctor had come to see her and pronounced her on the mend but not well enough to be up. Her temperature was still a bit high, but her throat was less sore which was more important as eating was less painful.

George and Sammy had come up immediately after school but hadn't stayed long. She wasn't sure if they were afraid of catching her germs or because they had a lot of homework to do.

Daddy was home as soon as it was dark now which was the only good thing about the winter. He came to see her immediately.

'Sweetheart, you gave us quite a scare. You look a lot better than you did yesterday.'

'I'm sorry, I blame sitting with wet feet in the shelter for an hour on Wednesday.' Her voice was husky and it hurt to talk.

'Just bad luck but getting cold probably made it worse. Now, if you feel up to it you can come down to listen to the wireless in the sitting room.'

'Dr Cousins said I was to stay in bed until tomorrow afternoon but I would really like to come down.'

'My house, my rules, my decision. If you feel up to it, that's good enough for me. I can always carry you back if necessary.'

'It won't be, I'm sure I can manage. When can I have a bath?'

'I've no idea, don't ask me silly questions, baths are your mother's preserve.'

He waited whilst Emily fumbled into her dressing gown and pushed her feet into her slippers.

'I'm going to walk backwards in front of you,' he said, smiling.

'Makes sense to me. You're so big that if I fall then you'll be jammed on the stairs and I'd be perfectly safe.'

Her first and most desperate need was to visit the WC. When she'd finished, she washed her face as well as her hands and risked a glance into the mirror. Who was that pale, sickly-looking girl with lank hair staring back at her?

It shook her that her appearance had changed so dramatically in so short a time. Maybe she wasn't well enough to be up after all. She found Daddy waiting a few yards down the passageway.

'I'm going back to bed; I'll get up tomorrow. Good night.'

'I'll come up behind you. Two flights of stairs are a lot after you've been so ill.'

Emily was exhausted by the time she flopped into bed. 'I don't need anything else, just sleep.'

'Your mother and I have decided that you're moving back into the empty bedroom. I know you like it up here, but it'll be more comfortable, warmer and safer back where you belong.'

'That's a good idea, I've been lonely and it would have been nice to have had a fire and an actual electric light.'

He didn't leave but sat in the chair beside her bed. There was just the oil lamp lighting the room and when this was off it was horribly dark in the attic. She hadn't minded until she'd been so ill.

Emily blinked back tears. War was beastly, those you loved had to go away and sometimes never came home again. Being a pilot was dangerous but at least Lucinda wouldn't be fighting the Germans, just delivering the planes.

19

Lucinda had to sit on the parcel seat behind Rose's bicycle on the journey from the cottage where she was billeted to the airfield. Unlike the other services, ATA members, being civilians, had to provide their own accommodation. Rose had told her the spare room was hers permanently if she wanted it and Lucinda certainly did if she passed the test this morning.

When they went over a particularly bumpy part of the lane, Rose wobbled and Lucinda fell off. 'Good thing I didn't land in a puddle. If I'm taken on I really need to get my own bicycle as I can't travel in and out like this every day.'

'That would be impossible even if we wanted to do it. We don't know where we're going or when, often have to either stay overnight or find our way back on the train lugging our gear. It's unlikely that the two of us will be flying anywhere together.'

Lucinda scrambled back on the bike and they completed the last mile without any further mishaps. The grumpy guard recognised Rose and waved her through, which was fortunate as if they'd stopped Lucinda knew she'd probably end up on the ground again.

Pauline was waiting by the Tiger Moth. 'I'm sorry, am I late?'

'No, I'm early and so are you. Are you ready?'

She nodded and tried to look confident when she was the reverse. 'I certainly am. You sit behind me whilst I do my circuits and bumps and then if I'm good enough I'll fly solo with you watching from the ground. Do I have that right?'

Pauline nodded. 'In you get, Lucinda, can't hang about as the weather might change and I've got a lot to do today.'

Rose had run through everything yesterday. Lucinda had sat in the front seat and her new friend had sat in the back and shouted instructions to her through the speaking tube. Lucinda was certain that her pre-flight checks would be perfect, that she'd be able to taxi the little plane onto the runway and take off when given the order from behind her.

Despite the fact that it was more than a year since she'd flown, it seemed like only yesterday. Perhaps flying a plane was like riding a bicycle and you didn't forget how to do it. Circuits and bumps were the technical words for going in a circle and landing and taking off on command.

She completed three, each one as perfect as the last. Pauline tapped on her shoulder when they taxied to a halt.

'Right, over to you. Don't go near London or you'll get entangled in the balloons if they're up. Go towards Hatfield town, fly around it and then return here and go in the opposite direction. No more than half an hour in the air.'

The rest of her test went swimmingly and she knew without having it confirmed that she'd passed and would be joining the ATA.

Lucinda taxied the Tiger Moth to the position it had been on the apron, switched off the engine and clambered out. Pauline was there but none of the other girls, who presumably had got their chits from the dispatcher and flown off to collect or deliver something.

'Well done, Lucinda, you couldn't have done better. You passed, of course you did, I never had a minute's doubt. There are a couple of lectures about navigation and so on you must attend but then you will be on the rota.'

'Do I get an official letter? Or can I start celebrating now?' She pointed at Pauline's smart uniform, practical long blue trousers and a smart jacket. Similar in style to the RAF but a different colour and far better cut. 'Can I order my own when I go back to London?'

Pauline nodded. 'It takes a week for them to make what you need. You'll have to wear what you've got until it arrives. You need an Irvine jacket, I expect Rose told you that already.'

'She did. I'm also going to purchase a Sidcot suit, I know exactly where to get both.'

'Good girl, just the ticket. As far as I'm concerned you're now officially on my books and I'll send your name and details off today to head office. You're lucky you didn't join until this year as when we first started they expected us to fly in skirts and stockings. Imagine having to bail out dressed like that? Ridiculous, but we're getting there.'

'I can't imagine having to bail out at all. I just flew for over an hour and nobody offered me a parachute. Do I get one once I'm one of you? I wouldn't have thought that we fly high enough for it to be safe to jump out.'

Pauline chuckled. 'It'd be a lot safer to jump than it would be to crash in situ. Come along, you've got a lecture about navigation to go to.'

'I'm good with a compass and map, with following railway lines and landmarks, I spent hours and hours going backwards and forwards last summer. My instructor said I should take my B licence but I couldn't see the point as a woman's never going to be a commercial pilot. However, I did all the studying and could have passed the exams. I've certainly got enough hours in my logbook.'

'I was going to ask you about that – how did you manage four hundred?'

'I flew semi-professionally for the flying school. I carried passengers to and from racecourses and so on. I wasn't paid so I didn't break any rules. This meant I was flying over a hundred hours a month.'

'Did you fly anything apart from a Moth?'

'An Avro Evian as well the Moth and I had a few hours on the bigger one but only circuits and bumps.'

'Excellent, if I'd known about you last year you'd have been in right at the beginning. But I think it'll be easier for anyone joining now we've ironed out all the wrinkles, got a decent uniform and have earned the respect of the male pilots and the RAF.'

On Saturday morning, Lucinda signed the requisite papers and became an official member of the ATA. She paid a month's rent in advance to Rose and got a lift back to the station. She'd a week to say her goodbyes, put the belongings she didn't need in an attic at Harbour House, and sign the papers for the trust fund and give it to Elizabeth and Jonathan before she left.

She'd put her small suitcase inside the larger as she'd left her flying gear in her new home. The Sidcot suit and Irvine jacket – a wonderful long leather flying coat lined with sheepskin that fighter pilots used – were paid for and would be delivered to the women's ATA headquarters at Hatfield. Sadly, her lovely new uniform wouldn't be ready for two weeks which meant the first week she'd be flying in her jodhs. There was a thaw, the snow turning to grey slush, which made walking through London unpleasant.

The train had no available seats so she was obliged to stand in the corridor squashed amongst a group of khaki-clad young men. Initially she was anxious, thought they would take advantage of her proximity, but the reverse was true.

'Right, you noisy buggers,' one of them said as the train pulled out of Liverpool Street. 'No funny business, we've got a lady present. Watch your language and no blowing fag smoke in her face.'

The speaker had a stripe on his arm so was possibly a lance corporal. She smiled gratefully at him. 'Thank you, I'm going to sit on my suitcase and pretend to be asleep so you go ahead and talk freely.'

'Here, you sit on me bag, love, it'll be more comfortable,' another soldier said with a friendly grin.

So she did, and there was absolutely no necessity for her to pretend to be asleep as they were polite, respectful, and jolly good fun to talk to. She discovered they'd been posted to what they called a 'cushy number' in Clacton and were very happy about it.

The train door was opened for her and her suitcase handed out after she was on the platform. 'Good luck, gentlemen, thank you for being so nice to me.'

Their response was a series of catcalls and whistles which turned a few heads, but she smiled and waved and made her way carefully over the slippery bridge and into Station Road.

Halfway down, she saw the front gate of Harbour House open and the boys rushed out to meet her.

She hugged both of them. 'You didn't have to come out in the cold but I appreciate that you have.'

'Emily's been really poorly, she's not allowed to get up yet,'

George said. 'She's moved down to the empty room next to ours so we're all on the same floor now.'

'I'm glad, I worried about her upstairs with no electricity or heating. I'm going to suggest to Elizabeth that I transfer up there. This would mean that I've got somewhere to think of as my home even when I'm goodness knows where.'

'We'll help you,' Sammy said. 'When do you have to leave to be a pilot? Will you be flying Spitfires and Hurricanes?'

'Goodness me, I shouldn't think so, at least not initially. I'll be delivering parts and transferring documents from one place to another in a Tiger Moth. Maybe, when the RAF have got used to us, they might let us deliver or collect a fighter.'

* * *

Ralph was given a week's embarkation leave by the major he was sent to and was told he was lucky to get that. Then he had to report to somewhere in Kent and prepare to be posted overseas. He headed home with his story ready and had almost begun to believe his lies. He telephoned to tell his wife he was on the way home and that he had some news for her.

She wanted to hug him when he walked in, but he retreated. 'No, darling, I'm cold and damp. I don't want to make you uncomfortable. I'll just sort myself out and join you in the drawing room.'

'All right, I'll have refreshments waiting for you. Do hurry up, I can't wait to hear your news.'

He was frowning as he dropped his coat on the chair in the boot room, kicked off his brogues and replaced them with his indoor shoes. Leone hadn't said she'd got good news for him which could mean she'd been mistaken and wasn't in fact pregnant as they'd hoped. There'd be no further opportunity to start one as God knows when he'd get home again.

He waited a few moments to recover his temper. With any luck, when she learned he was being posted overseas she'd forget about the bracelet. He walked into the drawing room, confident he looked relaxed and happy.

'I managed to get some decent coffee sent down from Fortnum & Mason, darling, so we've got that with a delicious array of pastries that Cook has just sent up. She's been busy all morning making your absolute favourites.'

This time Ralph embraced her, she softened into his arms, and they exchanged an enjoyable kiss. Once they were settled and he had his coffee he told her why he was home.

'I decided that being an intelligence officer in London whilst others are actually fighting Hitler made me a coward. Therefore, I spoke to the colonel and asked to be transferred to an active regiment. I join them in Kent next week and then we're being posted somewhere overseas.'

'Why? Why would you want to give up your safe position to go away to kill people and possibly get killed yourself? Doesn't your family matter to you?'

'I love you and my girls, Leone, but I'll be fighting for you as well as for King and country. I've ordered my uniform and will collect it in two days' time. I have some loose ends to tie up before I join my regiment so will be away for two nights. Then on my return I'll spend the remainder of my leave with you and the girls.'

She sighed and wiped her eyes. 'I thought you were issued with your uniform. Do you have to pay for it?'

'I get an allowance but officers, if they can afford it, have their kit made for them so it fits.'

'I'm proud of you, I really am, it's just such a shock. I really thought that our marriage had become a happy one at last. You won't be here when our baby's born.'

His coffee slopped into the saucer as he put it down. 'Are you sure? You haven't missed a second one, have you?'

'No, but I feel exactly the same way I did with both our girls. My breasts are tender, I'm nauseous in the morning and I seem to spend more time in the loo than out of it.'

'That's the most wonderful news, my darling, and I wish my conscience allowed me to remain at your side. I'm an officer, a junior one admittedly, but I'll soon prove my worth and be promoted.'

'Perhaps they'll give you compassionate leave to come home when our baby's born in the summer. Do you know what your role will be?'

'I'll still be an intelligence officer, although attached to my brigade I'll be moving about using my particular skills. I doubt that I'll actually be doing any hand-to-hand fighting. The major I spoke to was delighted to have me on board. I'm going to do a valuable job, a similar job, but as an officer and not a civilian.'

Leone gazed at him with love and admiration. 'I'm just lucky to have had you in England for the first couple of years of this ghastly war. Two of my closest friends have already lost relatives but, thank God, not their own husbands.' She smiled brightly. 'Perhaps one of them is in the same regiment that you're joining. William's a captain and Simon a major. You won't be the same rank but I'm sure that you'll use the same mess.'

Ralph hid his dismay. He hadn't thought this through properly – of course she was going to have friends who were officers and most likely in the army rather than the Navy or RAF. People like them would always be army officers.

'I'm afraid I can't tell you which regiment I'm joining, I think it quite likely my name won't even appear in any lists, I have to remain anonymous, or I can't do my job properly.'

'Silly me, of course you can't. My friends know that you're in intelligence so won't ask awkward questions when I tell them you're about to be posted overseas, and are now attached to a regiment, no longer a civilian.'

His fingers slowly unclenched. He'd got away with it. He didn't give a damn whether he had a son or not in the summer, he was likely to be blown up or die from some deadly disease, and what happened when he was gone didn't matter to him.

He gently told his wife that much as he wanted to he wouldn't make love to her as he didn't want to risk the pregnancy. This lie improved his standing. She'd not mentioned the jewellery and with so much going on he doubted he'd be asked again to produce it.

He'd always slept in the master suite, his wife through the communicating door. He kissed her good night and returned to his study. Another lie he'd told her was about having loose ends. His intention was to go to Wivenhoe, take a room at a place he'd researched, the Park Hotel at the top of the town away from Harbour House. He'd be in his uniform and anyone who saw him would scarcely notice another army officer. Lucinda didn't know he'd been forced from his sinecure, was no longer a civilian, so even if she somehow caught a glimpse of him, it wouldn't raise an alarm.

* * *

Emily was loving being back with the family, the novelty of the attic had worn off when the weather had turned cold a few weeks ago. She left her new bedroom door open so the boys could come in and out and tell her what they were doing. They knew that when the door was shut she was resting.

Lucinda spent an hour with her sitting on the end of the bed and telling her about her adventure in Hatfield.

'It seems strange that you had this secret past, that you weren't just a second cousin or something but a qualified pilot. I'm not sure I'd want to fly a plane but I'm very impressed that you can. I'm not even very steady on a bicycle.'

'I'm sure you can do whatever you want to when you're old enough to do it. Let's hope this dreadful war's over before you have to make the sort of decision I just have. Mr Hatch wasn't happy, said I was abandoning him, and I'm afraid we parted on rather bad terms.'

'Golly, you're going to be doing something really important, far better than wandering about doing very little in Wivenhoe. If you were an ARP warden in London or any other of the big cities that would be different.'

'Yes, you're right. Elizabeth has promised to ask around at one of her meetings. She thinks that if three women did it between them then it wouldn't be too arduous for any of them. I'm sure they'd all feel they were doing their bit for the war effort. Better than knitting balaclavas for sailors, I'd have thought.'

'Dr Cousins has said I can't go back to school for another week. I've got to recuperate. I'm allowed to get dressed on Monday – you don't have to leave before then, do you?'

'No, not until next Thursday. I start officially on Friday, 10 January. I'm really excited but I'm going to miss all of you most dreadfully.'

'And we'll miss you. Remember this is your home. Like anyone else who's in one of the services you'll be able to come back when you get some leave. Hatfield isn't very far from

London, Daddy told me, so if you get a forty-eight-hour pass you should be able to make it.'

Lucinda smiled. 'Actually, I don't know how things work in the ATA. I'll find all that out once I start but I'm definitely coming back for my birthday in February if I can.'

Elizabeth popped her head around the door. 'I think you should rest, darling girl, you mustn't overdo it.'

'Yes, Mummy, but I'll only rest for an hour. Daddy said I can come down for tea if nobody objects to me eating in my dressing gown.'

'I'll send one of the boys up to wake you if you're not down by five.'

* * *

Emily didn't mind resting even with the door closed as she could hear the family moving about in various parts of the house. It was strange how Lucinda had changed since she'd arrived last November. She was very much part of the family and they were all immensely proud of her. There weren't many young women who were doing what she was.

There'd been no necessity for anyone to wake her up as she came down early. Spending so much time in bed made it difficult for her to sleep and she thought if she didn't rest in the afternoon maybe she'd sleep better. Being awake when everyone else was asleep wasn't very nice.

If you were asleep, you didn't hear the bombers going over, didn't hear the Spitfires and Hurricanes roaring around the sky, didn't hear the bombs dropping or the big guns firing. When you were awake you heard it all.

Tonight they were having an early meal and Grace was going to join them. This would be the first time the baby had been up when they ate their evening meal. Emily hoped it wouldn't be anything too difficult to swallow as her throat was still rather sore.

'Hello, sweetheart, the fire's been burning long enough to make the dining room pleasant. The boys have laid the table, I've been watching Grace whilst your mother and Lucinda have prepared the meal,' Daddy said.

Emily was exhausted after all the fun and excitement of being with her family that evening. Lucinda had told them an extraordinary story about the man who'd not been very kind to her. Her brothers thought it smashing that he'd been arrested but Emily wasn't so sure.

20

Lucinda headed for Colchester on Monday to sign the papers at the bank that would confirm the small trust fund she'd set up for the three children. The train was crowded; it was the London train and not the local one. She'd mistimed her arrival at the station but thought she'd rather catch the bus from the main station into town than stand around on the platform at Wivenhoe or return to Harbour House.

A few times she had the strange feeling she was being watched and surreptitiously glanced around but saw nobody she recognised. Mostly soldiers, just a few shoppers and businesspeople. The weather was cold and dull – she couldn't remember the last time she'd seen the sun – no one wanted to be out unless they'd no option.

The hill from Colchester station was no longer snow-covered, instead it was icy, which was more dangerous. Several passengers overtook her as she made her slow way down. She wasn't usually so cautious, but she just couldn't risk a sprained ankle when she was about to start her new life as a pilot.

Fortunately, the road wasn't busy and she crossed without

having to hurry. Moving at speed in the treacherous conditions was a recipe for disaster.

She joined the handful of people, some suited gentlemen, a few women with capacious shopping bags, in the queue.

'Is a bus due soon?' Lucinda asked one of the women.

'Any moment, love, brass monkeys today, ain't it?'

'I wouldn't mind the cold if the skies were clear. We've not had any sunshine worth speaking of for weeks.'

An army lorry was approaching with the bus behind it.

'There it is, I can just see the bus. I hope it ain't too full, I ain't keen on standing even such a short distance. Me knees ain't too good nowadays.'

As the lorry was about to pass the queue, Lucinda felt a violent push in the small of her back. She hurtled forward, sprawling on her face in front of the lorry. Everything happened so fast. She was going to be crushed beneath the heavy wheels.

Her world went black, there was the most appalling smell, screaming, loud voices. She must be horribly injured so why couldn't she feel any pain?

Then the faces of two soldiers appeared in front of her. 'Bleeding hell, Fred, she ain't dead. It's a miracle. I thought she was a goner after going under the lorry like that.'

Her head cleared. Something about this accident wasn't right, but she couldn't think what it was.

'The coppers are coming, miss, and the ambulance, do you reckon we could pull you out?'

'Please do, it's cold and smelly under here.' She tried to move but couldn't for some reason. 'I'm stuck, I'm pretty sure I'm not hurt but something's holding me back.'

Lucinda didn't understand how she wasn't dead, how she was lying on her face beneath the lorry virtually unharmed.

Both soldiers wriggled under the lorry to join her. 'Bleeding miracle, that's what it is. One minute you was standing with them others waiting for the bus, the next thing you was in the road.'

'Someone pushed me into the road. I felt a hand in the small of my back.'

'That explains it, the bobbies will take statements. I never saw who it was, but I do know that there was a soldier, wearing a flat cap so not one of us, standing right behind you.'

The other soldier was fiddling about above her shoulders. 'There, that's done it, miss. The strap of your satchel was caught. Can you turn on your back?'

She didn't ask why, realising it would be less painful being pulled out that way than face first. 'I'll try, but for some reason my legs and arms are refusing to obey my instructions.'

'That'll be the shock. We could do it for you if you don't mind us putting hands on you.'

She lay still whilst they gently manoeuvred her. Then they carefully shuffled backwards, taking her with them.

'God bless you, love, I've never seen the like. By rights you should be dead. The good Lord is certainly looking out for you,' the lady Lucinda had been speaking to earlier said.

'Look at your poor face, all scratched and bleeding. Here, take my handkerchief,' one of the businessmen said. He was crouching down beside her as she lay on what looked like somebody's overcoat by the side of the road. Then a second coat was put over her and something soft put under her head.

How kind people were. There must be three of them prepared to freeze just so they could keep her warm. That was the last thing she remembered before she blacked out.

* * *

When she opened her eyes, she wasn't on the pavement but lying on a bed of some sort with a white-coated man and a nurse examining her.

'Good, you're awake. You fainted, Miss Somiton, shock can do that. I'm going to examine you to check you haven't received any thing more serious than cuts and bruises.'

Lucinda closed her eyes, couldn't find the energy to answer. The doctor knew her name – had she told him? She didn't remember doing so.

He stopped gently pressing and prodding. 'All tickety-boo. You might need a stitch or two on your forehead, and you've got gravel embedded in your hands, but superficial injuries only. Nothing short of a miracle considering you fell under a three-ton lorry.'

The mention of a lorry jerked her into full consciousness. She opened her eyes and stared at him. 'I didn't fall; someone pushed me. The driver of the lorry saw him do it. I need to speak to a policeman.'

'There's a detective inspector waiting to speak to you. I must admit I was puzzled that someone so senior had come to a road accident. I'll be as quick as I can, Miss Somiton, and then you can talk to him.'

'How do you know my name?'

He smiled and pushed his metal-framed glasses back up his nose. 'Your identity card was in your leather bag. Do you have family we should contact to let them know what happened?'

She gave them the telephone number for Harbour House. 'Please make sure whatever message is given doesn't make it sound as if I'm seriously hurt. Also, there's no need to mention how I fell. I don't want to worry them.'

'Understood. Now, please be quiet whilst I do my job.'

After what seemed like an hour of acute discomfort but was

probably only a few minutes, the stitches were in, the dressings on, the gravel removed and she was ready to speak to the policeman.

His sergeant took notes whilst she explained exactly what had happened. She also mentioned the feeling she'd had that someone was watching her.

'Your version, Miss Somiton, corresponds exactly with the witness statements of the soldier and one of the ladies who was standing next to you in the queue. I don't doubt that what you told me is the truth but for you to have been catapulted into the path of the lorry must have taken considerable force. I'd like the doctor to look at your back and see if there's any bruising.'

She nodded. 'I was going to suggest that as I've definitely got a sharp pain between my shoulders. My back hurts almost as much as my face.'

The doctor returned with the nurse. Someone had removed Lucinda's coat and boots, but she was still wearing her other clothes, a thick jumper over her warmest slacks.

The nurse carefully rolled up the back of her jumper and her vest and she winced as they did it.

'Yes, Inspector, you can see a clear imprint of a hand. The bruise is already spreading and will be causing Miss Somiton some discomfort.'

'Please tell me that there's nothing broken, that I'll be fully functioning by Friday. I've just joined the ATA, I have to be there on Friday and will be flying for them shortly after that.'

'Good for you, Miss Somiton. I wouldn't advise that you pilot any aircraft for a week, but you should be fully recovered by then,' the doctor said.

Lucinda didn't want to remain on the bed, and she certainly wasn't going to be admitted. She was shaken, bruised and cut by her near demise, but not sufficiently to keep her in hospital.

She saw her outer garments, bag, gas mask and boots on a chair in the corner of the cubicle. Whilst the doctor was conversing with the policeman, she collected them and, when the curtain was pulled back, she was ready to leave.

'I have an appointment at the bank, I don't wish to miss it. You have my statement – somebody tried to kill me – and I think I know who it was.' Lucinda was reeling at the thought that a man who she'd been involved with could do something so awful. He'd threatened her, but she couldn't believe he'd actually want to kill her.

'Matron has said we can use her office and one of the student nurses has rustled up a tray of tea and biscuits. You'll feel better after a hot drink and a couple of aspirins. We can talk in the office and you can tell me why you think someone might be trying to kill you.'

From his tone he thought her suggestion unlikely, had probably decided that she was pushed by someone who thought to do so was funny, the sudden impulse of an unbalanced mind.

He listened carefully, his sergeant taking down every word she said, and when she'd finished he wasn't smiling or looking sceptical.

'I agree, Miss Somiton. But the witnesses say it was a soldier, an officer, who pushed you. This Mr Castleton's a civilian.'

'Well, he was when I last saw him. Can you make enquiries at the War Office? That will either confirm or deny my suspicions – I sincerely hope I'm mistaken.'

'We have a car outside, Miss Somiton, where would you like us to take you?'

'I have an appointment at the bank where I just have to sign some papers and collect a document. Do you think you could possibly wait outside and then take me back to Wivenhoe?'

'I think we could manage that considering the morning

you've had. However, I shall return to the station and set my enquiries in motion and my sergeant will act as your chauffeur.'

* * *

Emily knew something was amiss and the telephone call an hour ago had been something bad. As soon as it ended, she heard Mummy ringing Daddy. Had Grandpa died?

Her door was open so she could hear the murmur of voices but not what they were actually saying. Lily arrived with tea and biscuits.

'Do you know what the telephone calls were about?'

Lily shook her head. 'I'm sorry, Emily love, I'm in the dark. It's something serious as Mr Roby had to be told. I don't think it's your brothers, maybe it's about Major Roby.'

'I thought that too. I do hope not. Grandpa was doing so well at Christmas and my parents said they were no longer as anxious about him.'

'I shouldn't have said that as you're not well enough to be worried about anything apart from getting better.'

'I expect someone will come up and tell me if it's something I need to know. Thank you for the tea but I don't want the biscuits. Save them for the boys – I think Grace enjoys a biscuit now so give one to her.'

'You'll not get better if you don't eat.'

'Biscuits aren't real food. I'll definitely eat my lunch.'

'Good, I'll bring it up in a bit. I'm just waiting for Miss Somiton as she said she'd be back before lunch. I wonder what's holding her up.'

'I'd come down and eat but I just don't feel well enough at the moment. It's not fair that you have to run up and down stairs. I'm sure a housekeeper isn't supposed to do that.'

'Go on with you, love, I do it because I want to. I love working here.' Lily smiled in a strange way. 'I've never been happier, who'd have thought that I'd be back with Patrick and things are even better than they were before.'

Emily looked closely at Lily. 'Are you expecting? Is that why you're so happy and look so well?'

Lily blushed. 'How could you possibly guess that? I can't lie; I've just missed my second monthly so it's definite. Patrick and I want another baby and this one should be arriving in August some time. I've not told your parents yet – I thought I'd wait until Miss Somiton has left.'

'Mummy will be sad that you're leaving but happy for you both. Will you be working here for much longer?'

'I hope so, for another few months at least. There'll only be the five of you by then and I reckon you won't need anyone apart from Enid to do the heavy work.'

'We don't need anybody really, having someone help in the house is a luxury. I'm sure we'll be able to manage when you do leave. I can cook, so can Mummy now and Daddy makes tea on Sunday already.'

'There you are then, nothing to worry about.'

There was the sound of a lorry pulling up in Alma Street. Emily pointed to the window which overlooked it. 'Please, can you see if it's something for us or if it's for the doctor?'

Lily hurried to the window. 'Goodness me, it stopped right outside our back gate. I'd better get down there and see what's what.'

Mummy called up the stairs. 'Lily, we appear to be having a delivery. Could you possibly come down and take care of it? I'm changing Grace at the moment.'

* * *

Emily was tempted to get out of bed and look for herself but knew she wasn't well enough. Instead, she had to contain her impatience and curiosity and listen to the banging and shouting of the delivery men as they brought a lot of things in.

The kerfuffle downstairs had only just stopped when she was pretty sure she heard a car pull up outside the front door. Her bedroom was on the other side of the house, but with her door open she could hear quite a lot and was pretty certain it was a car.

Minutes later the front door opened. Lucinda must be home and had somehow managed to get a taxi.

'Lucinda, darling girl, are you sure you should be home and not have remained in the hospital?'

'Elizabeth, it's superficial, the doctor wouldn't have allowed me out if there was anything seriously wrong. It looks far worse than it is.'

Emily ignored the fact that her legs were wobbly, that she had a temperature, and heaved herself out of bed and staggered to the door.

'What's happened? Why were you in hospital, Lucinda?' She now knew what the serious telephone calls had been about earlier.

'Emily, get back into bed, you're not well enough to be up,' Mummy said firmly.

'I just need to speak to Elizabeth, then I'll come up and talk to you. Don't look so worried, I fell on my face which is why I've got stitches. Very slippery out there today.'

Emily's heart stopped hammering. 'I'm glad it's nothing worse. Yes, please come up when you can. I'm going back now, Mummy, sorry.'

She flopped into bed and for a moment couldn't find the energy to lift her legs back under the covers. She hated being so feeble – as soon as her temperature was normal she was going to get dressed whatever the doctor and her parents said. Lying about doing nothing wasn't good for anyone in her opinion.

Lucinda appeared with the lunch tray and Emily was shocked. The scrapes and cuts might be superficial but Lucinda looked absolutely dreadful.

'I think you're the one who should be in bed, not me. What happened?'

'I told you; it was slippery. The good thing is that I'll be perfectly well by Friday and able to join the ATA as planned. If I'd broken an arm, twisted an ankle or something like that I'd have been devastated. I don't care what I look like as long as I can fly safely.'

'I'm really going to miss you. I think of you like a big sister. Do you think you'll be able to come home next month to celebrate your twentieth birthday with us?'

'I sincerely hope so, I know I'll be on the rota as soon as I start, but not how many hours we work before we get any time off. As civilians I doubt that we have to work as many hours as a WAAF.'

'Just before you came home there were a lot of boxes brought in. Do you know what that was about?'

Lucinda nodded and winced. Moving her head about like that obviously hurt.

'Yes, they're my belongings from the flat in London. I've rented it out to a very nice man for the duration. They kindly parcelled all my personal things up and arranged for them to be delivered here. I'm going to get your brothers to carry everything up to the attics as that's where I'm going to be sleeping in future.'

'I'm glad that you don't mind having to move, I prefer it down here. It was tricky doing my homework by candlelight and it was

very cold up there even with the chimney breast running through
the room.'

'The room I've got in a little cottage near where I'm going to
be flying from has electricity and running water but no bathroom
at all, outside loo, and no fireplaces upstairs. My attic bedroom's
going to be like a palace compared to that.'

* * *

Lucinda took the half-finished soup back to the kitchen, leaving
Emily to flop back on the pillows. Her brothers would be back
from school in a couple of hours and then it would be impossible
to rest with them going up and down carrying boxes for Lucinda.

There was something about Lucinda's explanation for her
injuries that seemed odd. Also, why would there have been
serious telephone calls if she'd just tripped and fallen? Emily
couldn't see how so much damage could have been done to
Lucinda's face if she'd just fallen on the pavement.

When she got up later she'd find out what had really
happened.

Lucinda put on a cheery countenance for the benefit of her family. Her face was stiff and sore but that didn't bother her particularly, it was the thought that a man she'd been in love with, had shared a bed with, had tried to kill her that was making her uneasy.

Emily was now asleep, the poor little lamb looked dreadful and had lost so much weight she looked like a scraped matchstick, as Lily would say. Elizabeth and Jonathan assured her their daughter was going to make a full recovery and would be back at school the following week.

The boys had just gone to bed, the baby was silent, so now she'd have to discuss what had happened in detail with them and she wasn't looking forward to it one jot.

They were sitting around the roaring fire drinking their nightly cocoa when the telephone jangled noisily. Jonathan said something impolite.

'I'll get it, it had better be important to disturb us at this time.'

Elizabeth gently admonished him. 'It's only eight o'clock, my love, hardly the middle of the night.'

He was chuckling as he opened the sitting-room door, letting in the freezing air from the passageway, and when they both protested he laughed out loud and shut it behind him.

They could hear him talking but not what he was saying. She exchanged a worried glance with Elizabeth. 'He's been out there so long his cocoa's getting cold.'

'I just heard him put the receiver back.'

Her stomach clenched when she saw his expression. He looked at her and she knew whatever he was going to say, it was about what had happened this morning.

'Lucinda, there's no easy way to say this. You were right, Castleton could have been the man who pushed you in front of the lorry. He's a soldier now.'

She listened with growing incredulity as he explained why Ralph was in uniform.

Jonathan resumed his seat but ignored his cocoa. 'This is why Scotland Yard are now involved. They know he threatened you and are continuing the investigation in London. They have his photograph and are showing it to guards, ticket collectors and so on at Liverpool Street.'

'Do you think that he'll try again?' Elizabeth said nervously.

'I think it highly unlikely. Lucinda's safe here, and with any luck either the Colchester police force or Scotland Yard will find sufficient evidence to arrest him.'

'His poor wife, she'll be devastated to hear what they've said and what they're suggesting. I'm sure she's no idea just how dangerous he is. There's something I don't understand, Jonathan, how they can prove it was him. I didn't see him, the lorry driver just said he saw an officer push me, there must be thousands and thousands of officers.'

'As I said, sweetheart, the police have the matter in hand. You just have to stay indoors until they've gathered enough evidence, circumstantial or actual, to arrest him and press charges.'

Elizabeth dabbed her eyes. 'I don't like the idea that a possible murderer is lurking about the place hoping to murder Lucinda. I'm also at a loss to understand why he should wish to do it in the first place.'

Lucinda had been thinking this very thing and believed she had the answer. 'He's a vindictive man. Because I didn't lie for him to the police when he was trespassing in my flat, he was arrested. Although he wasn't charged, the detective must have passed the information onto his superior so he was dismissed.

'I'm absolutely certain he never had any intention of being on active duty, bullies are always cowards, aren't they? He must have followed me this morning, I still can't believe he intended to push me in front of a lorry to kill me, it must have surely been a spur-of-the-moment decision.'

Jonathan was sceptical. 'In which case, why was he here at all? What sort of revenge was he intending?'

Lucinda shivered. 'You're right. I expect he'd put in motion something to stop me getting a good trade in the WAAF or even to stop me getting into the ATA—'

'He couldn't possibly have known that – you only knew officially on Friday. According to the detective inspector I just spoke to, Castleton spent those days at home with his wife. He told her he had things he had to finish at the War Office and would be gone for two days. So far, he hasn't returned home.' Jonathan looked grim. 'His wife hasn't been informed of the real reason for the enquiries.'

Elizabeth clutched Jonathan's arm. 'That means he could well be lurking about outside waiting to attempt a second attack on Lucinda.'

'As I said before, I think it was an opportunist attack, not planned. He's not going to break into the house, in fact, I doubt he's anywhere near Wivenhoe.'

Lucinda bit her lip. 'Do you think that he knows that we suspect it was him?'

'A good question, but not one that I can answer with any authority. I believe you said he was an intelligence officer – which makes his actions so far extraordinary to say the least,' Jonathan said.

'I now think what he did was carefully planned. He knows it'll be impossible to prove, the police will suspect it's him but as nobody saw his face, I doubt that will be enough.'

'I'm going to check that the doors are locked. I'm tempted to jam the scullery window shut but then Ginger won't be able to get in and out,' Elizabeth said.

'It's too small for an adult to come through so we don't need to worry about that window,' Jonathan replied.

Lucinda didn't want to talk about it any more. 'Excuse me, I'm going to bed. My face hurts and I ache all over from the fall. There's nothing any of us can do tonight and quite frankly I think Castleton will have already returned home to pretend to his wife that everything's tickety-boo.'

'Surely Mrs Castleton won't want him home if she knows what he's been up to – or suspected of being up to,' Elizabeth said.

'Why would they alert her to the possibility her husband's attempting to murder me? I hope for her sake he doesn't take out his anger on her or his children before he's shipped overseas.'

'Good point, Lucinda, I'd forgotten that he's not going to be in this country for much longer. You just need to stay indoors until you leave on Friday as the detective inspector said, Castleton has to report on the same day as you.'

Lucinda realised there was something even more important

she hadn't shared with them and that they deserved to know. She explained the truth about who she really was and Elizabeth was horrified.

'How could they have taken you in and then treated you so badly? I can't believe my cousin – your actual father – refused to speak to you.'

'I'm just grateful that my grandparents did adopt me, so to speak. The alternative would have been so much worse. I wouldn't have been a Somiton at all, would never have known you. I was upset when Pauline told me but I'm glad that she did as it explains a lot of the things I didn't understand.'

'Thank you for telling us, it makes no difference, you're absolutely part of our family,' Elizabeth said. 'Sammy is as much our son as George, family is who lives with you, who you love, there doesn't have to be a blood connection.'

'I'm hoping that you'll allow me to change my name to Roby if I can. I've also got something for the children. It's why I went into Colchester today.'

Lucinda handed over the document and both Jonathan and Elizabeth were overwhelmed by her generosity. They made a second mug of cocoa, unheard of under normal circumstances, and after drinking this she hugged both of them and retreated to her attic.

She enjoyed being at the top of the house surrounded by her boxes. Tomorrow, she'd unpack them as the clothes needed to be hung up or put away carefully if they were to be any use at all when she wanted to wear them in the future.

As the house settled into silence, she smiled. Notwithstanding the fact that her erstwhile lover had attempted to murder her this morning, she was happy with her life. She was lucky, had more than she'd ever thought she would, and couldn't wait to start the next chapter of her life.

* * *

Ralph enjoyed a decent supper at the Park Hotel in Wivenhoe and retired to his room, happy with how things had turned out. He'd timed his push perfectly, simple physics, and knew that Lucinda wouldn't be killed, just, he hoped, terrified that she might be.

As far as Leone was concerned, he was in London at the flat so as long as he was back by tomorrow evening, she wouldn't suspect a thing. He'd chosen this hotel because there were several army officers billeted there who were attached to the tank regiment stationed at Wivenhoe House.

He'd avoided any contact with them – had given a false identity, confident the landlord would take his word and not want to see his papers. The man had just assumed he was with the tank regiment and he hadn't disabused him.

Lucinda would be sleeping, uncomfortably he hoped, believing she was the unfortunate victim of an accident. Why would anybody suspect that she'd been pushed deliberately?

When she received the letter he'd posted yesterday, he was confident that she'd immediately reply and thus step out of the safety of the house and he could put his plan into action.

He intended to catch a train at lunchtime tomorrow – he'd checked the timetable – and was certain it would be packed with other khaki-clad individuals being posted elsewhere or going on leave to visit their families. He'd be anonymous amongst them.

This gave him ample time to complete his mission. Nothing could go wrong, this sort of thing was what he did, why he'd been an outstanding intelligence officer. He almost believed what he'd told Leone about his future in the army – his commanding officer would soon realise that his new lieutenant was somebody special and he'd be promoted and doing the work he was trained for, not in the frontline getting shot at.

* * *

Emily woke up for the first time since she'd been unwell with no headache, no temperature and able to swallow without difficulty.

She was still a bit feeble, but she hadn't eaten much for days. Daddy would be downstairs, it would be lovely to speak to him before he went to work. Warmly dressed in her thick winter slacks, she hurried downstairs and into the dining room.

He wasn't as pleased to see her as she was to see him. 'What the devil are you doing down here? You were told to stay in bed and rest.'

'I'm fine today, I'm not going to do a lot but I do need to be up and about. Feel my forehead and you'll see that my temperature's gone. I promise I'll have a rest after lunch.'

He grinned and hugged her warmly. 'Naughty girl, but you're right. You look different today. As long as you promise not to go outside, it's still freezing, then I trust your judgement.'

Lily came in with some scrambled eggs. 'I heard you getting dressed, love, and used up the last two eggs to make you this. I don't suppose you want any toast.'

'No, too scratchy, but I'm going to enjoy my breakfast, thank you, Lily.'

'I should eat that quickly, sweetheart, your brothers will be grumbling they haven't got eggs for breakfast if they see it.'

The boys came down smartly dressed in their purple blazers but they had to wear grey flannel shorts and long socks which meant like her that they got very cold knees. George pointed at her slacks and pulled a face.

'We can't wear long trousers, it's not right that you can. Girls aren't supposed to wear trousers, they're supposed to wear skirts.'

'I know, little brother, life's just not fair. Did you hear Lucinda getting up?'

'Not a peep,' Sammy said. 'I expect she's getting over the shock of yesterday.'

'I was going to wait until she was here to tell you,' Daddy said, 'but I'm going to tell you now. Lucinda has set up a small trust fund for the four of you. She used a third of her coat money.'

Emily tried to smile but hearing the word trust fund reminded her that she had this secret letter from Grandpa that he'd given her when she'd gone to Kent to stay with them back in October. He'd left her £10,000 and told her it was to be their secret until he was gone and then she could do whatever she wanted to with it. Emily had already decided that her inheritance would be divided equally between the four of them which meant that they were all quite wealthy.

'Emily, you've gone very pale. I think you've overdone it again,' Daddy said.

'I'm fine, I was just surprised. Lucinda is so kind and I'm going to miss her when she leaves on Friday.'

'We all are, sweetheart, your mother and I consider her very definitely one of the family. Lucinda said she wants to get her name changed to Roby and we couldn't be happier.'

This impressed her brothers. 'Smashing, imagine having a grown-up older sister,' Sammy said.

George was thinking. 'She's too old to be a sister, our parents would have had to have been sixteen when she was born. She's a cousin or an aunt – it doesn't matter which because as far as I'm concerned, she's our Lucinda.'

* * *

When Grace went up for her afternoon nap, Emily decided she ought to do the same. Lucinda was still busy upstairs completing her unpacking. It had been a really enjoyable morning helping Lucinda with her beautiful clothes, coats, frocks, silky underwear and the other things that had arrived in the tea chests.

Mr Hatch turned up with today's letters and as Emily was closest she opened the front door and collected them. She flicked through the half a dozen envelopes and saw that one was addressed to Lucinda; the others were business letters for Daddy.

'Mummy, I'll take this one up with me and put it under Lucinda's door. If I'm not awake when Grace gets up would you please knock on my door?'

She crept up the attic stairs and pushed the envelope under the door – there was plenty of room to do that as the house was so old none of the doors fitted properly. Emily thought that's why there were so many draughts whistling about the place.

As she drifted off to sleep, she heard Lucinda going down the stairs and wondered where she was off to. Lily had gone shopping and Mummy was in her own bedroom so she could hear Grace when she woke up. The baby now slept in her own room, a little box room next to Mummy and Daddy's, fine enough for now but when she got older she'd have to have something bigger.

She listened and was almost certain she heard the back door open and shut. Lucinda was supposed to be having a rest – why had she gone out? Was it something to do with the letter that had been pushed under her door?

22

Lucinda had been astonished to receive a letter from Mrs Castleton. She wasn't even sure how Ralph's wife had her address as she couldn't imagine that he would have shared it with her.

Dear Miss Somiton,

You must be surprised to receive this letter from me espe-cially after I caused you so much embarrassment by revealing your name and the relationship you had with my husband.

I do apologise for that – I was hurt and unhappy.

Ralph and I have reconciled and are trying to make our marriage work for the sake of our children.

However, I know that he gave you several pieces of my jewellery. These are family pieces and I'd really like them back. He pretended that they were at his flat, but I know you have them.

I've no right to ask you, especially after the way we both treated you, but could I prevail upon you to at least return the bracelet?

*This belonged to my grandmother and my parents are
visiting soon and will expect me to be wearing it.*

*The items are too valuable to be posted but if you could
bring them to London – I will reimburse your expenses, of
course – and treat you to a splendid lunch at the Savoy.*

I'll be there on Wednesday.

Yours very sincerely

Leone Castleton

She read it a second time and was incensed. This poor
woman had taken Ralph back, not knowing how truly evil he
was. Mrs Castleton needed to know what he was capable of and
divorce him for adultery.

Jonathan and Elizabeth had been most insistent that she stay
inside but this was a letter she had to write and then post immediately. The post office was only a hundred yards or so from the
front gate and she could be there and back literally in minutes.

She would also include the pawnbroker's slip so the jewellery
could be recovered. It wouldn't be cheap, but if the items were so
important then they would be redeemed regardless of the cost.

There was a stamp in her stationery wallet and she quickly
copied the address from the top of the letter onto the front of an
envelope.

Dear Mrs Castleton,

*It is I who must apologise to you as I'm going to tell you
exactly the sort of man that we were both involved with.*

*I didn't know that Ralph was married, he said he loved me,
he said that we would have a life together and I believed him.*

*Yes, he did give me three items of jewellery but I thought
that he'd bought them for me.*

After our affair became public knowledge and I was rejected by my family I came to Wivenhoe where I found a home.

I met Ralph briefly in the café at Liverpool Street when I still thought that I might have feelings for him. He asked me if he could use my name on a divorce petition, said that we could be married as soon as the divorce came through, said that he'd only married you for your money and there'd never been any love between you. I refused and he left, very angry with me.

Later he telephoned me here and I agreed to meet him in Colchester so that I could tell him that I didn't wish to see him again.

He was very angry and threatened me, said that I would regret my decision.

I thought nothing of this until...

Lucinda covered a second page giving Mrs Castleton every detail of the incident at her flat and that Ralph had pushed her into the path of a lorry. She ended the letter by telling this unfortunate woman that both Scotland Yard and the local police force were looking for witnesses who could identify him as having been in Wivenhoe and Colchester.

Satisfied she'd said everything that was necessary to warn Mrs Castleton about Ralph's true nature, Lucinda put the receipt from the pawnbroker's in with the two sheets of paper, sealed the envelope and was ready to take it to the post box that stood outside the post office on the corner of Queen Street.

She was well aware that it might be more sensible to ask Lily to post the letter when she left that evening but she believed it was imperative this information reached Mrs Castleton tomorrow, before Ralph returned home.

The house was quiet. Emily, the baby and Elizabeth were all resting and she'd heard Lily go out a few minutes ago to do her daily shopping.

Having seen the damage to her face, Lucinda used the poor weather as an excuse to muffle herself in a scarf so that only her eyes were visible, she also borrowed an old coat of Elizabeth's and hoped nobody, especially Ralph, could recognise her. She slipped out of the back door, ensuring that she closed it quietly behind her.

As she reached the corner of the street, Lily stepped out of Mr Moore's shop which was opposite. Lucinda felt a rush of relief. She hadn't revealed herself to anyone who might be in the High Street and now she could ask the housekeeper to take the letter for her.

'Goodness me, Miss Somiton, you shouldn't be out here.'

Lucinda held out the letter and shrugged.

'Here, you go back inside, I'll pop that up to the post office for you.'

'Thank you, this really needs to go in this morning's post because I want Mrs Castleton to get it tomorrow.'

If Lily thought it strange that Lucinda was writing to this person she didn't say so. She took the letter, dropped it on top of her basket, and walked briskly past the front of Harbour House, leaving Lucinda to dash back before anybody else saw her.

After carefully returning the coat to the peg, she unwrapped herself and breathed a sigh of relief. Nothing apart from a bomb dropping directly on the house would entice her out a second time.

Her heart was hammering – she was certain she'd caught a glimpse of a khaki-clad figure on the corner of School Road. It didn't mean this man was Ralph, it could be someone from

Wivenhoe House going about his legitimate business. But seeing an army officer so close had unnerved her.

She needed a cup of tea to calm her and was busy filling the kettle from the tap in the scullery when Elizabeth appeared behind her.

'You just went outside, Lucinda. What on earth were you thinking?'

'I only went as far as the end of the road, then I met Lily and she took the letter to the post office for me.'

'What letter? Why did you suddenly have to post a letter so urgently when you knew how risky that was?'

Lucinda busied herself with the tap and the kettle, trying to think of how to answer. 'I'll just put the kettle on, then I'll show you why.'

* * *

Elizabeth read the letter from Mrs Castleton, her expression incredulous. 'I don't understand how this woman has your address. I know that man is aware of your whereabouts, but I can't believe he'd have given this information to his wife.'

'I thought that too. In fact, I'm almost sure I saw him lurking just a few yards from here. I think he sent it deliberately to get me to come out. God knows what he had planned this time.'

'Wait there, my dear, I'm going to telephone the police. They need to investigate because if that was Castleton it proves our theory.'

The conversation was brief and to the point. Elizabeth replaced the receiver, smiling. 'They're sending a detective to make enquiries at the various hotels in the village. If that man stayed at any of them overnight, then this will prove our theory.'

'In a way, I hope they don't apprehend him today. I want him to arrive at his home after his wife has read my letter. She didn't write to me, that's obvious now, it must have been him and was part of his plan. I wonder what would have happened if I'd not seen Lily before I had to walk past him just now.'

'I thank God that we'll never know.'

* * *

Ralph couldn't remain where he was without someone noticing him. His ploy had failed; he'd been convinced Lucinda would immediately write a letter to Leone and want to post it.

Maybe she hadn't read the letter, possibly it was still with the others that were delivered and hadn't been given to her. Whatever the reason, he'd no option but to abandon the second part of his plan and catch the next train to London.

It had been his intention to bump into Lucinda and whilst doing so drop two stolen ration books at her feet and then loudly draw attention to them, emphasise the fact that they were somebody else's property.

Even if her new family wouldn't believe she was involved in the black market, not everybody in the village would think her innocent. People were suspicious and alert for wrongdoing, and mud would stick. He already had the story written and would post it to the same gossip column that had published the information about their affair a few weeks ago.

He was forced to abandon her final humiliation, but it wasn't worth risking being seen. He was already drawing more attention than he wanted. He pulled up his coat collar, pulled down his cap, and marched briskly towards the station. He was frustrated that he hadn't completed his plan, but confident eventually

Lucinda would read the letter and probably feel obligated to dash to London, recover the items of jewellery, and would then spend a wasted lunchtime waiting for Leone to appear.

That would have to do – with any luck there'd be an air raid and she'd become one of the many civilian casualties.

There was still an hour to wait before the London train steamed into Wivenhoe station. He couldn't risk being seen anywhere near Harbour House so decided to walk down to Station Hotel which he hoped would be open so he could wait in there and not conspicuously on the platform.

The door was locked and, swearing under his breath, Ralph crunched his way into Wivenhoe station. He already had his ticket so didn't need to go to the ticket office. The waiting room was empty, nobody with any sense wanted to sit in an unheated room for an hour when they could remain in their own home.

His breath steamed in front of him. Even with his thick army greatcoat over his uniform he was cold. He decided to march briskly on the spot, moving his arms in time to his feet in the vain hope that it would keep his circulation going.

He'd not been doing this for long when he heard the sound of a train approaching. This must be a local train, one that didn't go to London, but being on that would be better than remaining here.

It had come from Brightlingsea and was packed full of housewives, navy chaps and very few soldiers. He was going to be remembered if he got on but had no option as the guard had politely opened the door for him.

This journey terminated at a station called St Botolph's and he, like every other passenger, alighted here. As Ralph emerged from the station, he saw a bus approaching. That reminded him he'd caught a bus from the main station last time he'd been in

Colchester. All he had to do was find the correct bus stop and he'd be able to get where he wanted to be.

* * *

In the end, he caught a train that had come from Norwich rather than Clacton but there were so many servicemen and -women on the train he was able to relax, knowing he was now all but invisible.

Eventually he arrived at Liverpool Street and was fortunate to find a taxi to take him to his flat near Horse Guards. He'd told Leone he'd be gone two nights so couldn't go back until tomorrow, but there was a decent hotel close by where he could get a meal this evening.

Ralph was about to enter the building in which his flat was situated when someone called his name. He turned and two military policemen approached him. One of them, a sergeant, saluted and then attempted to arrest him.

'Begging your pardon, sir – I have orders to place you under arrest for behaviour unbecoming. Will you come with me, please, sir?'

'What the devil are you talking about? I've not done anything unbecoming.'

'Sir, I must insist. You are under arrest by authority of the Corps of Military Police. You have no option but to accompany us. We are carrying out our duty as instructed and I suggest that you don't resist.'

They were attracting a lot of attention from passersby so Ralph had no option but to cooperate. Whatever they thought they were arresting him for he would soon disprove. It had to be something to do with Lucinda and the lorry, but the evidence would be circumstantial, and he was sure he could talk his way out of it.

He was hustled into a military vehicle and taken to the Military Provost's office to be interviewed. He was asked to empty his pockets – the normal procedure – but as he reached his hand into the first one, an icy chill ran through him.

He dropped the stolen ration books on the table. It didn't matter what he said, it didn't matter what they thought he'd done, just having these on his person was a criminal offence.

His life as he'd known it was over. If he was lucky then he'd have his commission removed, be reduced to the ranks and forced to serve alongside the hoi polloi. If he wasn't, then he'd spend time in a military prison.

He'd hoped to ruin Lucinda and without even trying she'd ruined him.

* * *

Emily was fully recovered by Thursday, which was fortunate as the family had decided to give Lucinda a big send-off with a party tea just in case she didn't manage to get home for her birthday in February. There was a cake, it even had real eggs in it, scones, jam and actual butter. Lily was amazing and had also made rolls which would be filled with cheese and pickle, Spam and piccalilli, and for the boys some would be filled with Marmite.

Something momentous had happened and the grown-ups had been talking and laughing all evening. It was something to do with Lucinda, but Emily didn't know what. As long as her adopted older sister was happy then so was she, and she didn't need to know the reason.

The tea was super, they played silly games afterwards and her parents joined in. Grace toddled about getting in the way, falling onto her bottom and screeching with laughter. Emily couldn't remember having such a wonderful time before.

Lucinda would be leaving on the first train so she could report at nine o'clock for her first official duty as a member of the ATA. Emily was disappointed that the uniform wouldn't be ready for another week but Lucinda had promised she'd come home wearing it when she could so everybody could see.

She'd been absolutely thrilled with the gift they'd clubbed together to buy her. She now had her very own bicycle so she could get to work and back without having to sit on the back of her friend's cycle.

Ginger woke her up sometime after five and for once she was pleased as this meant she could get up and say goodbye to Lucinda again. Emily flung on her clothes and crept downstairs. There was noise coming from the kitchen, so she wasn't too late.

'Good morning, Emily, I thought I heard you coming. I didn't want anyone to get up and see me off, it would be too upsetting.'

'Well, I'm here now. I'm going to walk down to the station with you too. I wish you'd come to live with us earlier, I've loved having an older sister even for so short a time.'

'If I'd come earlier then maybe I could have avoided the beastly business with that man.' Lucinda bit her lip, her cheeks were pink, she knew she shouldn't have said anything.

'Please, tell me what happened? I'm old enough to understand that you had an intimate relationship with this horrible man, that it was written about in the papers. I've worked out for myself that he had something to do with your accident.'

'Then I don't see why I shouldn't tell you the rest but you must promise not to say anything to the boys as they really aren't old enough.'

Emily nodded. She listened avidly and laughed when she heard what had happened to this Mr Castleton. 'They knew that he'd used a false name when he stayed at Park Hotel. The fact that he was in Wivenhoe hanging about near this house when he was supposed to be in London was enough evidence to charge him with attempted murder?'

'It certainly was. The police managed to get two witnesses to identify him getting off the train at Colchester just before my accident. But it was the stolen ration books that clinched it. He must have intended to plant them on me somehow. When they searched his bag, they found a letter addressed to the gossip column with all the details.'

'Then it serves him right. I hope he stays in prison for a long time. I do feel sorry for his wife, it must be hard for her.'

'She will have read my letter and be aware that he deserves everything that happens to him.'

'Do you think you could ask someone to take a photograph of you in your uniform standing by a Tiger Moth? I'd like to show off with it at school and I know the boys would too.'

'I don't think they'd be too impressed by me flying a Moth; however, if I ever get to deliver or collect a fighter then I'll definitely have a photograph of that for them.'

* * *

Emily stood on the icy platform waving until the train steamed out of sight. She didn't envy Lucinda having to travel in the guard's van as she had a bicycle as well as a suitcase. She'd have to cycle from Hatfield station to the RAF base with her suitcase tied on the back.

The house would be different without Lucinda, and she was going to miss her. They'd promised to exchange correspondence and this would mean Emily would receive a letter addressed to her for the very first time.

Tomorrow was Saturday and both her friends were coming over. George and Sammy had managed to catch the girls before they caught the bus home yesterday. It had been far too long since she'd seen them and she wanted to know how Jimmy was doing. She hoped he wouldn't be put into an orphanage; even though his life wasn't very jolly, at least he had more freedom than he would in such a restricted place.

23

Lucinda couldn't take her precious bike on the underground so unless she was incredibly fortunate and found a taxi she'd have to cycle the five miles with haversack, gas mask and satchel over her shoulders and her suitcase attached to the metal shelf behind the saddle.

As she wheeled her way out of the station, a taxi pulled up right beside her. 'Excuse me, I need to go to Paddington. Could you possibly fit me and my bike into your lovely taxi?'

The ancient cabbie grinned. 'Don't see why not, lovey, no one else hanging about waiting. It'll cost you a few bob and take about an hour, though.'

'I'll give you three shillings – is that enough?'

He touched his cap. 'That'll do a treat. I ain't getting out so you've got to get your bike in yerself.'

Luckily this cab was one of the old-fashioned vehicles and much roomier than the more modern ones. Those black cabs were almost gone from the streets as they'd been requisitioned by the War Office and had been camouflaged and were being used by the Auxiliary Fire Service.

The bike was heavy and cumbersome but Lucinda was fit and strong and with a bit of pushing and shoving she accomplished the task in a couple of minutes. The sky was grey, the temperature below freezing and London smelled of smoke and water. The taxi had to do several detours, reversed twice, in order to find a clear route to Paddington but he didn't complain.

When he pulled up outside the station, she was ready with her money and had added an extra threepenny bit because he'd managed the journey in less than the hour. There were two businessmen waiting to jump in. Neither of them offered to help with the bicycle, which she thought typical of men like them.

The cabbie tipped his hat, nodded and with crunching gears and a strong smell of burning oil he took off to somewhere in the city with his new passengers.

There was a train waiting and Lucinda now knew the drill and scooted her bicycle to the guard's van. She was greeted by two friendly young RAF pilots who were also travelling with bicycles.

'Here, miss, we'll put that in for you,' the fair one said.

'Thank you, that's very kind. I've already barked my shins twice getting here from Essex.'

The van was full of parcels, wicker chests on wheels, but there was just room enough for the three of them to perch on one of the big chests.

'I expect we're going to the same place,' she said brightly to the fair-haired RAF officer.

'We're getting off at Hatfield.'

'As am I, I've just joined the ATA and will be flying from tomorrow. Are you there to complete your training?'

'No, we bally well aren't. Fully qualified, the pair of us. You're the first female ATA pilot we've met.' He held out his hand. 'I'm Jack Ross, this is Roy Riley, we're test pilots.'

She shook hands with them and introduced herself. 'I have four hundred hours in my logbook.'

'Crikey, a veritable expert. What happened to your face?'

'I slipped; the stitches should come out in a couple of days.'

'Good show, don't want to scare the horses,' Roy said as he expertly flipped open his silver cigarette case and popped a fancy cigarette into his mouth.

The guard popped his head out of his little cubicle. 'No smoking in here, sir, too many combustibles.'

The cigarette was carefully returned to the silver case and that vanished back into a trouser pocket.

By the time they steamed into Hatfield, she'd learnt a lot about what to expect on an RAF base and that not all of the boys in blue were as friendly to the ATA women as these two were. They were experienced pilots who'd recently been attached to de Havilland for ferrying duties and test flights on Oxfords and the new Mosquito. The de Havilland factory was based at Hatfield so it made sense for them to be heading there.

They wheeled their bicycles out onto the forecourt and the two of them looked around as if expecting there to be signposts.

'Follow me, gentlemen, I know exactly where to go,' Lucinda said.

By some miracle they arrived at the base without anyone coming to grief. There was the sound of an aircraft doing circuits and bumps, but also planes taking off on the main runway. It might be grey and freezing cold but it was obviously not bad enough to ground the planes.

The RAF pilots pedalled off in the opposite direction to her, calling out cheerful goodbyes as they tore across the tarmac. She wondered if she'd see them again, but thought that perhaps regular RAF didn't mix with the ATA.

She propped her bicycle up outside the hut and was about to go inside when someone shouted at her.

'Don't leave that there, some bugger will pinch it, take it in with you, that's what the other girls do.'

She turned and saw the speaker was the fair-haired mechanic she'd met when she was here last, Sergeant something or other, but she couldn't remember his name.

'Thank you,' she called and waved. She certainly didn't want to lose this precious bike as walking two miles every morning would be absolutely beastly. The only drawback to this two-wheeled miracle was the fact it had no lights, therefore using it in the dark might be rather hair-raising.

She elbowed open the door of their office and wheeled her bicycle in, seeing at once that there was a small room set aside for just this purpose, and there were two others already in there.

Pauline came out to greet her. 'Welcome, well done for finding that. I was thinking Lucinda's a bit of a mouthful, would you mind if we called you Lucy?'

'Not at all, I don't want to remember anything about my past. I'm in the process of having my name changed by deed poll. From now on I want to be known as Lucy Roby, I hope that won't cause confusion as my documents will still read Lucinda Somiton.'

'You can call yourself anything you want, common usage and all that, but until you get your legal ducks in a row we can refer to you by your new name.' Pauline pointed at her damaged face.

'I bet there's a story behind that. I've managed to snag some real coffee from the officers' mess, it's just brewed. I'm not flying today, join me in my office.'

'Thank you, I'd love to,' Lucinda replied. It was going to take a few weeks for her to think of herself as Lucy Roby, but a new life demanded a new name. In future she wouldn't hesitate to say who she was, wouldn't have to watch them flinch and look disapproving when they recognised her name.

* * *

Three hectic days later, she'd just returned from her third short hop, this one had been to White Waltham, in a Moth and was hanging up her flying gear in the locker room when one of the girls poked her head around the door.

'Lucy, there's somebody here to see you. Pauline said you can use her office.'

'Okay, I'll be there in a minute.' Lucinda didn't ask who it was, assumed it would be someone from head office wanting her to answer a few questions about her change of name.

Her uniform was being sent by train in a couple of days and she just had to cycle to Hatfield and collect it. She felt a bit out of place being the only one not wearing navy blue – also Pauline had told her there were several suitable applicants coming to be tested at the weekend and she didn't want to be the odd one out when they came.

There was a youngish woman, expensively dressed, waiting to speak to her. It wasn't anyone Lucinda had ever met before.

'Sorry to have kept you waiting, I don't know who you are, I apologise if I should recognise you.'

The young woman was clutching her handbag as if it held something precious. Lucinda hadn't realised how nervous her visitor was.

'Please, sit down, I'll ask one of the girls to make us some tea.'

'I don't think you'll want me to stay to have tea. I'm Leone Castleton.'

Lucinda put out a hand to steady herself. 'What on earth are you doing here? I can't think that we have anything at all to say to each other.' She frowned. 'How did you know I was here?'

'Pauline told me. I'm sorry, do you want me to leave?'

'You've come to tell me something so I might as well know what it is.'

The young woman nodded. 'I don't blame you for hating me, I should never have done what I did. Please, can I sit down, I don't think my legs are going to hold me upright much longer.'

Immediately Lucinda stepped forward and guided her unexpected guest to the nearest chair. 'We both definitely need a mug of tea.' She was about to go in search of someone to make it when there was a knock on the door and Rose came in with a tray.

'We thought you might need this,' she said and placed it on the table and left them to it.

After a few reviving mouthfuls, Lucinda was ready to listen. 'I'm sorry that your husband has got into such dreadful trouble—'

'He deserves it, if you hadn't written to me I wouldn't have believed what I was told. My parents are supporting me. I've already instigated divorce proceedings.'

Lucinda couldn't help her shocked gasp.

Leone shook her head vehemently. 'I won't be naming you, don't worry. A private detective has found another young woman he had a relationship with who's only too happy to be named in return for a substantial remuneration.'

'Then I'm glad for you. Do you know what he's going to be charged with?'

'The army are taking a very dim view of one of their officers doing what he did and whilst wearing a uniform. Attempted murder and possession of stolen ration books, using a false name are the main charges.'

'Golly, I suppose that means I'll be wanted as a witness.'

'Actually, he admitted that he pushed you. He thought telling them he'd planned it carefully and was aware that you'd not actually be run over would make it just a misdemeanour or something.'

'I thought him an intelligent man, I was obviously mistaken. Will he go to a military prison?'

'They've already held a court martial and he was given the option of going to prison for ten years or going to Africa as a private to serve on the frontline.'

'I'm sure he took the second option. One thing Ralph doesn't lack is self-confidence. I'm sure he believes that somehow he'll rise to the top, regain his position in society.'

'Yes, that's what he chose. I thought you'd want to know. I also thought you'd like to know that my family and his have made sure that he'll never be promoted, and will have to remain in the army for the same duration as his prison sentence would have been.' Leone smiled. 'He's a regular, signed up for ten years, not a conscript.'

Lucinda laughed. 'I bet he didn't know that when he took what he thought was the easiest option. Thank you for coming all this way to tell me. I've grown up a lot since last summer, I'd never have been taken in by him if I met him now.'

'I'm sure you wouldn't. I think you should also know I'm having a baby – he wanted a son so that the title and the entailed estates will remain in the family. So I hope I have another daughter and so does his brother.'

Lucinda then discovered that the stolen jewellery had been recovered which was another reason for the visit.

'I have to go, my chauffeur Robertson is waiting outside. I really don't want to be out in the blackout.'

There was a smart blue Bentley already purring quietly outside the office. Lucinda walked out with her visitor. 'Good luck with everything, Leone. Thank you for coming, now I can get on with my life and put an unpleasant episode behind me.'

She didn't wave the car away, not sure she understood the reason Ralph's wife had made the journey but decided that, like her, Leone wanted closure.

* * *

Emily checked the dining room for the umpteenth time. The cake was in pride of place in the centre of the table, there were sausage rolls, dainty sandwiches, and a variety of other luxuries that Lily and Mummy had managed to obtain for this special double birthday party. Not only was it a twentieth celebration but also for her little sister who'd been one year old a week ago.

The weather had been absolutely beastly at the end of January, then milder for the past two weeks of February, but now the temperature had dropped dramatically, there were blizzards in the north of England and heavy snow already falling in most places. This was why Lucinda, now legally known as Lucy Roby, had managed to get a few days' leave to celebrate her birthday with her new family.

'She's coming, she's coming,' Sammy yelled from the window. 'I just saw her crossing the road. She looks ever so posh in her uniform.'

'Don't shout, Sammy, I'm only standing three yards from you,' Emily said, laughing.

Daddy had taken the afternoon off for this special day. Grace was wearing her best smocked frock, the boys were in their Sunday best, as was she. Mummy always looked smart so hadn't needed to change.

George had the front door open and an icy blast whistled

down the passageway. Emily ran to the door and all three of them hugged Lucy.

'I can't tell you how pleased I am to be here. It was an absolutely ghastly journey, but worth it to see you all,' Lucy said.

Emily pulled George and Sammy away, took Grace from her mummy, which meant that her parents would now welcome the new member of the Roby family.

She stood with the youngest member in her arms and a bubble of happiness swelled in her chest. She was so lucky, she had so much, and seeing Lucy – now her actual big sister – standing there looking smashing in her smart ATA uniform made everything just perfect.

One day, when she was grown up, Emily decided, she was going to make her family proud, by doing something as amazing as Lucy.

* * *

MORE FROM FENELLA J. MILLER

Another book from Fenella J. Miller, is available to order now here:

https://mybook.to/Harbour6BackAd

BIBLIOGRAPHY

A to Z Atlas Guide to London, 1939 reproduction
Wartime Britain by Juliet Gardiner
One Child's War by Victoria Massey
How We Lived Then by Norman Longmate
Growing Up in the War by Maureen Hull
The Home Front by Marion Yass
The Story of Wivenhoe by Nicholas Butler
River Colne Shipbuilders by John Collins and James Dodds
The Wartime Scrapbook by Robert Opie
Oxford Dictionary of Slang by John Ayto
Waiting for the All Clear by Ben Wicks
The Longest Night by Gavin Mortimer
Spitfire Girl by Jackie Moggridge
Golden Wings by Alison King

AUTHOR'S NOTE

I always check dates and events and my aim is to be as historically accurate as possible, but sometimes in order to fit my story arc dates have to be moved and small facts changed. When this does happen, it is deliberate and not an error.

ABOUT THE AUTHOR

Fenella J. Miller is the bestselling writer of over eighteen historical sagas. She also has a passion for Regency romantic adventures and has published over fifty to great acclaim. Her father was a Yorkshireman and her mother the daughter of a Rajah. She lives in a small village in Essex with her British Shorthair cat.

Download your exclusive bonus content from Fenella J. Miller here.

Visit Fenella's website: www.fenellajmiller.co.uk

Follow Fenella on social media here:

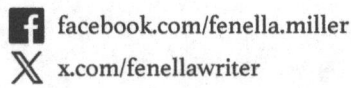 facebook.com/fenella.miller
x.com/fenellawriter

ALSO BY FENELLA J. MILLER

Goodwill House Series

The War Girls of Goodwill House

New Recruits at Goodwill House

Duty Calls at Goodwill House

The Land Girls of Goodwill House

A Wartime Reunion at Goodwill House

Wedding Bells at Goodwill House

A Christmas Baby at Goodwill House

The Army Girls Series

Army Girls Reporting For Duty

Army Girls: Heartbreak and Hope

Army Girls: Behind the Guns

Army Girls: Operation Winter Wedding

The Pilot's Girl Series

The Pilot's Girl

A Wedding for the Pilot's Girl

A Dilemma for the Pilot's Girl

A Second Chance for the Pilot's Girl

The Nightingale Family Series

A Pocketful of Pennies

A Capful of Courage

A Basket Full of Babies

A Home Full of Hope

At Pemberley Series

Return to Pemberley

Trouble at Pemberley

Scandal at Pemberley

Danger at Pemberley

Harbour House Series

Wartime Arrivals at Harbour House

Stormy Waters at Harbour House

All Change at Harbour House

Blitz Spirit at Harbour House

Trouble Comes to Harbour House

The Duke's Alliance Series

A Suitable Bride

A Dangerous Husband

An Unconventional Bride

An Accommodating Husband

A Rebellious Bride

The Duke's Bride

Standalone Novels

The Land Girl's Secret

The Pilot's Story